PAPER TARGETS

PAPER TARGETS

Art Can Be Murder

Steve S. Saroff

Paper Targets is a work of fiction. Any resemblance to actual events or persons, living or dead, is entirely coincidental.

Flooding Island™ Press

ISBN: 979-8-9857038-1-8

FloodingIsland.com

Flooding Island and the Flooding Island logo are trademarks of Flooding Island LLC

Front Cover Painting "Mixed Drinks" by Doug Meier

Rear Cover Photo by Steve S. Saroff

A sincere thank you to Eric Forrest Hutchins, Stacy Lear, Howard Heffelfinger, Ira Byock, and Michael Fitzgerald, for inspiration, encouragement, and for helping this drop-out dyslexic find and fix the multitude of typos and editing mistakes that will forever trouble my written words.

For Karen Cairn, with love.

Several chapters of an early version of this story (*The Lie and the Aether*) were read on the podcast, *Montana Voice*. Thank you to listeners who provided me with editorial feedback and encouragement.

Praise for Paper Targets

"This book is flat-out genius, the best novel I've read in years. The first five pages are absolutely gorgeous, as good as it gets, well worth the price of the book if you don't read another word. Then it's as if Kurt Vonnegut, Larry Brown, James Crumley, Scott Turow and Patricia Cornwell all decided to throw in together, like an all-star team of authors combined to do a greatest hits project. The novel is that good, that remarkable." - Martin Clark, Author of *The Substitution Order*, *The Legal Limit*, *The Plinko Bounce* and more.

"An astonishing page-turner of a novel. Fun page-turning mystery but also mildly terrifying. I read it in 2 sittings. I'm a mud slow reader. Highly recommended to everyone, especially those interested in noir, art, a blazing narration, and all of our deeply unsettling subconsciouses." - Michael FitzGerald, Author of *Radiant Days* and founder of Submittable Inc.

"Atmospheric, poetic, tragic, dark and light, crazy and sad. Intricately deep characterizations and entertaining to the end." - Mahayana Dugast, Author of *The Return of the Sovereign Heart* and Top Goodreads UK Reviewer

"Infused with nature and solitude. Readers will be immediately invested in Enzi's fate, and Saroff expertly intensifies the plot through unfolding backstories and quiet tension. Lyrical yet succinct, Saroff's first person narrative is well crafted, granting readers an inside view of Enzi's sentiments." - Publishers Weekly / Book Life

"A wonderfully written thriller with Big Sky country as a setting. His tale has something of the spirit of Hemingway stories. His spare prose seems designed to step out of the way but is arresting in itself." - Kirkus Reviews

Chapter 1 - Helen

Secrets that are shared but still not understood remain secret.

My first secret was that I could not read. And yet my earliest joy was listening to the murmuring of my mother as she read to me. We sat on a couch, a book shared between us, and I remember leaning against her. I also remember trying to touch the words, their shimmering mystery, as she held and guided my hand back and then slowly forth, beneath the lines. This was in a room connected to the garage where my father sometimes spent his evenings drinking and tinkering with his car. I remember looking up and seeing him through the open door. My second secret was that I could feel the sadness that swirled between my parents.

Sometimes, after my mother put the book away, I would go into the garage where my father was. He also guided my hands, helping me lift the heavy wrenches and showing me how they could take apart and put back together broken things.

And so, I grew up with the soft sounds of words and the metal hardness of tools. But as I grew, letters kept flipping, reversing, and tormenting me. When I tried to explain, I st-stuttered. But looking at trees, the clouds, or the cracks on the sidewalks, I saw patterns that did not have to be deciphered or explained. And those patterns flowed into each other. Looking up, through the branching limbs of an oak, into the turbulence of a storming sky, then looking down at the rain splashing at my feet as I walked home from school, I felt connected to what I then had no words for.

I have words now. And as I touch this keyboard, and if you are reading here, then you and I are not so far apart. But my lonely story will share better if I first tell you some of where I came from. Far enough back, all of us must have a connection, a history, to those who struggled and left. It might be great grandparents. Or closer. It could be your father or your mother. Or maybe, like me, it might have been you who had to run.

My parents were immigrants. My father, as a young scientist, was invited to become part of a university, and my mother, a professor of literature, came with him. So I was born in America. But my mother became sick, and she died when I was twelve years old. Then I was alone with my father, who had started to drink as my mother had begun to die.

It was my father then who would wake me each morning before he left for work, not returning until he was drunk, the sky long past dark. I would hear the car tires crunching on the gravel where he parked. I would hear him stumbling into the house. Lights would go on. Sometimes he would sing, though mostly, he was quiet. But other than his not being there, he was not abusive.

He would always check on me -- a few moments, some brief talk. The 'Hey Enzi, how was your day' interactions perhaps made him feel everything was still good. He had a great job in America, and he had a son. We were not hungry. But my days alone, facing the bullies at school who were drawn to stutterers like me, or, conversely, being ignored by teachers who avoided those of us who struggled to read and talk, made me fidget. My inability to read or write, my dy-dyslexia that turned my vision into a forever migraine-aura, and frightened my speech into a st-stutter.

When I wasn't in school, I would walk in the woodlands that divided the suburbs near where we lived. Among the trees and brush -- the White Oaks and the Tulip Poplars, the Sumacs and Dogwoods -- I found something that substituted for friendship. In the green and yellow light that filtered through the summer foliage, or among the shadows of the grass-dry mottled autumn days, patterns and shapes would form and dissolve as I walked. In those narrow strips of neglect behind the houses and the apartment buildings, those places where forgotten kids went to throw rocks and bottles or smoke weed, I fit in by walking by. I wanted to stop, to talk and listen. To learn the names of the other lost kids I saw, but instead, it was enough struggle to learn the names of trees.

Sometimes before going to bed, I would look at my mother's books on the shelves that still lined a hallway in our apartment. Often, I would take a book down, hold it, open it, and remember. The books she had held, the pages she had turned, and I would try to see the words that she had so easily read to me. But, as I tried, the letters would move and swim. Still, I would often bring a book to bed and slowly try to read in the light from my bedside lamp. Migraine sufferers can close their eyes on the confusion of their auras and clench their teeth at the throbbing pain. I did not have any pain, but my auras were constant, and peering through their confused centers, I looked for clarity in my solitude.

But I still tried to read. And I liked best the children's books, with drawings and stories, which my mother had read to me. She would come back then, an arm around me, another holding the book. I remember her deep accent, though she only spoke English with me, "put your hand here," she said, "look at the word and stop trying to see the letters. Look for the shapes." And as most kids start with 'a' then 'b' followed by 'c,' my learning moved slower because I was slow. I had to find words one at a time -- 'sky,' 'rock,' 'tree,' -- among the multitude of drowning letters.

My father, who had studied the molecules of cancer in rooms filled with glassware and centrifuges, had been unable to do anything for my mother as she faded away. Then he had been unable to do anything for me. In his sad despair, maybe like the letters that I struggled to see, he began to drown too. Then after one-too-many DUI's he was fired from his job. Finally, in the self-created legal clockwork of his ruin, I was taken away from him.

There were other schools then, different bullies, more poorly paid teachers, lots of cinder block walls, fewer trees, less sky. And, when I was fourteen, I ran.

I slept against wire fences. I always tried to hide. I stayed out of the cities, and I found jobs further away from everything. I made it through a winter, then another. I lied about my age until I was old enough not to have to lie anymore.

I hitchhiked and found jobs that lasted a few days or a week: picking apples in Washington state, stringing fences on ranches in Wyoming, working and sweating on road crews everywhere. I found the West and nights in bunkhouses, with the sounds of men coughing and drunks talking in their sleep. I found filthy motel rooms with stains on the walls and the forever miles of highways and roads. But I also found the sky, the rivers, and the wind, and I knew that the rooms were only for sleep, that the work was to be able to keep moving. Cities collect the runaways who are afraid of openness. The towns in the West collect the runaways who are afraid of not being able to keep leaving.

But I found something else. Never being able to clearly speak more than the few words needed to get work and rent rooms, in my solitude I picked up books and held newspapers and looked for company in what was printed. And, by doing as my mother had told me, giving up on individual letters and working to see the patterns of complete words, I learned to read. Then, when I had accumulated enough word-shapes, when I had moved away from trying to understand the shifting letters, I was reading full words in the same time that the single 'a,' 'b,' and 'c's' used to take. And what was in the books came in a fast rush. And the math books I found gave names to the shapes and the numbers I had always seen. But the swirl that I still see in the aura of my periphery is where I have found answers to secrets. In those repetitions that are never the same, math hides in the patterns. And math is what gave me the un-asked-for edge in this world of stainless steel and autonomous machines. The secrets I learned in the patterns that I saw, the patterns that I felt, opened the wide doors to money but also pushed me up against the rusted fringe of too much lonely and bloody greed.

As I drifted, I would look for libraries in college towns and read math books. The best days of my life -- like this memory: the University library in Missoula one September. The fluorescent ceiling lights blinked on and off to warn of its closing in fifteen minutes. I looked up at a clock and realized seven hours had passed. I had been studying the mathematics of automata and trying to find a combination of linear equations that could explain chaos. My thoughts now filled the notebook, but none of those written thoughts were words. They were math symbols, and like Kangi – pictographs of concepts – the symbols carried more meaning than what 'a,' 'b,' and 'c' take pages to explain.

When the library closed, I went outside into the autumn darkness. The air had the woodsmoke tinge of coming coldness. I swung on my pack. I walked across the road that circles the campus. Right there, right next to the library, there was the mountain. Mount Sentinel. I walked partway up, high enough so that I could see the Missoula lights. Up where no one would bother me, I fell asleep in my sleeping bag, with nothing between me and the sky. My dreams had no words. My dreams had only ideas. The following day when I woke up there was an inch of snow on top of me, and I was cold and wet. But I was happy. I walked back down the mountain to the library and books filled with symbols.

I kept drifting, hitchhiking, but when I was eighteen, I bought my first car for three hundred dollars. It was a wreck of a thing, and I expected it only to last a month. Instead, it lasted a bit more than a year and took care of me for thousands of miles. That year, whenever I got any pay, I would buy a few more tools and fix things. I replaced the thermostat. I replaced the alternator. I changed the tires. I fixed the brakes.

The second winter that I had the car, I was working in the northeast corner of Montana, near the Canadian border, on an oil rig.

My job was melting the frozen mud and water from the catwalks beneath the derrick. I did this with steam from a pressurized hose. It was the lowest paid, worst work. The steam screamed against the metal decks and shrouded me in a mist that soaked into my clothes and kept me covered in a thin, crackling glaze of oily ice all day. By that time, I had learned about work clothes. I had good boots. I had heavy gloves. I wore wool covered by denim. That winter, though, was sleet followed by wind, and no matter how much the crew boss yelled, I couldn't keep up with the ice. Then, one morning there was another man there. He stood shivering and stamping his feet as I showed him how to connect the hoses to the steam fittings on the pipes that ran like electrical conduits all over the rig. He wore thin shoes and a nylon bowling jacket. He wore jeans. He had a cotton stocking cap under his hard-hat. He had on a pair of the lousy gloves available in the trailer office next to the time clock. He cursed with each sentence, "The fucking cold. This fucking shit."

We worked all day into the early winter darkness, until the whistle blew. I turned everything off, coiled up the hose, and hung it in a tool closet, but the new man left his lying there, still connected to the steam fitting. Then he climbed off the deck and walked into the office trailer.

I could hear him yelling, "This is fucking shit." Then he came out holding a check for his one day of work.

While getting into my car, he came up, opened my passenger door, and got in the front seat. When I looked at him, he said, "Brother, give me a fucking ride into town. The man in there says to fuck me," and he gestured with his hand to the trailer, "So fuck him." We were about thirty miles outside of Plentywood, with the only thing for miles being the rig. Other workers were getting into their cars and trucks. I'd been on the road then for years. I knew that I didn't like this person. I wanted to tell him to get a ride from someone else, but instead, I looked at how he was shivering, how thin all his clothes were, and I said, "Sure," and we drove off.

I didn't talk, but he kept repeating how "fucked up" the day's work had been and how "fucking cold" he was. Then he started saying how "fucking much" he needed a drink, and how "fucking stupid" I was not to have quit as well, since by quitting, he had gotten paid for his day's work, while I would have to wait until Friday for my paycheck.

He also kept twisting the radio dial back and forth between stations, rolling his window up and down, looking at me like he was waiting for me to start talking and smacking the dashboard in time with the music from the radio. Finally, I asked him where he had come from. He answered and said that he had come down from Calgary, where he had been in jail. He had come into Plentywood the night before, had spent his last money at a bar, and was told that he could get a job in the morning if he showed up at the Conoco station. He said he had been told, "Anyone can get a job if they show up early."

Then he said, more of a demand than a question, "Brother, where are you staying?"

I had a motel room in Plentywood, but I said, "I sleep here, in the car." He answered, "Well fuck that. Drop me off at a bar. Someplace that will cash my check."

Ten miles from town, there was a restaurant on the highway at a crossroad, with a bright neon sign in the window and streetlights showing the empty parking lot. He looked at it as we drove, and as we passed, he said he wanted me to stop and turn around. He said he was hungry and wanted to get some food, "Before I spend all my fucking money in the bar." So I stopped and went back.

After I parked, he rummaged on the floor by his feet and found a sheet of newspaper. I wasn't paying much attention to him. I had told him I didn't want anything, that I would wait to get food at the grocery store in town. After he got out of the car, I thought about driving away, about leaving him there. It had been twelve hours straight of work. My arms were tingling, and my thoughts were not moving fast. I was listening to the radio, and I was feeling the warmth from the heater - with the engine running - parked there, waiting.

Then he was back in the car, startling me, and he was saying, before he had even slammed the door shut, "Brother, get the fuck *moving, now.*"

I pulled back on the highway and started toward town, and he was quiet for nearly a minute until we were well past the restaurant and onto a stretch of the road that was straight and empty. Then he said, "Change of plans. Drive through town. No need to stop at no bar in this fucking place. We're going over to 'North D' tonight."

I looked at him. He pulled his left hand from his jacket pocket and held a fist-full of cash, maybe a hundred dollars. I stared at the cash, and he looked like he thought I was impressed. He said, "It was fucking too easy. I wrapped my hand in that newspaper, went up to her, and said, 'Fucking blow you fucking away, give me the fucking money,' and she god-damned did. Everything in the register. Check it fucking out," and he waved the money in my face. Then he said, "Brother, it's half yours. Easy money. Fucking half."

I braked hard and pulled over right there, not even a shoulder. I stopped the car. He told me to keep driving. I told him that I didn't want the money. I told him to get out. He said, "This is easy, this is half yours," and he held the cash toward me again. He said, "Fucking drive me to Williston." I said no. He said, "You were out of there *fast*, man. You are *clean*, my brother. You get this for being here. For driving," and he waved the hand full of cash toward the east.

I could have done it. I could have driven him to North Dakota, and maybe he would have given me money. Perhaps we would have been parked in front of some bar in Williston, that most western of towns in that most desolate of states, and he would have gotten out. Then I would have driven the 110 miles back to Plentywood. Back to my motel room. Maybe sleep for an hour, then show up again for work. My exhaustion not even noticed because everyone at those winter workplaces was always exhausted or hungover. Instead, I said, "It's not right. It's not our money."

I said this, and then, with a twitch, like I have poked him in the eye, he fidgeted and exploded. He yelled, "Fucking froze all day." Then he reached into his pocket and had a large, folding knife. Open. "Get the *fuck* out of the car," he said.

I knew right then that he would try to kill me if I didn't get out of the car. I knew this because I saw, in the light from the radio, that he was moving his knife hand back, but more than that, I saw that his eyes were open wide and that his face was smiling. His teeth were all there, white and clenched. He was about to stab me. Then I opened the car door, and I fell backward out onto the road. I kicked up with my feet, and I thought that I somehow must have kicked his arm. Doing this meant that I was okay, that I was not cut. But he slid over fast behind the wheel, and was driving my car away.

I laid there watching the red of the taillights dim until, about half a mile away, they disappeared. I was in darkness. Not even a light in the distance, just a road at night in winter, with no trees, no houses, no people. I rolled onto my back and looked up. There were the stars. A moonless, cloudless night. Stars thick like a blanket. My stars. The stars I had seen from many places. Stars whose names I knew. Stars that were familiar and comforting and which showed me ever richer, ever better patterns. I looked up, and I saw places where I would be happy. I saw mathematics.

I walked the rest of the night. No cars stopped. And in the early morning, I was explaining my story to the police. They asked me over and over to repeat again and again what had happened. Even though no one blamed me, I had then been awake nearly two days. Back in my motel room, I slept hard and solid, and when I woke, I had nothing but my wool and denim clothes that I was wearing. I had no car, no tools. Through the rest of that winter, I stayed there in Plentywood. I went each pre-dawn to the Conoco station and rode with the other daily-work bums into the fields, to different derricks, to the steam, to the ice.

Seasons changed, and I worked in other oil patches and sweated on other summer road crews, and I found more of the less and less. But I also kept studying mathematics, with no idea of why. Then, for a brief, perfect time, I had stability which calmed all the other variables. I thought that my constant had found me. Is it only once in a lifetime, then forever a search for what was lost? Preparing, and working, so that mistakes that ruined the first chance will not be made again?

Wanting what was good. Wanting what is gone. The morning warmth of a clean kitchen, with bread going into the oven. Wanting a garden behind a rented house on the railroad side of town. Talking about good things to do with tomatoes. Pulling weeds from near the young basil plants. Her going to the university, and me working my labor job. Evenings. She with classwork, me with math books. The studying I was doing on my own, not knowing where it would lead.

She would come over and say to me, "Put this away. I will rub your back. Let's drink beer and dance. Here. In our home."

It was after another drifting and homeless winter. I had saved and bought another old car. It was a springtime, and I drove to Missoula, the town where I had been before, the town with the library and the mountain. And I found work, and rented a room. Then Helen found me.

Helen. I met her in Maloney's, an Irish bar on Main Street. A bar with bright lights, Jameson's whiskey, Guinness beer, and not much else. I was in there after a day of work. She was in there with a group of students, and when she was next to me, ordering a beer, she touched my arm, she said, "Hey."

Once in a lifetime?

She asked me if she could eat some of the peanuts spread on the bar in front of my beer. She leaned on her elbows. A jean jacket that was a size too large over a white tee shirt. Long, loose hair. High, Irish cheekbones, sad, Irish eyes. She asked me if I was going to the university. I told her no, that I was not a student. She asked me where I was from. I told her that I was not from anywhere anymore. She said, "We all have to be from someplace."

I was shy, not knowing what to say to her. Not understanding why she was talking to me. Instead of answering her, I asked her where she was from. Then I asked her why she was in Montana. She sat down on the barstool next to me. She said, "I looked at a map, and Montana seemed a good distance from where I was at the time." Then she asked, "You want to cross the street? You want to dance with me?"

She told me later that she liked my hands, how rough they looked, and that I didn't remind her of anyone she had ever known. Such a small, uncontrollable thing, and forever then, I was lost. We were dancing in the Top Hat. She was spinning with both her feet in the air. I was holding on to her, my arms around her waist, her arms around my neck. Her hair was across her face and brushing against mine. She smelled like coffee and lilacs. I told her this, and she said that I smelled like dust. She said, "Maybe we fit each other." Between songs, we were sweating and laughing. We found out each other's names. I told her that I was not planning on being in town long and was staying at a motel near the river, where I paid for a room a week at a time. She asked me to take her to the room, to show her the river. I told her that the river there was muddy. She said, "Then show me your bed." I told her that the room's bed was lumpy and narrow and that I slept in a sleeping bag. "Then show me that," she said, "get me out of these bars."

That first night after leaving the Top Hat, I remember walking with Helen down to the Clark Fork River. We were behind the Sweet Rest Motel on Broadway on the edge of downtown. She was drunk, but I was not. She was standing on the point of a large, angular rock, a beer bottle in her hand, saying, "Watch me now." Then she tried to spin on one foot, like a ballerina. She said, "I can do a pirouette. My mother made me take lessons. Watch." She spun. She fell. Her hand with the beer bottle did not let go, and the bottle broke in her hand, and the glass cut deep. Not a metaphor, not some fiction. Real blood and a wound that nearly took her hand.

When Helen and I first went to my motel room I had been frightened of her directness. She pulled my shirt as I was unlocking the room's door. She kissed my neck. When I opened the door and turned on the light, she walked past me, straight to the table where I had my books.

She picked one up, opened it, sat on the bed, and said, "Yuck. I hate math. I thought you weren't a student?" Not knowing how to explain, I took the book from her and said, "Let's walk along the river."

Now she was sitting in the mud, holding her hand, crying. I sat next to her, saying, "It doesn't look bad," saying this because in the dark, I couldn't see much except the mud. However, when I touched her hand, I felt her blood splashing out on me. I stood her up. I walked her to my car. She said she was going to pass out. I opened the back door, and she lay down on the seat, on top of the few changes of clean clothes I had back there. I told her to squeeze the cut hard and drove fast to St. Pat's.

At the hospital, I parked next to where the ambulances parked. I opened the back door, but Helen couldn't sit up. She seemed unconscious. There was blood everywhere. I crawled in next to her. I held hard onto her hand and wrist and pulled her to a sitting position. Then I got her outside the car and onto her feet and dragged her into the emergency room.

She had lost a lot of blood, but the doctor said she had probably passed out because she had been so drunk. They took her into a room where they cleaned and sewed her up. The broken bottle had cut an artery and a vein in her palm, but no tendons, no nerves. A nurse brought me a clipboard and asked me for information. I said all I knew was her first name and that I had just met her. The nurse sat down next to me then and said, "Can you wait here and take her home? Do you know if she has medical insurance?"

I reached into my pocket and brought out my wallet. I looked inside, and I said to the nurse, "I have some money. You can have it, but I have no idea who she is."

The nurse smiled, patted my arm, and told me to put my wallet away. "When she can talk, we'll find out what we need."

I spent six hours in the waiting room. A nurse finally came in with Helen. She was pale and had a bandage and splint on her left hand. The nurse gave me a list of instructions about changing the bandage and some prescriptions for medicine. "You need to get her home now," she said.

I brought Helen back out to my car. It was now daylight. I was supposed to be at work. She sat down in the front seat. I said something about her mother not doing a good job with the ballet lessons. I asked her where she lived, and she told me. I drove her home, stopping first to buy the prescriptions.

She lived in a small house on the north side of town. I parked in front of the house, and she got out, wobbly, still drunk, and drugged. She leaned against the car and said, "Oh my." So, I got out and went around to help her. When I got to her, she was still leaning against the car and looking at my clothes in the back seat. She said, "Did I do all that?"

"You were bleeding," I said.

"No kidding," she said, "I ruined your clothes. I'm so sorry for all of this."

I got her arm over my shoulders and helped her into the house, helped her lie down on her bed. I put the medicine where she could reach it, got her some water, and told her that I had to go. "I have to see if I still have a job," I said.

She nodded, said she was sorry again, and I left.

That is how I met Helen. All these years later, these girls with their blood. Helen's blood long ago, Kaori's blood soon. And their paint. Helen's then, and Kaori's soon... their paint... and their sadness, and their way of showing with no words.

I lost my job. I showed up after being awake all night in the emergency room and got fired for being late. I didn't care. I went back to the motel room, lay down on the bed, and slept. When I woke up late in the afternoon, I drove to a laundromat and washed the clothes that had been in the back seat. Then I came back to the room and started packing the few things I had left there. I was going to drive to Idaho; I was about to leave again.

I was putting my stuff into the trunk of the car when a car pulled in next to me. It was Helen. Her window rolled down. Her smile. Her sad eyes. Her bandaged left hand.

"Hi," she said. "I tried to call. They said you checked out. I need to apologize and thank you for taking care of me."

She stayed in her car. I stayed where I was. I didn't know what to say, so I said nothing.

"Here," she said, "I was out of it this morning. Here, take this. You paid for all my drugs." She was crossing her good right arm over and out the window, holding some cash.

I told her I didn't care, that it hadn't been much, but she kept telling me to take it. So, I walked over and stood there, took the cash, and put it in my pocket.

I asked her if she hurt much, and she said she did. I looked at the size of the bandage and asked her how she was going to get along. She answered that she hadn't figured out yet how she would get dressed. She was wearing the jean jacket from the night before, except that it was draped over her left arm. She was still wearing the white tee shirt that she had on in the bar. But now, it was stained with blood and river mud.

"You took my shoes off," she said, "I put them back on, but I couldn't tie the laces. Could you tie them for me?"

She opened the car door, swung her feet out onto the parking lot, and I knelt and tied her shoes, her muddy shoes. Then I stood up and told her I was leaving town.

She said, "But we just met," and tried to brush the hair out of her face, but she used the bad hand and said, "Ow. Damn, this hurts."

I asked her if she would miss many classes, and she said she would but it didn't matter. Then she told me that it was a good thing that she hadn't injured her right hand.

"You wouldn't be able to write, then?" I asked.

"No," she said, "I wouldn't be able to paint."

"Do you paint houses?" I asked, not understanding.

"No," she said, "I'm an art student."

Blood and paint. I remember how I stood there, in the parking lot of the Sweet Rest, talking for more than an hour as the evening got dark. She asked why I had the textbooks that she had seen the night before. I told her that I read them to look cool. She told me that she didn't believe me. I told her that I liked math because it was something that I could understand. I told her that sometimes when I worked on problems, it felt the same way as listening to music. She talked about music then, saying that when she drove from Detroit, she liked the AM radio stations that came through at night. She said she liked the way songs would fade away before they were done and that sometimes the static was the best ending.

She said her parents were angry with her for coming to Montana. She said that her father told her not to study art. But, she said, "Why study at all if it isn't what you want, right?"

I had sat down on the pavement. I was touching her shoelaces, wondering about when I would get up, get in my car, and drive away. Then she said that her hand hurt, that she had to get home and take her pills. I stood up, said it had been nice talking with her, and I started to get into my car. I didn't know anything.

She almost let me go, but she said, "Wait. We should talk more."

I stopped and looked at her. It was dark, nothing but flashing neon from the motel's half-broken sign. She continued, "I'll need you to help me with my shoes for a few days. Is that okay?"

I parked my car in front of Helen's house. I helped her with her shoes. I cut the stained shirt off of her with scissors, her bandaged arm resting on my shoulder, me trembling, her saying, "I couldn't do this myself."

I helped her on with another shirt. I buttoned it for her. She asked me to light a candle, and she turned off the lamps. Then she swallowed pills and drank from a bottle of wine. She lay down. I got my sleeping bag from the back seat of my car. I came back into her room. I lay down on the floor next to her bed. She moved to the bed's edge so that we could see each other. She said that I didn't have to sleep on the floor. I told her that I wanted to. She asked me why, and I told her that I am comfortable on the floor. She yanked all the blankets off her bed then lay on the floor next to me.

I didn't know where to put my arms. I didn't know how to lie next to someone. Helen said, "Here, come here," and with her good hand, she pulled me until I was wrapped about her, both of us on our sides facing each other. She whispered, "Talk to me."

I wanted to tell her about trout from the Yellowstone River caught with a piece of string, a hook, and grasshoppers. I wanted her to understand the fires made from river driftwood and all the stars in the perfect sky. Instead, I said, "I don't know, I don't know, how, how, to talk," I said, "I don't know," I said, "I don't know where to begin," I said, "I don't know anyone, I don't know anyone," all this in a stammer, a nervous and shy voice.

She nodded, brushing her head against mine. She whispered, "I don't know anyone either. No one knows me. Tell me things."

That night, that first night with Helen, I told her about how I remembered names of rivers, all the rivers I had slept next to. "Tell me," she said, and she fell asleep as I strung together names, moving from the east to the west, Shenandoah, Susquehanna, Missouri, Wind River, Columbia.

I found another job, pushing a vacuum cleaner, emptying trashcans, and doing the other things that a janitor does.

For a while, I kept sleeping on her floor. There was no rush, and I eventually started sleeping in her bed. I would sometimes wake in the night and listen to her breathing next to me. I would wake and feel her arms around me. In the mornings, she would get out of bed and open the windows. That spring sunlight, the scents from the flowering trees in her backyard, all of it pouring in.

It had been a month from the night she cut her hand. The bandages were gone. The stitches were out. She told me that I was not camping now. She said that I was living with her. She told me that I didn't have to keep everything I owned in my car.

She went to classes, painted, and pulled me into a place I had never been before. A place with no struggle. We were both sitting cross-legged on her bed. She reached and touched my hands and leaned forward so that all her hair was spilling into her lap. She wanted to know what I would do with my life. She said that I couldn't only be a janitor. I asked her why not. She told me that I must be more. I asked her again why, and she stared at me.

I didn't get it then. The hint of what was coming. Instead, all I cared about was how every afternoon, leaving work, I would be happy. I would be coming back to Helen's house to share with her.

She bought me presents. A bottle of Spanish olives. Bottles of wine. I also brought her things. Loaves of bread from the local bakery. Flowers from the sides of mountains: Shooting Stars and Lupine, Arrow Leaf, and Larkspur. In the evenings, she would come home from classes and put the flowers in a vase. I would light the candles along the window ledge, the candles on the table, the candles near the bath. She would turn off all the lights and paint. Canvasses leaning against the walls, Helen sitting cross-legged in front of them, a long brush in her hand, the colors muted and orange in the dim light. I would soak in the tub - the grit of my day's work coming out of my pores - until she would say, "Enzi, come here and tell me what you think." I would bring one of the candles and sit next to her, moving the flame close enough to see brightness in the wet paint.

She also gave me warmth and touch two and often three times a day. She'd pull her shirt off and tug at my hands. Me barely into the place, the door hardly closed. "Let me wash first," I said. She smiled, then unbuttoned her jeans and asked, "Why?"

And in the dark too. Me still so close to the road, my solitary nightmares coming at four in the morning. Gasping, awake, I think I am lying by some highway. I'm so young that the barking dogs are terror, so young that I'm hiding from police, so young that I am scared of the older bums who will beat and rob me. It is raining hard; I'm soaked and cold. But it's only sweat, and the barking dogs are chained down the street, and I'm not a runaway. Instead, I am lying next to a beautiful woman who has told me, "Wake me whenever you want." I am warm and safe, and I reach across the bed's darkness and hold her, my heartbeat going from panic to peace. She calms me, she tells me I am dreaming. She puts her mouth against my ear. She tells me how good things are. She tells me how happy she is. I fall back to sleep, listening in the dark to the whispered plans of our shared life. I wanted nothing else. There should have been nothing else.

I wanted to grow with her. I would meet her parents and impress them with my devotion; this was the plan. We were drunk in the kitchen. Drinking wine from the bottle that we were passing back and forth. She invited friends from her art classes, and it was a simple party. Then she said, "I'll say, Dad, meet Enzi, he v-v-vacuums," and all the fun evaporated because she was laughing and her friends were laughing, and it was hilarious to them.

Chapter 2 - The Lie

The years, as years do, spun me forward. Soon, in these words pulling me towards a confession, I will explain how I changed from an honest laborer into someone else. I learned how to turn my ability with abstract ideas into money, and with that money, I moved away from the drifting hardness of the road. But I still was runaway-lonely. And the money, which would become dirty, was not enough. I should have stopped. But at the deciding moments where I could have done something as simple as ignoring a stranger, or a phone call, I didn't. Blame it on the sidewalk crowds, the starkness of grey buildings in a strange city, or on the rain falling from a Montana sky. Blame it on quiet nights alone.

At three in the morning, the phone rang. I let it go to voicemail and didn't listen to the message until the next day. The call had been from Kaori, a woman I had met at a crowded party more than two months before. Kaori had told me then that she was an artist and had come from Tokyo to Montana to "become famous." Now she was calling me because she was in jail. Her voice message said, "Please. I have no person now. I in the jail. I find your name in my pocket. I wait for you." Nearly six feet tall with red-tinted, jaw-length black hair, I first noticed her because she was standing by herself with her back to the crowd, looking out a window. Then I saw her hands, long and thin, her fingers stained with blue paint.

The people I worked with had brought me to the party, but I was weary from listening to technical talk and money stories. When I saw Kaori, I wanted to stand next to her, next to someone I didn't know. So I went over to where she was. She turned and looked at me for a moment before returning her gaze to the darkness outside. It was the start of September, and outside it was raining. I tried to watch the rain through the darkness. But all I could see - all I was able to pay attention to - was Kaori's reflection. Her eyes were large and dark in the paleness of her face, and she too seemed to be looking at my reflection, looking at me. So, I spoke to her reflection. "You have paint on your hands," I said. "What have you been making?" She didn't answer. She didn't move My eyes relaxed, focusing past the window now and into the darkness. I was about to turn, leave the window, and go back to the kitchen or another crowded room. Suddenly she looked directly at me, her face less than two feet from mine, and said rapidly and with a strong accent, "My boyfriend, he student. He love me. I come to Montana for him. For him I paint. For him I artist. For him I be famous."

I asked her, "Is your boyfriend here?"

She shook her head, a silent 'No,' and turned her gaze back to the window and said quietly, "No, no. He go. He go."

"Who do you know here?" I asked.

She answered, "I come here to find my boyfriend, but he go now. He love me, but he forget me."

Then she continued, "I paint all week for him. I finish this morning." She nodded her face toward her hands, "I bring painting to house this afternoon, but he no take it."

"Your painting," I asked, "what is it of?"

She looked at me quietly and asked, "You understand art?"

I nodded, yes.

"How you know art?" She asked. "You study it?"

"No, I do not paint," I said, "but I think I understand making things, like why we try to show ourselves. But why wouldn't your boyfriend take your painting?"

"You ask what I paint. I made myself," and she put a hand up, pulling her hair above her head, "I paint my hair in colors of how I feel for him. I paint rainbow. I paint sad thing like storm. And he not take it. He say he will not look at it. He close door on me. He have other girlfriend now. He break my heart." She was looking out the window again, and continued speaking without looking at me, "I come here because I knew of party. I think maybe he come here. But he does not come." She looked at me again and said to me, "You understand art? You understand why I trash painting?"

"Trash it?" I asked.

"Yes. Take knife, cut face. Throw painting in can by street."

Her English was beginner-flawed, but her meaning was a song. I remembered when my stutter was strong, and I used a handful of words that would not twist or bounce. She spoke like this, careful with her sounds, precise with her meaning, but with the 'so what' to the syntax that never really matters. I understood her perfectly. I felt nothing was hidden, and I wanted to hear more.

In the world of the lie, in a place where I had been for years, no one is honest, and no one risks weakness. In the world of the lie, people stomp each other with proud complexity, like they are competing for grades in classes, and where stutterers like me are pushed, row-by-row, back until we are pushed out. Even if we understand what matters most.

In these few sentences exchanged with Kaori, I knew that I didn't want to be at the party anymore. I didn't want to listen to anyone else except her. And what I suddenly wanted was to try to save her "trashed" painting.

"Hey," I said, "I don't know you. You don't know me. But will you let me keep that painting for you? Can we find it?"

She didn't answer right away, and when she did, she didn't say 'yes' or 'no.' Instead, she asked, "You have car? You drive me home now? He not come here. I go home."

And without saying anything else, we left.

She lived in an apartment building on Arthur Street, near the University. When I parked next to it, she turned to me and said, "Thank you for drive home." Then she added, "My name is Kaori. Painting in can behind building," she pointed, "I no want to see it again."

She opened the car door and was about to close it when I said, "Wait. Can I see you again? Can I talk with you sometime?"

"No," she answered, "I have boyfriend. He no love me anymore, but I have boyfriend."

"Ok," I said, "But if you do want to talk sometime, or if you want to show me paintings, here, call me," and I wrote down my name and number on a scrap of paper. She took the paper, and without looking at it, shoved it in her coat pocket, closed the car door, and walked into her apartment building.

I waited a few minutes, got out of the car, and went to the back of the building. In the alley, there was a dumpster with a hinged metal cover which I lifted. I looked inside. In the light from the streetlamps, on the top of the garbage, was an abstract portrait of Kaori. It was about three feet square, painted in blues and reds. Her hair was a sprawling rainbow, and her skin was white with highlights of silver. There were two diagonal cuts through the canvas. One went through an eye, and the other across her cheek and through her mouth. I pulled the painting from the dumpster, held it so that its surface was away from the falling rain, then took it to my car and put it in the back seat. It was an oil painting, and some of the paint was still wet. As I drove back to my house, I shook my head and smiled. There was now blue oil paint on my hands.

She didn't know anything about me. She hadn't asked. And because I was sick of the lie, I had written my name and number rather than handing her a business card. I did not think she would call me, but I kept thinking about her. I had taken the painting and hung it on the wall in my bedroom. The two cuts had not ruined anything; rather, they gave an expression to the face that I had seen in Kaori's. Wildness with a hint of desperation.

I was awake two months later, early November, at seven in the morning, listening to the message she had left. I boiled water and made coffee. I listened to the message again. And again. She did not know English well, but she had given me enough words to understand what was happening. I found the number for the county jail, and I called. Yes, they had a girl named Kaori. They also told me that her bail was set at thirty thousand dollars, she was being held for committing four felonies - breaking and entry and three assaults - and that her scheduled court date was two months away. Over the phone, they wouldn't tell me any details of the assaults. And when I asked for specifics about what bail means - having never bailed anyone out of jail - they told me to call a lawyer or a bail bondsman. In the background, there was yelling and noise. The person on the other end of the phone abruptly hung up.

These years in the lie have made me hate lawyers. So I called up a bondsman, the first one listed on Yelp. I told him what I knew, and he explained that I could go to the jail myself and hand over thirty thousand in cash which I might get back if she showed up for her court hearing. Or I could give him three thousand that I will not get back. I asked him why I might lose the thirty thousand even if she made her court hearing, and he explained that the judges often used the posted bail as the fine - in addition to prison time - for people found guilty. "What did she do?" the bondsman asked. I told him I had no idea, and he said, "A Fella could hire a lawyer. Find out." I thanked him for the info and told him I would think over the options, and we ended the call.

I went to work. I read and deleted several messages. I spent a few hours on the phone. It was all politics about who will control things. O'Neill came into my office and complained about work being done in Seattle. He told me that I needed to go there as soon as possible. In the last two weeks, I had already been to SLAM four times. But I said, "Ok," and I went home to take a shower and get some clothes. I caught the afternoon flight, got into a rental car, then into the traffic, spent the night at a motel, and at six the following day - in the dark - went to SLAM and talked with executives most of the day. There was no discussion of what was broken or impossible. Instead, everyone was worried about the auditors that their principal investor had on site. The talk revolved around how we would describe "person-hours" spent on "designated projects." It took hours to get to any point, and even then, I was not sure what I had said or what anyone had said. I caught the evening flight back to Montana and got back to my house near midnight.

All the concrete, the fractured motel sleep of the night before, the day in the glass-palace rooms with whiteboards and assistants, the diagrams and convincing, the ego talk, then the furious freeway traffic in the winter dusk - too many trucks - nothing soft. Ugly machines. Too fast. The airport, the shuttles, into and out of the crowds, back onto a jet. Back. Unlocking my door. It always feels like weeks.

I turned around and walked back outside. In the dark, close by, are mountains. I breathed the cold air deeply. To be stirring a fire someplace up high, counting stars. I went back into my house, where there was no welcome home, which meant it was no home.

It was now a few days since Kaori left her voicemail. In the morning, I went to work and spent hours with O'Neill explaining what went on in Seattle. Then I had to spend hours on the phone with people in London. Then more phone time with people in Seattle, who asked me if I would come back there the next day. Now it was four in the afternoon and already getting dark. A nothing day. A day in the lie.

All of a sudden, I wanted to know what she had done. I picked up the phone and called the bondsman. He remembered me. "We can do it right now," he said, "Meet me at the jail in half an hour with three thousand in cash," and he gave me driving directions.

I left my office and went across the street to the bank and got the money. I then drove down Broadway to the jail. The bondsman was already there. He was dressed like a working cowboy, the boots, the long black coat, and the hat. When he shook my hand, I saw a revolver under the coat, like a cowboy. He asked me for the money. I gave it to him, and he said, "Thanks, I like hundreds."

We went into the lobby where, behind thick glass and through a speaker, a guard asked, "Who is it today?" The bondsman explained, and then we sat and waited for half an hour. He told me again that I wouldn't get my three thousand dollars back, and he had me sign some paper that said if she didn't show up for the court hearing, I would have to pay him more than thirty thousand dollars.

"A Fella trust this gal?" he asked me.

"I really don't even know her," I told him.

He stared at me. He seemed impressed when I handed him the money, and from how I dressed and what I drove, I knew he thought that I didn't have much money. Which was fine. But then he warned me, threatened me, "A Fella needs to make sure she shows up for the hearing. I don't want to be coming after no Fella." He was silent for a while, then said, "Usually I check a bit more to make sure a Fella is good for all the cash, but what the hey, right?" and slapped his knee, like he did this sort of thing all the time. Like he hoped he would have to chase somebody down for a bad debt.

There was a buzzing sound, and a steel door opened, pushing damp and stale air into the waiting area. A jailer came out, escorting Kaori by holding her elbow. She was wearing blue jeans and the coat that she had on that night we met. On her feet, she was wearing orange paper slippers. Her pants and her coat were stained with dark and dried blood. She was looking at the floor, her head bowed, her face hidden by her hair. Both her hands had bandages on them. The right hand had a gauze bandage wrapped about her knuckles, and the left had a bandage near the wrist. The bondsman had Kaori sign some paper too. Kaori did not say anything and did not look up at any of us. Then as we were going out, the jailer said to me, "She can keep those slippers. She wasn't wearing any shoes the night she came in."

Outside, the bondsman shook my hand again, this time letting his coat swing open, so I got a good look at the holster around his waist and the long-barreled pistol. In his free hand, he was holding the papers that Kaori signed. I glanced at them and asked if I could get a receipt for the cash I had given him earlier. He looked at Kaori, then looked back at me, and said, "She's your receipt. You keep your eye on her."

It was dusk outside. The county jail was on the west side of town, near a pork processing plant. The place smelled like bacon, and the knapweed-filled fields surrounding the jail were spotted with scraps of newspaper and other wind-blown trash. Kaori and I were standing next to each other. I looked at her, but she was still looking at the ground. I turned away from the bondsman. I said to Kaori, "This is an ugly place. I'll drive you home."

Neither of us said anything as I made the ten-minute drive from the jail to the University district. When I got to her apartment, I parked and turned off the engine. She was still looking down, and I had not been able to see her face at all. "Here we are," I said, "you're home now." But she didn't talk, and she didn't look up either. Then she said, quietly, "I wait three days for you. I do not know if you get my message."

I didn't say something like, 'Hey, I have almost no idea who you are and no idea of what you have done, so why should I risk who-knows-what to get you out of jail.' Instead, I said, "It was a lot of money."

"How much?" She asked. I told her and I also said - and I am not sure why - that I didn't care about the three thousand that I had given to the bondsman, but I did care that she made it to the court hearing in two months. She nodded, said, "I got it." Then she opened the car door, stood there for a moment, and said to me, "Come inside."

I got out and followed her into her building. Her apartment was on the ground floor. She took a wallet from her pocket and got her key, opened the door, turned on the light, and said, "Please, come." The apartment was one room. There was a kitchen nook in one corner, a bed in the other. The center of the room had a table with one wooden chair. Next to the table was a painter's easel. Leaning against the walls were dozens of paintings, most of the canvases the same size as the one I took from the dumpster.

The place stunk with the smell of rotting food from dishes in the sink, mixed with fumes from the oil paintings. Kaori went to the window and opened it. Then she said to me, "Please," and gestured to the chair. I sat down, and she took out her wallet, asked me how to spell my name, wrote me a check for the money I had given to the bondsman, and handed it to me. I took the check but then asked her, "Didn't they tell you that you could have bailed yourself out? Didn't they explain that if you had money - if this check is good - that you could have called a bondsman yourself?"

She was looking at me. There were dark circles under her eyes. Her lower lip was swollen and cut. Her straight hair was tangled, and wisps of it were curling into one side of her mouth. I looked at her. She was crying. Slow, slow tears in the corners of both her eyes, slow, slow tears down her face.

Then she said, "If no one want me out, then I do not want come out."

"But you don't know me," I said, "We don't know each other at all."

She nodded and said, "You take my painting. In my culture we know without much word."

I still had no idea of what she had done or of who she was. But I said to her, "You need to wash up, change and get some sleep. Is there a shower here?" She nodded 'yes' and pointed to a door that I hadn't noticed. I asked, "Do you want me to leave?" She shook her head fast, no. Stay, she told me. She said, "Please, no leave me alone."

She got some clothing and a towel from a dresser and went into her bathroom. I couldn't stand the stink anymore. I drained the water from the dishes, which got rid of most of the smell right away. She came out of the shower about the same time I was finishing washing the dishes and started to tell me that I shouldn't have cleaned, but I shrugged. She sat down on her bed, and I went back and sat on the chair. "What did you do?" I asked, "What happened?"

"I so sad," she said. Then she lay down and pulled her blankets over herself. "I tell you in the morning."

I got up to go, but she sat up and said rapidly, "No, no, please stay." I went back to the chair and sat down, and she smiled at me. It was the first time I had seen her smile. Then she pulled the blankets up to her face. She had changed the bandages on her hands, replacing the gauze wraps with band-aids. Now she didn't look like a felon. Instead, she looked like a girl from Tokyo, living alone with her paintings. I said, "Ok," and she closed her eyes, sighed several times, shuddered, then seemed to be sleeping.

There was a lamp in the apartment's far corner, near the window, and I turned that on and turned off the overhead light. I paced quietly about the room, looking at the paintings, gently pulling them from where they leaned against each other, one at a time putting them under the lamplight. They weren't like a student's work or from someone whose hands and eyes were trying to kill time. There was a style, a consistent mood between all the paintings. Faces with their eyes closed and figures huddled against walls on the outside of row houses - house after house after house - with tall buildings behind and elevated railroads overhead. Tokyo. The railroad edge of Tokyo, where school children commute four hours a day between their cramped homes and distant schools while their parents work. Same sort of stuff as the rusting oil barrel fringe of Montana towns, the emptiness past the sprawl, but in Tokyo, it was a sanitized and crowded emptiness.

I spent an hour with the paintings and forgot about Kaori, who was sleeping a few feet away. At about seven, I decided to leave, but when I was opening the door, Kaori said, "Don't go." I closed the door and went and sat down on the floor and leaned against the bed.

"Did you sleep?" I asked.

"Yes. But I wake and watch you. You like my art?"

"Much," I said. She put her hand on my shoulder.

"Sleep next to me," she said, and then again, "I so sad."

Maybe because I had been desperate too... I laid down next to her, five hours earlier than I usually try to sleep, and we held each other, two strangers, and our eyes closed. Then I was asleep as if I were drugged and drunk. Roaring trains turned to softness, her breath on my neck, my mouth against the top of her head, dreamless and still.

I woke up alone in Kaori's apartment. I put my shoes on, used the bathroom, then waited. After about a half-hour, I wrote a note asking Kaori to call me, and I left. Instead of going to work, I drove onto the interstate and headed west. I pulled off at the Fish Creek exit, fifty miles from Missoula, then drove about ten miles until I started getting worried about getting stuck if it started snowing. I turned the car around and parked where the road was wide enough for someone to get past. I walked up a south-facing slope until I was out of the dense lodge-pole, to where the land was open and high. After an hour of walking, I made it to the ridgeline. Then I continued uphill for another hour. It was a brilliant late autumn day, warm enough that I didn't need gloves or a hat and cool enough to be comfortable. I sat down and leaned against a large Ponderosa Pine, waited for my breathing to slow back to normal, then took my phone out of my jacket pocket and turned it on. There was a clear view down into the Clark Fork valley, so the phone worked fine. I called the office.

"Where have you been?" Suzzy asked, "You've got a bunch of messages."

"I'm having a slow day," I said, "I'm going to keep working here, from home. Give me anything you think is important, otherwise, I'll deal with phone messages when I next get to the office."

Suzzy said that nothing seemed important, and I thanked her and said that I would be in the next day. Then I turned the phone off. I sprawled out in the sun, lying on the deep layer of pine needles. The warm vanilla-like smell made me feel good. It was silent. No breeze, and too late in the season for insects or birds. I tried to sleep, but couldn't, so I sat up again and took out a small notebook and pencil from my coat pocket and made a list of things I knew for sure about Kaori. I wrote, "Artist. Sad." Then I made another list of questions. I wrote "Get a lawyer? Call the court? Find out where her boyfriend is?" I ended the list with, "Did she try to kill him?"

I laid back on the pine needles, but I couldn't relax, and not only because I wanted to know more about Kaori. I was also thinking about Tsai, someone I had met in Seattle several months before. Since then I had been doing his illegal computer work. Code hacking that I knew could get me put into federal prison.

I sat up and turned to a blank page in my notebook, and at the top, I wrote, "What I Know About T," and made a shortlist on that page. I wrote, "Montana connection? Global networks. Texas drawl. London business."

When we had first met, Tsai introduced himself by sitting down and saying, "Hello Enzi. You and I have a Montana connection." It was a late evening in Seattle, and I had gotten to a café after leaving a dinner meeting with SLAM's chief financial officer. I was going to read for a while before going back to the hotel for the night. But the stranger sat down. I asked what that connection was. He told me that both of his grandfathers had worked "in the Butte, Montana mines." I asked him to tell me more about that, but he waved his hand and said, "Painful time ago." Then he talked briefly about the global financial network that he was involved with, saying that he was a vice president of British Telglomerate. He also said that he had flown up from Houston, Texas, specifically to meet me. When my expression showed surprise, he told me he had followed me from my earlier dinner meeting, saying that he knew the person I had been talking with. He said, "You will see, Enzi, that our world is a small one. I already know about you, and now you will start to learn about me. My name is Tsai."

I closed the notebook, turned the phone on again, and called Tsai. He answered by saying, "Yeah, what?" and I could hear traffic noise.

"Where are you?" I asked.

"Driving," he said, "In Manhattan. It sucks."

"Park," I said.

"When was the last time you tried to find a parking space in New York at five? And where are you? You're not in your office."

I told him. Then he said, "Last time we spoke, you were outside too. Do you ever sit at a desk anymore?"

"Whatever," I said, "What's up? You wanted me to call you."

"You and I need to meet. You did a good job. I need to see you in person. Come to New York. Tomorrow."

"I can't make it," I said.

"Why not?" he asked.

"Personal stuff." Then I added, "Why don't you come here, to Missoula."

He was silent for a while, with only the sound of slow, congested traffic, horns, and wind.

I asked, "Something wrong with you coming here?"

"Yeah, there is something wrong with me coming there. Like maybe I don't want to do the carrying. But you, you have reasons to come to New York, all of which would stand up well under cross-examination. Meet me tomorrow night at eight. Meet me in that deli we both like. The one where they don't serve milk."

"Katz's," I said. Then I asked, "And my personal situation? Do you even want to know why I think I should stay here?"

Tsai said, "Bring your 'situation' with you, Enzi. You are only going to be gone for two days. When you fly back, it will be safer traveling with someone." I was quiet. Then Tsai added, "Bring her with you."

One of the things I noticed about Tsai was that he could correctly guess most of the time, by how well he listened to people talk, underlying reasons. And how he paid attention to what wasn't said. I decided then that it would be good to be in New York and try to bring Kaori. It could help. It could make it easier for me to relax as I checked my bag. Also, Tsai and I were both breaking serious laws and acting like it was clean business, so it would be a bit of a reality touch to have someone with us who was fresh out of jail to remind me of what he and I were risking.

I told him, yes, the personal situation was a girl, and yes, I would come to New York. Then I turned off the phone again and sat and listened to the silence before walking back to my car.

I drove straight to Kaori's, parked, went in, and knocked on her door. She asked who it was, and after I said, "Enzi," she opened the door, but only a few inches.

"Yes?" she asked as if she didn't know who I was or why I was there.

"I'm hungry," I said, "I spent the day outside and haven't eaten anything. Will you come and eat with me?"

"You funny," she said. "You act like we are friends. You should go away. Why should we eat together?"

"Maybe because you are hungry, or maybe because you called me to get you out of jail. I don't know, like, remember me? I was here with you last night?" Then I asked, "Can I come in?"

Then she said, "I go eat with you. But you wait." She closed the door and came out in about a minute, carrying a jacket and a large sketchbook and wearing dark sunglasses, even though there was almost no light in the hallway. I didn't say anything. I walked out of the building, and she followed me, and we got in the car. She said, "I spend all my time in apartment. I should go out. You help me again, even though I tell you go away."

I asked her what kind of food she wanted, and she told me it didn't matter. I started the car and was about to drive south on Arthur when Kaori touched my arm and said, "Please, not go this way. Jim house this way. Turn around. Go other way."

I told her sure and made a U-turn.

A day of walking in the hills and sitting in quiet had given me what it always did, patience. I was in no hurry to ask her who Jim was and was in no hurry to try to find out why she had been in jail. Instead, I was happy to feel hungry and tired but knowing that I would soon be eating good food and would be near this art girl with her dark glasses and sketchbook.

I was content to be quiet, but then she asked me, "What you do today?" We were pulling into the parking lot of a restaurant. I parked and looked at Kaori. "I can't see your eyes," I said, and I reached over and took off her sunglasses. She did not move, did not seem even to blink. It was dark now, and the only light was from the streetlights.

"I left your apartment this morning," I said, "and I drove out of town and up a dirt road. Then I walked for a few hours and thought about you." I said this, speaking like I had been telling myself I must speak – only saying true things – but I still felt, as I looked at her, foolish and thought that she was about to laugh.

But instead, she said, "I have liked to go with you. I sit all day in apartment, like jail, and think about Jim and how he hate me, how he bad for me. I should go walk with you." Then she reached and took the sunglasses from my hand, put them back on, and said, "I no want to see much. Come, we go inside. We eat, then talk," and she got out of the car, carrying her sketchpad, and walked into the restaurant.

We sat down in a booth, she on one side, I on the other. Kaori took off her dark glasses and picked up her menu, and said, "menu hard. Better when visit friend." I didn't understand, but then she explained that it was strange to her that when going to restaurants that she had to decide what to order, but when going to a friend's house, everyone had the same food. She also said, "I think much already today. Not think here."

I got the waiter's attention and asked him, "Could you please bring us whatever is good?" The waiter answered, "Sure," asked a few price questions, and then went back toward the kitchen.

Kaori said, "We play game now. We wait. No talking. Then food comes. Then we have good surprise. Then we eat. Then you ask questions."

I started to say something, and she said, "Shhhh! This is wait time."

So, I waited.

I had sat day after day, month after month, in classrooms where teachers demanded attention to what they could not explain. I would turn my head away from their prattle to look out a window, but then there would be a yell, or sometimes a loud slap on a desk. I had stood by the sides of freeways in the evenings, trying to hitchhike a ride before dark. Holding my thumb out as cars rushed past while the roar of the traffic, often in the rain, mixed with the hiss of thousand-mile loneliness. I had been in rooms with the long tables and the whiteboards and the dry markers. I had tried to understand strutting words that became nothing other than the noise of ego. I knew how to wait.

Sitting quietly with Kaori, it was not a classroom, not a highway-side, not a meeting. It was two people who had noticed each other. The paint on her hands, the moods that she drew, and she had noticed that I had seen her colors and her essential lines between the space.

When the food came, Kaori, smiling, said, "Now we have good surprise," and told me that she had not eaten all day. I said I was hungry too. Then she said to me again, still smiling, "Shhhh! We both only eat now."

I said, "sure, then questions, right?" She nodded but answered again, "Shhhh! Eat!"

When we were both finished, she said to me, still smiling, "Now you ask questions." She then took her sketchpad out from its case and held a pen, poised in her hand.

I thought she wanted some silly game lightness. I looked at her without asking anything. I looked long enough that I saw a seriousness in her eyes that was not hidden by her smile, and since I did not want silliness, I asked, "Kaori, is Jim your boyfriend?"

Then her smile, and the game, was gone. Her eyes showed a bit of widening, a flash of rage. She looked down at the sketch pad and began drawing. After about a minute, and without looking up from her drawing, she answered, "He was my boyfriend. Today I decide that I no have boyfriend now."

"Were you in jail because of him?"

"Yes. Him and Elizabeth. And police. I attack. I bite Jim. I hit police." She kept drawing, not looking at me, and continued, "It raining. I run out of apartment. I forget shoes. I call him. He hang up phone. I call and call. I run to his house. I run in rain."

"Does he live close to you," I asked. "When you asked me not to drive down Arthur, is his house near your apartment?"

"Yes," she said, "It was house of ours. My apartment only for paint. It was my room. It was my bed. It was my window. I stood by window. I in back yard that was my backyard. I could see in window. My candle burning. My bed. My boyfriend. She not right in my bed. She wrong to be on my boyfriend."

Kaori stopped talking and concentrated on the drawing, her arm moving fast and smooth. I said, "You do not need to tell me anything else. I don't need to hear anything that you don't want to say." But she looked up at me and said, "you can see answer here," and she turned the drawing pad toward me.

It was a pencil and ink sketch, all dark except for accents with red and blue ink. The fast lines of three blurred figures in motion. A naked woman being pulled by the hair across the floor by another, barefoot woman, whom I recognized as Kaori by the red in her hair. And a naked man was waving his arms next to the two, his face outlined in blue. Behind them was a large, sliding glass door with the window shattered. Streaks of gray looked like rain. Red marks on Kaori's hands were blood. There was a lit candle next to the bed. There was a bottle of wine, colored blue, next to the candle. Kaori let me look at the drawing for maybe five seconds, then yanked the sketch pad back, ripped the drawing out, crumpled it, and started on another.

"He was drunk," she said, "and he call police when I break window."

"When the police came," I asked, "What happened?"

"Jim put hand on my face, he pull me. I bite his finger. Police put hand on my shoulder. I hit police. Here," she touches her own nose, "Police push me. Put cuffs on me. Elizabeth say I say, 'I kill Elizabeth'. She is liar. Jim drunk. He drink wine. He drunk. Elizabeth was on Jim. That wrong. Jim call police on me. That wrong. It was my window. I pay for big window. It was my big bed. I pay for big bed. I pull Elizabeth to make her leave. Pull out of bed. But she not understand my way. She think I try to kill her. It my blood. It my blood on her hair. It my hand break window. It not her boyfriend. It not her blood. "

She told me all this between rapid breaths, nearly in a whisper, but still, I was left with a feeling that she had been yelling at me. Her English moved back and forth in tense and correctness, but I understood. I was suddenly afraid of her. Afraid of her question-and-answer game. Then she was quiet again and drew in her sketchbook. The waiter returned to our table, and I asked him to bring some wine, whatever he thought was right. I asked Kaori if she wanted some too.

She looked up and said, "I think for self now. I ask easy question now." She asked the waiter, "Do you have Raspberry coolers?"

The waiter said yes, they had wine coolers. Kaori put her dark glasses back on and said again, "Raspberry," a word that was difficult for her to pronounce, and she smiled again and looked for a moment like a high-school girl, absolutely innocent.

The waiter asked her what she was drawing, and she said, "Here, see," and turned the sketchbook toward him. I was watching the waiter's face, wanting to see his reaction to whatever Kaori might show him, but he said, "Very nice," then went back to the kitchen.

I asked her, "What are you drawing now?" and she let me see. It was a sketch of a huge, half-full wine glass in a clearing in a forest. There was a crescent moon in the night sky that was reflected on the surface of the dark wine. Sitting on the base of the glass was a naked woman, her knees up under her chin, her arms wrapped about her legs, and her long hair hanging in front of her face. I was amazed by the drawing, amazed that she drew it in less than ten minutes using nothing except a pencil and a sheet of paper. But it was not her technical ability that touched me. Instead, the simple emotion of the drawing made me shiver for an instant, made me want to hug my tired legs, the way the ghost-like woman in the sketch had done. Emotion that came from a hand to paper, then to my eyes, in a way that no one yet has figured out how to do over the Aether of computers.

She ripped the drawing from the sketchbook, handed it to me, and said, "For rescuing me, this for you." I took the drawing from her as the waiter brought our drinks. She sipped from her cup, giggled, and said, "I like sweet purple drink. I like bars where they have pink drinks and cream that floats. I like straws and little hats. Have you been to Karaoke bar? I sing American song."

I heard all this, but I was looking at the drawing she had given me. I was drinking rain that had fallen from Australian clouds, moved through the earth, up into a vine, and turned into fruit half a world away. I was drinking dark wine that had aged on a ship as it crossed oceans, and mysteriously, stayed delicious. And I was sitting with a girl who had punched a Montana cop in the nose. But who was sipping her sweet purple drink that was spiked with industrial ethanol fermented and distilled from North Dakota corn, but who was also able to show her feelings simply by sketching onto paper. Someone who was able to make me frightened one moment and foolish the next.

"Kaori," I said to her, "I have to go to New York City tomorrow morning. Will you come with me?"

"Why you go New York? I never been there," she said.

"It's a good place," I said. "We can stay in a hotel in the middle of the city. Up high, look at the lights at night. Lots of bars there with sweet drinks. I have a meeting tomorrow evening. Work stuff. Then we can go to galleries."

She took off her dark glasses and asked, "You have job?"

I started to laugh. "Yes," I said, "I have job."

"What kind of job? You don't dress like you have job. You look like student. You have old car."

"Oh," I said, still laughing, "You can't tell what someone does by how they dress."

"In city you have job, you wear tie."

We looked at each other for a while, not speaking. Then I said, "Come with me to New York. I have money, but this isn't Tokyo, and I don't care about ties or cars. Keep showing me your drawings. I want to see what you draw next."

"What you do?" she asked me then, "Why you go New York?"

"Software," I said, "Networks. My job. Come to New York with me, talk with me."

She had finished her wine cooler and said, "I decide. I want another. This." She waved for the waiter, and he brought us more to drink. Then she said, "I don't know computers. But I like talk. What will we talk?"

What do we tell, what stories do we use to show ourselves? Should I have told her about leaving home when I was young? Should I have told this girl who went to karaoke bars in Tokyo about the Canadian plains at night, the thunderheads in the far distance, the silent, flashing lightning? Should I have told her about being so hungry that, waking up, I would cry, no place to go, no one anywhere to talk with? I could also have told her stories about the good things. About rivers and sun-warmed rocks, and the way I found Montana, the first summer. Trout from the Yellowstone River, fires at night, stars in the sky. But I knew she wouldn't want to hear about those things, so I said to her, "I will tell you stories about going up in buildings and finding stairways to the rooftops of skyscrapers, and getting up there where no one is allowed, and you will tell me stories about the buildings in Tokyo."

She asked, "In New York, we go to the roofs?"

I said, "Are you scared of heights?"

"Yes," she said. "When I walk across the bridges I want to jump off. I am scared of myself much then."

"Then we will not go to any roofs..."

"No, no, you do not understand. Take me to places. I will not jump when I am with you. In New York, I will buy you tie. You will look so nice."

None of this made sense. I was driving Kaori home. She was leaning against my shoulder. She said, "I am drunk, but I not call police. Jim calls police. I not call police."

At her apartment, I put her into her bed. "New York tomorrow," she said, "rooftops of skyscrapers. Bars with sweet drinks," and she giggled.

"Yes, New York tomorrow. I will be back here early. You sleep now. I have to go home and pack." I left.

Back at my house, I leaned her sketch against the wall underneath the slashed painting. Then I bought two tickets to LaGuardia. As I was putting dirty socks into a suitcase, I thought about the cash that Tsai would be giving me, and I got scared like I was the one needing someone to keep me from jumping.

Chapter 3 - New York

Six-thirty in the morning, I knocked on Kaori's door, expecting to wake her up, but she was already dressed. She stepped out into the hallway carrying a jacket, a small duffle bag, and a zippered portfolio case. I knew she was not allowed to leave Montana before her court hearing, but I didn't tell her that. Instead, I asked her if she had some ID with her because she would need it to get on the flight. She said she had her passport. Then she locked her door, and we went out, got into the car, and made the seven-mile drive to the airport without talking.

At the airport, I parked in the long-term lot, and we went in and got our boarding passes. I checked my suitcase, and Kaori asked me why I did not have a small bag to carry on the plane. I told her that I liked bringing one bag with enough room to fit whatever I might buy in New York. We then went through security and waited at the gate for our flight.

Scattered details come up like this. Remembering where I left the parking stub on the car's dash. About the way the TSA agent unzipped and looked inside Kaori's portfolio case. Glancing at the sketch pad and pencil sharpeners. I also remembered touching the keys in my pocket. The key to my car. The key to my house. The key to the suitcase. I remembered those things but could not remember what Kaori was doing. I knew she was sitting next to me and that we were both facing large, dark windows. I knew that outside, our flight was parked at the gate where it had been since the night before. But I couldn't remember looking at the plane, and I couldn't remember feeling anything except tired.

During the two-hour flight to Minneapolis and the brief layover, we didn't talk at all. However, on the next flight, to New York, she told me about how children in Tokyo learned to read and write. I took the notebook and pencil from my coat pocket and asked her to teach me some Japanese, and she spent the next two hours - until we landed - writing the phonic sounds for some simple Japanese words. She laughed at my pronunciation. She had me say things like "Tomodachi" and "Neko." Friend and cat. She also taught me to say, "Kitanai furui okami," getting me to pronounce it perfectly before she told me what it meant. "This means, 'I am dirty old wolf,'" she slapped my arm gently. "When you see Tokyo girl at party, you say to her."

"Why should I do such a thing?" I asked.

At first, didn't answer. Then she leaned close to my face, putting her mouth against my ear, and whispered, "Because you like my body. Because maybe I be nasty girl with you." Then she sat back in her seat, and closed her eyes, and was a young woman I didn't know at all.

After landing in New York, we got my suitcase, caught a cab, and went into the city. It was late afternoon. The traffic was absurd. Kaori wore her dark glasses and looked out the cab's window without commenting. The taxi dropped us off at the New York Palace, fifty-five stories of excess. As we walked into the lobby, I asked Kaori if she wanted her own room. She said, "No."

I got an expensive room on the thirty-sixth floor with two large beds. It was still a sterile hotel room to me, but Kaori seemed happy. She turned off the room's lights and stood near the windows. The entire wall was glass. The view was toward downtown, with dusk coming on and a clear sky, with building lights starting to show. I was laying back on one of the beds, my feet on the floor, my arms behind my head. She came over and sat next to me.

"Four days ago I in jail," she said, "and now I am in New York. You need tie. You confuse me."

"I don't need a tie," I said to her. "But I do need to go and meet the person I came here for. Come with me. He is interesting."

"Where you go?" She asked.

"Rough kind of place," I said. "No sweet drinks, but interesting."

"Will you talk about computers?" she asked.

"No. I think we will talk about almost nothing. Maybe we will talk about you. You can tell my friend, his name is 'Tsai,' about the trains and the buildings you showed me in your drawings."

Kaori turned her head away from me and said, in better English than she usually used with me, "I am more than what I draw. You remember what you hear me say. You remember what I show you in art. But I have secrets you have not heard or seen. Maybe I tell your friend my secrets."

I heard Kaori say this, but I was mostly thinking about Tsai, thinking about why I had come to New York. And when Kaori then stood up, picked up her coat, and put her hand out to me, saying, "We go then," I forgot about her, even with her being next to me, even as we held each other's hand and headed to the elevators and the street.

It was a short cab ride to Katz's. Lower Eastside, Houston Street. We changed worlds from excess to grit. Young men leaned against payphones, and there was graffiti on most flat surfaces. We went into the deli, and Tsai was already there, sitting at a table in the corner. He was reading a newspaper but looked up when we walked in the door. He nodded to me and we went to his table. He was wearing an expensive suit. He immediately handed me a briefcase and said, "This is yours."

It is possible I could still have backed away. I once had kicked with my feet and rolled out of my car and lost everything I owned because I did not want to take what was not mine. But in Katz's my hand reached out. Tsai's and my hand momentarily touched. Then I was holding the briefcase, and doing what was wrong.

I introduced Kaori to Tsai. They shook hands, and Kaori said, "Pleased to meet you," and she smiled.

Tsai asked, "Are you hungry? Do you like kosher sandwiches?"

Tsai had a big Texas accent, but all his grandparents had been Chinese immigrants. Then his parents ended up in Austin, where Tsai was born. The briefcase Tsai had handed me was a test, and it contained half a million dollars. He had given me this illegal money in exchange for the security holes I coded into SLAM's global network. Security holes that Tsai had been using for several weeks to steal financial information. It was the first illegal work I had ever done.

Tsai had already explained that I would be getting more. Instead of the cash, we could have easily worked out a way to pay me with something less cumbersome, like crypto, but he had told me that he needed to see how serious I was. "If you will risk checking a suitcase full of cash onto a plane – which will be easy if you have the right attitude – then we can keep working together."

He told me this two months before, during our first meeting at Katz's. When I had balked about getting onto a plane with a suitcase of cash, Tsai said, "I've got a collection of old hundred-dollar bills. The ones that don't have those metal security stripes and fibers. Of course, don't try to carry it on. Make sure to check the stuff. Large suitcases work well. Put the cash into dirty socks. Pretend you are living in a dorm. Save them up for a month. Then travel with someone. Don't worry, that's important, don't worry." He went on, "And when you are home, convert the paper. I like gold bullion coins myself. Take about nine thousand dollars at a time and go to coin dealers. Wear a cowboy hat. Smile a lot. Get the dealers to keep getting more for you, and if you're buying, they don't ask for ID. Then bury the metal in different places. Steep hill slopes on public land where it would be hard to log or build a road are good. I scatter steel and lead shot, you know, shot-gun pellets, all around so that a good-old-boy with a metal detector won't mess up the plans. And keep some kind of map. Have a bit of pirate fun about it all."

"You're serious?" I had asked. He answered, "Why wouldn't I be? I've got coins all over the hills in the desert. Of course, they don't do as well as the S & P, but my wife thinks I'm a rockhound. And I do collect rocks too, by the way. Quartz crystals. Pyrite rocks from mine-tailings. Anything that glitters. I'm especially fond of malachite from near Bisbee." Tsai stared at me for a while. Then he said, in that first meeting, "You and I work in a world of the abstract. But there's no point unless some of what we do is tangible and makes us sweat."

That was two months ago. Now Tsai and Kaori were at the counter together, and Tsai was explaining the food. Pointing at the pastrami and matzo ball soup. He was saying, "There are thousands of expensive places to eat in the city, but only a few like this." The counterman had already tried to hurry them up, saying, "Make up yo' mind, come on now," but it was a joke, there was no one else waiting for service, and the counterman was cutting slices of meat and handing them over the counter so that Kaori could taste the difference between pastrami and corned beef. "Of course, there is no ham here," Tsai said, "Not kosher. And no cheese either since we don't eat meat with milk." Kaori looked at him and asked, "You Jewish?" Tsai laughed and answered, "Of course. I am a Jewish American Chinaman from Texas." But when Kaori cocked her head slightly, Tsai said, "No, no, I'm kidding with you. I'm mostly like all of us, a mixture of everything."

Katz's was bright and square. White linoleum and cafeteria chairs at industrial tables. Tsai, Kaori, and I ate pastrami sandwiches. People came in and out, and outside it was dark, without much noise of traffic. Tsai was enjoying talking with Kaori. He was asking her all the normal questions that I had not. He asked about her family, what her father and mother did, about brothers and sisters. She explained that her father owned a business in Tokyo, and she had one younger sister who still lived at home. She said her mother, "Keeps house."

Tsai asked her what she was doing in America. Kaori said she was living in Montana because "Sky reaches forever. Mountains good for art."

Tsai asked her if she was an artist, and Kaori nodded and said, "Yes. I paint." Then Tsai said he would like to buy a painting from her. "I will buy from you whatever you think is your best," he said, "I will pay you a thousand dollars."

I saw that Kaori was impressed. She told him, "But you have not seen, you do not know if you like."

And Tsai answered, "Enzi has told me that your work is excellent." Then he said, "Come on, let's get out of here, let's go to midtown."

We got up and walked outside. I was carrying the briefcase, and it banged against my legs. I wanted to put it under my shirt. I wanted to make it invisible. I wanted to find an ATM with a slot big enough for a leather briefcase. But instead, I walked behind Tsai and Kaori, who were chatting like close friends, and who walked calmly by the several groups of men leaning against lamp posts and walls. Tsai didn't just go to the curb and wait for a cab or call an Uber. Instead, he took his time, sauntering from the corner of Houston and Ludlow. Kaori turned to me, "Your friend is most nice," she said.

Then Tsai waved his hand, and almost immediately, a cab stopped. We all got in the back seat with Kaori in the middle. Tsai told the driver to take us to the NBC building, and the driver said, "Rockefeller Center," and we were driving.

I had the briefcase in my lap. Kaori asked, "What is in there?" and touched the case. I flinched, and I saw Tsai smile. I looked at him and hoped he was going to say something, but he kept smiling at me, like he was watching to see how I would answer. I still didn't know for sure what was in the briefcase. I was guessing -- right as it turned out -- that it was cash, but I hadn't known for sure. "Work stuff," I said, "Manuals. Papers."

Kaori was okay with that answer, and she turned to Tsai and asked, "Where are we going?"

"Top of the NBC building," he said, "Nice views from there. Nice drinks."

"Can I jump off top?" she asked. I explained to Tsai that Kaori feared heights because they made her want to jump. She slapped my hand and said, "It not true. I not scared when I not alone."

"Then we won't leave you alone," said Tsai.

All the flashing darkness between the passing lights, the car making its hard turns, the noise from the cab horns, everything was confusion. As I had done ever since I was a young kid who became lost in classrooms where the words and the writing moved fast, I went somewhere else that was slow. In the ride from Katz's I went to where it was quiet and to where I had sweat on my face from walking uphill. The sun was shining, and I was trying out an idea. A way to encrypt data streams by doing cyclic redundant checksums on every 1,024 bits of data. Matching each data block against a matrix of set numbers, taking the set of numbers as the operands from the computer's own processor. Making the key to the code be in the computer itself, in the order of its own instruction set. Like a 'book-code', where you can decipher messages only if you have the same edition book as the person who created the code. And by using the computer's own instructions as the key to that code, it would be like hiding valuables in an unlocked drawer next to the big, obvious safe.

Then Kaori pushed her leg against mine, and like the kid in the classroom when the teacher suddenly has called his name, I was back to the noise and the flashing darkness. But I was also next to Kaori.

I liked her legs; I loved her hands. Her smell, the way her red-tinted hair looked in the light which came and went in the cab. But mostly, I wanted to see her paint more. I wanted... I wanted... not what it was that she wanted, and definitely not what Tsai wanted.

Kaori was looking at Tsai. I unfastened the latches on the briefcase and opened it enough to get my hand in. I felt envelopes, letter-sized envelopes, and I took one out and closed the case. Kaori had not turned away from Tsai. I put the envelope in my hip pocket. It felt like a fat wallet back there. It felt good. I pushed my left knee and thigh against Kaori's leg. She giggled slightly and returned the pressure. And maybe that was all I wanted. To feel good and to not be alone.

The cab dropped us off in front of the NBC building, but Tsai pointed to a men's clothing store that was still open, one block down. "You need different clothes to get in," he said to me.

"Then let's go somewhere else," I said.

"Nah," said Tsai, "There's a view up there, and besides, it is the best place for talking."

Kaori nodded at Tsai and said, "He needs tie. He needs look nice like you."

I shrugged, I didn't care, but I followed them down the block and into the store where Tsai found a clerk to help us. In five minutes I had on a dark linen suit with a black cotton shirt and a blue tie. I was laughing then, thinking, "This is silly." But I had the clerk throw out the clothes I had been wearing, and Tsai nodded his approval. When I paid for everything, taking some cash from the envelope that had been in my back pocket, I saw Kaori looking at my hands with an expression that reminded me of how she looked when I bailed her out of jail: face down, hair covering everything, sad. "You do have job," she said to me. And Tsai, not missing anything, put his hand lightly on Kaori's shoulder and said, "Enzi has important job."

We walked back to the NBC building, and we took the express elevator to the Rainbow Room. In the elevator, Kaori leaned against Tsai, looking like she was an older sister, being so much taller than him.

"You are quiet, Enzi," Tsai said to me, "Still waters running deep or are we in a quagmire?"

"Thinking," I answered, "about deep quagmires."

The elevator opened on the sixty-fifth floor. It opened to velvet blackness in a narrow hallway. A man in a tuxedo was standing next to the door of the Rainbow Room. We walked up to him. Tsai asked if we could get an "upper" booth and handed the man a hundred-dollar bill. The man took the bill and said, "I'll see what I can do." He told us to wait and went into the bar. He came back in a minute and said, "Your booth is ready, have a good one." We went into the bar, and a waitress greeted us. She was all smiles, and it was obvious that she had been told about the large tip and expected the same.

Money makes things easy. Clothes and attention from strangers. Stuff. But none of it feels real because there is no work and no ideas. And without the work or ideas, stuff becomes junk. But I was holding the briefcase, and I was wearing the clothes. And I was looking at a view, at the top of an elevator ride, a view that was bought, that took no work, no sweat, to get to.

Take away the money, though, and it became a dark bar.

We were all getting drunk. I had been drinking cold vodka. Tsai was drinking scotch. Kaori had been sipping pink stuff through narrow, blue straws.

We were sitting in a booth that was against a windowless wall. The booth was several feet higher than the rest of the tables, and we had a view directly out the windows behind the bar. The view was of New York City, and it was a clear night. We were higher than most of the other buildings, and we were looking down, instead of up, at a blanket of stars.

I had put the briefcase on the floor against my right leg. Kaori looked at the view and talked with Tsai, who was sitting against her left side. I had mostly been silent. Kaori kept her leg against mine and was holding my hand, so I tried to talk to her with my hand. Stroking her fingers, touching her wrist, turning her hand over, palm up, and putting my hand flat against hers.

The waitress brought us another round, but I gently lifted Kaori's hand before I drank mine. I dipped two of her fingers into the ice-cold vodka. For a moment, she let her fingers linger in the shot glass, then she yanked her hand away, turned from Tsai and looked at me, and said, "What you do? You crazy?" I didn't answer. Instead, I drank the shot and then held the empty glass against the palm of her hand.

She and I looked at each other for a moment. Then I said, "Not everything makes sense. I wanted to taste your fingers, but..." She interrupted me with a laugh, pulled her hand away from mine, but then touched my face. Then she said, "You kiss my fingers, here," and she moved her hand down near my mouth.

We drank more, and I got up and went down to the bar. I got closer to the windows. Tsai and Kaori stayed in the booth. There were not many people, but it was still crowded and had the universal reek of a bar. I looked at the faces in the dark, trying to decide if there was anyone I could like. But it was a money place. The drinks were money. Even the chairs were money. I was standing at the stainless bar, and behind it, a door opened, and the bartender came out carrying a box. For a moment, I could see into a place where I felt like I could belong: the back room, the clutter of a small kitchen. A young man was there leaning back against the steel counter; a white towel draped over his shoulder. He was smiling and was saying something in Spanish - I heard the fragments of a few good words, "Bueno.... hasta...." The bartender's expression changed as the door swung shut behind him. He was back into the room of money and lies, and his face became a mirror. His face became like mine. I looked at the people sitting near me. I looked at their hands. Hands holding drinks, hands on the bar top, hands limp like the bartender's rag that he was now using to wipe up the vodka that I had just spilled.

"No problem," he said to me, "Let me pour you another."

"I'm sorry," I said, "I don't need another. Let me have some water instead."

The bartender replied, "What kind?"

I wanted to say, 'water,' but I caught myself. I remembered where I was, remembered that I was so drunk that I had spilled a drink, and realized that my voice was slurred. So I said, "Any type," and the bartender opened a blue bottle and poured the blue liquid into a glass filled with blue ice cubes. I took a blue bill out of my pocket and handed it to him, and he turned to get change. I said, "Keep it," and he smiled a blue smile and he put the bill in his pocket and asked, "Where you from?"

I wanted to say, "I am from there." And I wanted to point toward the kitchen door, but I didn't want to have to explain anything true. I wanted to say, "There's been a mistake. I am on the wrong side of things." But instead, I pointed to Tsai and Kaori and said, "From up there, that is where I am from." And I walked up to the booth, back to my strangers, back to what I was becoming.

"We are surrounded by chance and also by opportunity," Tsai was saying to Kaori. "Like how I met my wife. I'm not so tall. My wife, though, is tall. Like you," he touched Kaori's head, "but not Asian. It was a hot day, and in Texas, hot days mean a hundred degrees with humidity. I was on my motorcycle on the highway. Houston. Five in the afternoon. Traffic stop and go. Then all stop. Six lanes not going anywhere. There was a classic Mustang next to me, a convertible with the top down. She was driving and had the radio up loud. She had all this blond hair. The car was black. Man, it was perfect. I started talking. You know, about how the traffic jam sucked and the heat. She sort of leaned out the window even though the top was down, and I sat there on my motorcycle. I wasn't wearing a helmet. She said, 'you have nice eyes.' When the traffic started moving again, I gave her a card, and she called me, and we got married a few months later. Never delay. There are no second chances."

Tsai then abruptly said to Kaori, "Okay, Now explain why you are in America. I don't believe it is only because of good sky for art."

I thought Kaori would laugh or ignore him, but instead, she said, "My father wants to go to America when he is boy. But he cannot. He makes me and my sister to study English. He says to study all the time, this important. But all he read is magazine with porn picture. My mother sleep in one bed. My father in other. My father drink beer each night. My mother cry. Sister and I fight. All the time I paint. I plan revenge on father. I will go to America because he did not go. Then I meet college student. American. And he take me from Tokyo. There is nothing else."

Like her hand moving over paper, it was a fast sketch. She had put on her dark glasses again. She looked away from Tsai, looked toward the windows of city lights, the buildings in the night, and she said, "No, there is more. I go to jail because boyfriend stop love me. Then I rescued." She leaned against me. "Now I here, and you buy painting of mine you have not seen. Soon I become famous. You are wrong. I have second chance."

Tsai said, "Tokyo to America to jail to here. You are doing well." He stopped talking and looked at Kaori for a few seconds, then moved his eyes past her and to me. He gave me a look that, in my blue-light drunkenness, said, "We should not be drinking more. We should not be mixing our crime with this girl's fragility."

"You should watch her draw, Tsai. " I said this because I meant it. I wanted Kaori to do something like reach over and take the gold-plated pen that Tsai kept in his shirt pocket, click it, reach for a napkin, then show what she could do. But nothing happened.

I was drunk, and I remember the fragments of conversation. But Tsai suddenly said, as I thought he would from his expression, "We should not talk anymore. We must say goodbye and goodnight."

Kaori was clumsy and had to lean against me in the elevator back down to the street. She had kept a "little umbrella" from a drink of hers. Tsai had become a Zen Buddha, small and calm. He looked like he had always been that way. But I was not fooled even with all the vodka in me. Tsai was forever thinking about complexity. About things as abstract as the space between numbers far past the end of their limits of precision. Or things as hard-wired as the data links at the Cayman Islands. I was going down, down the express elevator, with the tall suicide girl leaning against me. She was trusting me. I felt that in how she was breathing and how she had an arm around my back. But instead of thinking about her, about what was good, I was thinking about Tsai, and how he was controlled by greed, and how I was becoming like him.

Months before, the first time I had been in New York with Tsai, he and I also sat down in Katz's. That first time Tsai had explained to me about the London security market, data connections from there to New York through the Cayman Islands. He explained then how SLAM was a sloppy company that could be exploited. He got me excited because I had started to catch some of his greed and had started to think like him and the other executives at places like British Telglomerate and SLAM. Tsai said, "Business is whatever you can get away with." Then he talked about what he needed, wrapped in engineering words and logic. Tsai had said, "It will be perfect. Some developers in Montana. You, working for SLAM, build the flaws initially, and I will have other people take it from there. No one will know each other. You start the process, make the weakness possible. So we get to have a few moments of head-start on all the rest of the world for the rest of time. It will be big business."

The elevator reached the ground floor before I could think myself out of the sadness that I was falling into. I was in a city. But I looked up, and even though it was only a narrow slit, there was air and sky and a few high stars that had managed to compete against the fallen New York lights. Seeing those stars washed my sadness away -- and I knew where I wanted to go. Instead of words, instead of talking, I wanted to go to the top of a tall building. I wanted to be in the air above the glass and concrete.

Tsai got us a cab, and he said goodbye again. And as I looked out the back window, I saw Tsai walking on the street, strolling deeper into Manhattan.

Then we were back at the hotel. And we were back in our room. I put the briefcase under the bed and said to Kaori, "Come on, let's try to find the roof."

I thought she would not want to leave the room again -- it was about two in the morning - but she surprised me. She said, "Yes, a high place. Now." And like that -- snap, snap -- I was glad I was with her.

Her hands touched and un-touched mine. I was happy, then I was scared, then happy again. She was not a sweet-drink-drunk then. Instead, she was moving like the lines in her sketches, cat-like and ready. Ready for finding a Manhattan rooftop in the middle of a clear night. We went up the stairway, but our way was blocked by a locked door on the fortieth floor. We were both panting because we had run up five flights. She had been holding my hand. We still had fifteen more floors to go. We went back down one flight, and we went through that door, and there was a bar, which was still open, though there were only two or three people there. I looked across the bar to the corner of the building opposite where we were standing. There was another door. We walked to that door. No one noticed or cared about us. We tried the door. And it was unlocked. We walked through the door and closed it behind us. We were in a dim hallway that led behind the bar. We walked down that hallway, and there were several more doors.

I tried all the handles. Most were locked. A closet. Another closet. Then, yes, what I was looking for. A narrow service stairway. Steel stairs. Fluorescent lights. Steep steps. We went up. Fourteen flights. We weren't running anymore, but we were still climbing fast. Then there was a door marked, "No Entry," the door that I was hoping to find. Like a lot of things in forgotten places, it had been left unlocked. It opened with a "whiiissssshh" sound as the pressure difference in the stairway sucked the night air down on us.

We were on the top. Cell antenna masts and ventilation units. I heard Kaori gasp. Not because of the height --- she couldn't see that yet since we had come out of a doorway that had put us roughly in the center of the rooftop --- but she gasped because she knew we were someplace where we were not allowed.

"Someone comes?" she asked, whispering. I put my arm around her, and I said, "I will tell them we are guests in the hotel, and I will say I am sorry, and they will tell us to go back. It would not be much trouble. We did not unlock doors." Then I walked her to the edge.

We were walking on loose gravel that crunched under our feet. There was also the noise from the metal boxes that housed industrial fans. The fans were pushing air to the rooms beneath us. We stepped past these. We also stepped around the antenna masts, and we stepped over the cables that snaked about. There was some light - red, flashing light - from beacons on the antenna masts, but it was mostly dark.

We got close to the building's edge, and the street sounds came up to us like vertical wind. Kaori gasped again. Her knees were against the concrete rail. She leaned over it, looking down. I stepped back a bit, holding her by the waist.

I said, "Sit down." And we both sat so that it was safe, resting our chins on the top of the railing that was only about two feet high. Our faces were next to each other, and both of us were looking straight down onto Madison Avenue. She turned and looked at me. Our foreheads touched. We played tricks with our eyes, moving our heads so that we were looking directly into each other. Her eyes that had no color or shade in the darkness. We moved our heads again, and we kissed while we were still looking into each other's stare. I liked the way she tasted, the alcohol sweetness of her lips. I liked the gravel that I was sitting cross-legged on. There was no bartender to interrupt us. I liked the girl. I liked the city from up high. I leaned my head far back, and there were stars. Light from that place where there is no sadness. I was finally high enough.

She put both her hands on my shoulders. She said, "I do not love you. I am not girlfriend. But I be with you tonight." She lifted her arms behind my head. I put my hands under her shirt, turning them so that both my thumbs were pointing down and my fingertips were touching. I pushed against her, starting near her waist, as she pulled against me. My hands moved up, lifting them briefly over her breasts and out the opening of her shirt. I crossed and closed my hands gently and entirely around her neck. I felt her strong pulse and her breathing. She kept her arms around my head. Then she got to her knees in the gravel, straddled me, sat on my lap, and brought her knees up under her chin. She kicked off her shoes, and her stocking feet rested on my legs. She moved her face again close to mine but far enough back so that I could see the city lights reflected in her wide-open eyes. All those thousands of lights reflected in her darkness. She said again, questioning, "Only one night, yes? You not ask again?"

I moved my head forward, and said, "I will not ask again."

She whispered back to me, "Okay. You do everything tonight. Love me on these stones."

She fell asleep there, on the roof, lying naked on top of me. Not for long, maybe a few minutes. My hands moved slowly over her, touching and remembering, with the gravel underneath my back being a perfect contrast to her perfect smoothness. Then she shuddered, pushed herself up, and put her clothes on. "I cold," she said. And she said, "Get up, Enzi. Take me to room with window and soft bed."

We went back the way we came, through the unlocked service doors and stairways, down to our floor and our room with the wall of windows. We left the lights off and lay together on the bed closest to the windows. It was then four in the morning, and I was no longer drunk, and I was tired. I wanted to go to sleep. But Kaori took off her clothes again and said to me, "Now you be naked," and she pulled off my tie and helped me take off my shirt and my pants. Then she said, "You on your side," and she pushed at me so that I had to turn away from her. I was then curled on my left side with my face toward the windows and my back toward her. Then she said, "Stay. Do not move." I felt her getting off the bed. Then the bathroom light was turned on so that a dim glow filled the main room. I heard her rummaging about, and then she was back on the bed.

Next, instead of feeling anything, I heard her sketching, a soft scratching over the surface of the paper. "I draw you," she said, "I draw man who love me one night only."

I didn't move. I closed my eyes and began to fall asleep, but in a few minutes, I felt Kaori get off the bed, then the bathroom light went off so that it was dark again. I heard her tearing the paper from her sketchbook, then she was back on the bed, and I felt her hand on my shoulder. I started to roll over, but she said, "Please, no move." Then I felt something strange. She was tucking the large sheet of paper from the sketchpad under my shoulder and hip and was wrapping it over my back. She did this, then she laid down against me so that the sketch that I had not yet seen was trapped between us. Then she pulled the blankets over us. I was sore from the roof's gravel, sore from where it had pushed and bruised me through the new linen jacket and shirt. The paper against my back was cool, and it took the sting of the gravel away. Then, as we both fell asleep, our movements caused the paper to make sounds, which mixed with and became my dreams. Dreams of Kaori tearing and crumpling sheets from her sketchbook and throwing them at me. The crumpled drawings hitting more solidly than could be possible, little hard fists beating at my back, beating in time with the code to my heart.

I woke up alone. I woke up to the sound of a hotel maid pounding on the door and yelling, "Housekeeping." We had forgotten to hang the "do not disturb" sign on the door. I shouted, "Come back later," and the maid went and pounded on the next door. My mouth was dry, and my head hurt from the vodka. I got out of bed and looked in the bathroom. She wasn't there. I pulled the briefcase out from under the bed and opened it. The cash was there, along with a new burner, a flip phone. I took the briefcase of cash, and the near-empty suitcase, into the bathroom and locked the door. As the ever-practical Tsai had suggested, I had brought a few dozen pairs of unwashed socks with me. Sitting on the toilet, I distributed the ten-thousand-dollar bundles, putting one or two into each dirty sock, which I then rolled and wrapped into balls.

After finishing with the socks and the cash, I closed both the suitcase and the briefcase and took a long shower. When I came out of the bathroom, Kaori was back in the room. "You must wear clothes," she said to me, turning her face away. "You must not be naked near me," she said, "You and I not be this way." I picked up my clothes. The only clothes I had were the linen ones from the night before, which were now so dirty that I decided I could not wear them.

"I need to call someone and have them go buy me some more clothes," I said, "I can't wear these." I put on one of the thick, white bathrobes provided by the hotel.

I would not have cared about how the clothes looked, even if they had been torn or filthier. Still, I was remembering what Tsai had said about not looking unusual. So I said to Kaori, "You and I wore these out quick, didn't we?"

Looking out the window, she answered me, "I no understand you. You made me drunk. I wake up. I confused you in bed with me. In future, be careful of good clothes." And still, facing away from me, she continued, "You have big luggage. Wear other clothes from your big luggage."

Loneliness mixed with throbbing paranoia. My mood became a mixture of her contrasts. Her love for me the night before. Her apathy for me that morning. And to escape what did not make sense, I tried not to care what Kaori thought of me. I said, "I didn't bring any other 'nice' clothes." I walked over to the closet, and there I found a thick Manhattan Yellow Pages. Probably the only place in the world where yellow pages can still be found. I remembered the name of the men's store from the night before, and I called them. When I asked if they could deliver more clothes if I paid with cash, they said, "No problem, sir."

With cash in Manhattan, everything flows. I told them I had been in the night before and said that I was in a room at the Palace. I read the sizes off the labels, and they said someone would be at my room shortly. This time with two suits and even a few black tee shirts. When done with the men's store, I called room service and ordered two breakfasts.

When I hung up the phone, Kaori, who was standing at the window with her back to me, said, "Now I see you are big-shot. Now you are a stranger. Now I see you not care about art."

I ignored her and stretched back on the bed, and turned on the television with the remote. I was still watching it when half an hour later there was a knock. I let in the room service person and he put the tray of food down on the table that was near the windows. Then I gave him a hundred-dollar tip. He thanked me and flowed out of the room.

All this time, Kaori had been standing by the windows, looking out at the city. I was expecting more of the same coldness from her, so I was surprised when she turned around, sat down in the chair across the table from me, and asked, "What sort?" She lifted the metal covers from the plates. Nodded, smiled, and said, "I like omelet. I like coffee. You take care of me even when I am mad at you. Jim never take care of me when I mad."

I sipped from my coffee. "Did you get mad at Jim a lot?"

"Yes. I did it. Mad when he not listen me. Mad when he not see me. Mad when he not see my meaning."

We ate for a while in silence, then she said, "I most mad when he called police. When I break my window. My big window." Then after a moment said, "I lied. I tell you that Elizabeth was liar. But she not. I the liar. I say, 'I kill you.' I do think I kill her. But in Japanese. Not in English. In English everything I say is not what I feel. In English I be other people. You learn Japanese and you will know me. You will know my secrets."

Kaori stood up from the table and walked back to the wall of windows. She looked out over the city and said, "Tokyo sky not blue. Tokyo sky gray."

I said that New York's sky was often gray as well.

She said, "Tokyo sky seem gray all time. My bedroom Tokyo window, near ground. Only could look up, but not see sky. Too many buildings close. I grow up. I think that sky is always gray." She made a fist, and pounded lightly on the window and said, "I always want to break Tokyo window. Want to hit and hit." She said, "In Montana, in house with Jim, I say, 'We put big window in room,' and we did. I buy. I wake up and look every morning. I remember colors of Montana sky, of flower, of tree. I take memories to my paint place, to apartment, and try to paint color. But all I paint is Tokyo color. Memory of Tokyo window last forever. Gray cover everything."

She sighed, then turned around and came back to the table and the food. "Maybe I go back to Montana and kill Elizabeth. Maybe I go back into jail."

She was smiling like it was a joke, but her hand had picked up a fork and was clenching it tightly enough that her entire arm trembled.

I said to her, "Don't think about hurting anyone. Remember these New York colors."

She said loudly, "I pretend! Okay?" and giggled. "I don't care anymore about window," her voice sounding like a little girl's. She repeated, "I don't care, I don't care," her head leaning first to her left, then to her right, moving with each syllable which she pronounced in a singing lilt.

Then there was another knock on the door, which I was glad to get up and answer.

It was the clothing. $2,463. I paid the man and tipped generously, and then he too flowed away.

I took off the bathrobe and started to put on the new clothes, and as I did, Kaori came up to me, put her hands on me, and said, "Wait. Be naked longer."

"I thought we weren't going to be 'this way.' I thought last night was the only night," I said.

She didn't answer me. Instead, she pulled my hand, leading me to the windows, where she turned away from me again. She faced out over the city and put both her hands flat against the glass at her shoulder level, and said, "You such silly man. You must see more than I say. Love me again. Please."

My sadness, and especially my joy, one moment was solid, but then the next it was empty space. The city, in the brightening daylight, the city in front and underneath us, was waking up from dreams of stars and dreams of promise and was becoming a maze of lies. Less than twenty-four hours in

New York, and I missed Montana terribly. Kaori turned, looked at me over her shoulder, and said, "You kiss me. Now. You must." And her eyes closed, as the blue sky faded into concrete gray.

Chapter 4 - Money

New York City. The morning after the night at the Rainbow Room with Tsai, and after the rooftop with Kaori. She was showering. I called back to Missoula.

My assistant, Suzzy, answered. "Where have you been?" she asked.

"Don't ask. I'll be back in a day or two. Any events?"

She tells me, other than normal messages, there was a "scary one." She tells me that I had been "scheduled" to be in Seattle on Friday, in two days, to meet with the transport coders, the developers at SLAM who are hostile to me.

"That guy, Dave Cheat, he said to tell you that he found things in our code that he doesn't understand and that he doesn't see documented anywhere. So he's pissed that he couldn't reach you."

I thanked her and told her that I would call Dave Cheat soon and ended the phone conversation.

When Kaori came out of the shower, I said, "Let's stay in New York today and go visit art galleries. We can go back to Missoula tomorrow." She smiled.

The hotel concierge jotted down the addresses of several nearby galleries for us to visit, and we walked out into the daytime. It was a fall day. The temperature was perfect. And there was even a breeze that had polished the sky into a bright hue of hope.

I was not wearing a tie. Instead, I had on one of the black tees under the linen jacket, but Kaori still said to me, "You handsome now. We walk to art," and she entwined her right arm with my left, almost like we were happy.

We visited galleries and looked at paintings, drawings, and ceramic vessels on pedestals. Though, the general theme mainly was blank walls and emptiness, which in contrast to the crowded sidewalks was refreshing. We were greeted by people who answered Kaori's questions about media – oil or acrylic, porcelain, or stoneware – and her questions about whom the artists were – local or distant – and she was answered with well-dressed politeness. But the few times I asked about prices, I was answered with enthusiasm.

In one of the galleries, there was a display of small paintings in hand-forged iron frames, which Kaori stood close to and studied and said, "I like." The paintings were abstract and colorful. I asked Kaori if I could buy one for her, and she pointed to the one she was currently looking at and said, "Yes. You can buy," which I did.

We walked more on the streets. I asked Kaori why she liked the painting we had bought, which showed nothing but color, while the art she made was of people and places which I felt told stories. She said, "I do not want to see stories when I look at art. I have own stories. I want other art to say nothing."

And to this, my response was to entwine our arms, as she had done earlier. Almost like we had no secrets.

The evening dusk came quickly, along with the noise of honking cabs and braking trucks. And that, mixing with the expressions of the people on the sidewalks who were leaving for their daily struggle to return home, exhausted us. We went back to the hotel, ordered room service, and ate. Kaori turned on the TV and clicked rapidly between channels for several minutes before turning it off again. "I close eyes now on everything," she said, and I nodded. As I fell asleep, I realized the day had been a rare, almost normal one. Hours without decisions to make or drama to try to forget.

The following day we checked out of the hotel and got a car to the airport. At the ticket counter, I checked the suitcase through to Missoula. The airline agent wrapped an adhesive routing slip around its handle, and I watched as he placed it onto the conveyer belt. It disappeared into the machine-greased bowels of LaGuardia. The briefcase that had held the cash, the one which Tsai had given me in Katz's, I carried. It now contained the burner phone, a paper pad, a pen, and the small painting I had bought. When Kaori and I walked through airport security, the TSA screener took the painting out of the briefcase and scowled at it, probably trying to decide if the heavy frame could have been a danger. But he put it back into the briefcase and let us proceed to our flight.

Was it going to be this easy? I kept thinking that someone would walk up to me and yell, 'Sir! Please stop!' because maybe the suitcase, on its convoluted conveyer ride, had to have gone through some inspection scanner, something tuned to find old bills, a scanner which would then flash for attention. Or maybe it would be a TSA worker who had been told to open every X number of bags and look randomly. With each breath, I felt a pang of anxiety, a feeling that I would soon be trying to explain an impossible reason for soiled socks full of cash. But that didn't happen. Instead, we were on the flight, then in the air.

On the flight, Kaori became curious about me. She asked questions about my 'business.' I spent time trying to explain private Internet networks and computer coding. I found that the more detailed her questions, the less I thought about the suitcase full of cash.

I said, "You know when you use a credit card at a bank machine?"

She nodded.

"You are using a computer network then. One that connects to banks. To the places where money is stored. But there is not much paper money anymore in banks. Almost all money is only numbers on computers. And changing numbers moves the money. The work I do lets people do things with their money. Like buy art from a gallery with a credit card."

She nodded again. She understood.

I continued, "Bank machines, and credit card machines that stores use, don't give many choices of what you can do. They have confusing interfaces. I make easier interfaces so people can use their phones in stores and use bank machines without being confused. I do this and write secret codes too, so money is not stolen."

She asked what the word 'interfaces' meant.

"What is between two places," I said. "Like the beach at the ocean. Waves come up. Then the water washes backward. In one place, there is only water. Further up, there is only dry sand. In between, there is a place where there is sand and water. The wet sand on the beach. That is the 'interface' between the water and the land."

"Interface. I got it," Kaori said.

"Two nights ago," I said, "the drawing you made that you put on my back, that was an interface between us." I had said this hoping that she would tell me what she had done with that sketch. I had not seen it but I wanted to.

"No, that was not interface," she said. "That was art." She smiled, and before I could ask her directly about the sketch, she said, "Talk more about your 'interface' business. Talk more about the work that you do with no tie. Talk about work that is water on sand."

I tried to explain. The parts of code that you see on screens, the buttons, and the words. Places where people enter their names and passwords and choose what they want to have done with their money.

"So, you work for bank?" She asked.

"No," I answered, "Not for a bank, but for a company that makes computer codes – apps – that banks use."

She asked then, "How come you in Montana? How come you not in New York?"

"A friend and I started a company in Montana," I said. We wrote computer codes. Algorithms and apps to make secret codes. Then a big company bought our company. It is what American companies do. They buy small companies then take big credit."

I also told Kaori that when SLAM had offered to buy our company, they wanted to move it to Seattle. But when I told them that I wanted to stay in Montana, they bought us anyway. Then they sent employees to Missoula.

"But I never wanted to be boss," I said, "I never wanted to wear a tie."

She said, "You look nice in tie. But I get now. You write 'secret code.' Sister and I write 'secret code' that our father not know. My father wear tie. Maybe better you just wear you. You be a secret."

Then she leaned her head against my arm and said, "You are like TV last night. I turn you off now and close eyes."

I looked away from Kaori to the darkness that was growing beneath us the further west we flew. Then we were flying over grids of rural roads lit by occasional cars. Towns as clusters of lights. An intersection with neon from a gas station. Then another town. Looking at lights from five miles up usually calmed me, but I couldn't relax.

I was thinking of TSA and getting stopped at the airport after we landed. And I was thinking about having to be in Seattle in two days. In a room with other coders, most of whom had advanced degrees, and all of them resentful of my being self-taught and now being a director at their company.

These would be the coders who had spent a decade building their big-company technology, which now streamed numbers and moved money. I did not know what Dave Cheat's programmers might have discovered in my code, but they could demand explanations that would have to be more than the fluff of what I had said to Kaori. I would not be able to talk about the ocean and sand. Instead, I would have to explain code in specific ways that would make sense. But at the end of every lie, there is no sense. So, I would try to explain my code in confusing ways that would match the expectations of what corporate coders love: the language of complexity. And when language of any type becomes complex enough, chaos merges with the lies and they both hide in confusion.

What I had added to the interface code after O'Neill and after the other Montana programmers had finished with it was not much. A few de-referenced pointers to functions that were hidden in graphic files. The graphics were the buttons and the backgrounds, and the logos on the screens. A graphic file is a three dimensioned grid of numbers. X and Y, and sixty million shades of color to each Z. I had taken some of those Z locations and hidden my code there. My coded numbers had changed the shades of the buttons and logos so slightly that I trusted that no one would notice. But I also had to change the checksums of those graphic files and modify the dates of those checksums. And my illegal work, which Tsai had convinced me to do because I wanted to be convinced to do it, could, of course, be discovered. Just as a suitcase of cash could be found if it was opened. But first, it must be noticed. And had Dave Cheat noticed?

Kaori was sleeping. The grid of lights beneath us had changed, and there was deeper darkness as we flew over mountains. Nearly back to Missoula. I had started thinking about what I was doing and how it would also destroy O'Neill and everyone else who worked in the Missoula office if I were caught.

O'Neill. He and I had in common being self-taught. He and I did not start with code or jargon. We started with juggling. Years ago, I met him as I watched a group of jugglers in a Missoula park. They were tossing clubs between each other, and I watched the patterns and the timing. O'Neill said hello and asked if I juggled. When I said I didn't, he told me that I should learn. We started talking then about moving objects. He said, "Juggling is ordered disorder." And as our talking moved into math and specifics, neither of us had asked the other where, or why, we had learned what we had. But we both talked math and fractals. Things that repeat but are never quite the same. I took out a notebook and drew a sketch and tried to write an equation. O'Neill took my pencil and completed the equation, saying, "Look at it this way."

He was ten years younger than me and was spending the summer traveling across the country with two other jugglers, the three of them doing street performances to make money for travel expenses. He and I then talked about using computers to model vastness. The edge of distant things and how subtle motions could have significant effects, such as how a wrist flick changed the juggling clubs' timing. We talked about the computer languages we each had learned and used. He had a laptop computer in his bag, the screen duct-taped together. He turned it on and showed me the simulation software that he had written. Software that could be used for scrambling information sent between computers in a chaotic way that could be elegantly un-scrambled.

"Throw the data. Then catch the data. I got the idea," O'Neill said, "by thinking how juggling patterns work."

Then I suggested that we could make money with software like that, and he asked, "How?" And that is how we started working together.

His traveling friends went on without him. He and I started a software business in Missoula, writing graphic interfaces and encryption algorithms. Then selling those algorithms over the Internet, first to other programmers, then to banks. O'Neill would say, "They are buying their safety from a clown and a bum."

And I thought, "Is it this simple? I could have started doing this years ago."

Then there were no more lights. Kaori was still sleeping, leaning on my shoulder. We were coming into the Missoula air space, and I was going back and forth between in the gray spaces between near panic and near peace. None of SLAM's technical managers had wanted a little Montana company to create their interfaces. But no one at SLAM had the fast clarity demanded by the rush of rapid competition. Like workers at most large corporations, SLAM's coders were stuck in the comfortable ways of what had always worked for them. As I had explained to Kaori, SLAM had bought my company because big companies buy small companies. That is how they become big. Big companies buy what they need. But that also meant that SLAM's coders were resentful because they hadn't been quick enough. And those resentful coders were looking for what was wrong in the code coming from the small companies. Such as the simple interface software developed in Montana by a juggling clown and a stutterer.

SLAM had found out about O'Neill and me because several of their bank customers had been using our software. An owner at SLAM decided that if they bought our company, SLAM could then jump into competition with other companies immediately. So, we were each paid five million dollars' worth of SLAM's private stock for the interface code and encryption methods we had developed.

But we couldn't sell our stock until SLAM completely integrated our code with their existing network, which we would have to help them do. So, O'Neill and I were then hired by SLAM, given executive job titles, and put in charge of the coders who were sent from Seattle to work with us.

From the beginning, SLAM's technical managers did not like us because it had not been their idea to buy our company. It had been their bosses, the company owners' idea, which the technical managers weren't aware of until after the purchase had happened. Then those managers, Dave Cheat and others, tried to make us work in the same ways as they had. They required structured protocols and layers of project oversight and corporate slowness.

Instead of coding and working on algorithms, I used my new executive title. I moved into the world of business and manipulation. I spent most of my time convincing SLAM's owners to give O'Neill and me control over our work. I explained to the owners of SLAM that to rapidly invent, it was necessary to work without 'corporate' hindrance.

This took a month of flying back and forth between Missoula and Seattle. I would wander the hallways at SLAM, waiting until I 'chanced' into other execs, then talk a bit about Montana - trout fishing or the weather - and ask, "What are you doing for dinner?"

I would eat and drink with the executives, owners, and board members, continuing with stories. Still, always the talk turned to how much wealth was going to faster competitors. Then I would describe ideas for changing SLAM, and they would listen and say things like, "Merrill has put the pressure on us to be flexible. Can you build flexibility for us?"

I would answer, "Yes. Yes." Then for effect, I would draw sketches on napkins and say, "See? This is how it will work."

Sometimes I would scribble part of an equation and say some gibberish, like, "We can calculate the vast audience we will reach. Everyone has a bank account. We will be part of all transactions."

Afterward, when whoever I had been having dinner with would go home, I would catch a ride and find a coffee place up on Capitol Hill. Then, I would sit by myself, reading and drinking coffee for a few hours before going to the airport and catching the midnight flight back to Missoula.

Tsai met me during that time of lobbying after he had followed me to the café in Seattle. Most of what I had started explaining to SLAM was the truth. Even some of the equations. I had wanted my software to be used and becoming a company director would make it much easier for this to happen.

Tsai sought me out because he had first sought out SLAM. He knew about the banks which had been using my software. He viewed SLAM as a company whose employees could not rapidly understand the new financial networks because of their layered and bureaucratic management.

Tsai picked people he needed, and he picked me. And I did what he wanted me to do because I liked being needed. Also, I had been intrigued by the fortune that he said I would get.

"Enzi," Tsai said, "it will be beyond that small word you use all the time. It will be far beyond 'stuff.'" Tsai said this to me, leaning close, during that first meeting in Seattle. He said, "You will still get crumbs, but those crumbs will be from the largest of pies. Three-point one four out to as many numbers as you want."

Tsai explained that he spent time with the technologists of many different world banks. He had seen the encryption algorithms that were used by some of the banks that had been using my software. He explained that he wanted to meet me because he knew that I had created those algorithms.

Tsai said he was impressed with what I had managed to do from a place not known for technology or business. He said he had heard -- telling me this before anyone at SLAM had even hinted of it -- that I would become one of SLAM's directors. "You are their 'entrepreneurial boy'," he said. "You are going to help them raise a few hundred million dollars more in venture money. You have the buzz, buzz. You've got them excited. And that's hard to do. And very, very good."

Tsai made me like him, but he was not specific about what he was after our first meeting. Tsai explained that he was interested in any new technology that I might learn of or develop. Tsai said he had a "personal interest," an interest that did not concern the global company where he worked. He called it that, saying, "The global company," instead of saying BTG. Tsai also asked me if I was interested in making money on the side by doing work for him. "It would be 'serious,'" he said with his Texas drawl, "All cash."

I knew he was talking about breaking laws, but I underestimated the scale of what he wanted. That first meeting in Seattle, I thought all I would be doing for the man from Texas would be letting him peek at new ideas, and I hadn't been scared at all.

About a month after our first meeting, Tsai and I met again, but this time at Katz's in New York. I learned then what Tsai wanted. It was the middle of summer, the sidewalks on Houston Street crowded and sweaty. I remember Tsai saying, "You can tell the tourists in this city by how they look up at the buildings and how they pronounce street names. They come to this street because it is listed as a place to 'see,' but they don't even get the name right. This street is not pronounced like the city in Texas." He taps his fingers on the table and continues, "Fitting in matters most. Become your environment. Say 'yes' to everyone who wants to hear a 'yes.' Never say 'no.' You can always get out of a 'yes' later, but when you say 'no' you will never be asked in again."

Then he explained everything, somehow trusting that I would not turn him in, somehow understanding that I would say 'yes' to him. I had become a Director at SLAM two weeks before, and I was impressed that Tsai had predicted this. Then he said in a hiss with a drawl, "Now you can get close to SLAM's core technology and make changes to it for me. This isn't science fiction; it isn't even complicated. It's mostly bluff and internal politics. No one will get in trouble."

He went on, "SLAM paid you with stock, but they lied to you. They ripped you off. They will never finish integrating your code with theirs because their managers will never let that happen, so you will never be able to cash your stock. They are bullies. But I will pay you cash now. And crypto after you have all the cash you need. No trouble. A few key presses. Done."

Tsai had said the word 'bullies,' and I was back in grade school, my mother dying, my drunk father seldom around. My hair never combed, my clothes not fitting quite right. The wrong styles, the wrong colors. And I stuttered. So, the bullies swarmed and poked and prodded in and out of class. Bullies had taken from me. Bullies had helped push me onto the road. I did not want it to happen again. Tsai had my attention.

I asked Tsai then how much anyone could steal from individual banking transactions. He answered, "Nothing. People keep close tabs on their bank accounts. But we aren't interested in people's bank accounts, no matter how many there may be."

"What are 'we' interested in?" I asked.

Then Tsai made it clear that he wasn't kidding. He wanted me to do something that would help him steal thousands of millions. He wanted me to help him steal billions of dollars. He said, "You and I are interested in something that SLAM doesn't even know about yet. SLAM will get a contract with the London Stock Exchange. My company is already making that deal. I've been working on it for three years. Connecting London with New York. BTG is working on the interface too, but that part will get messed up at the last minute. Like next week. I'll make sure of it. Then I will suggest that we look at SLAM's interface. The part that you and your group have built. British Telglomerate will then have to form an alliance with SLAM. Then the interface between the exchange, the traders, and the rest of the world? Well, you will make it so that I can siphon off information whenever I need it. You just press a few keys."

And that is what happened. SLAM's user interface, my software, merged with the British Telglomerate's and connected with the New York and the London Stock Exchanges. The owners, the lawyers, the investors at SLAM were pleased. My new position at SLAM as a Director was looked on as fortuitous. And the executives who had given me that position had no reason to suspect anything other than ambition on my part.

The suitcase of cash had been taken off the New York to Minneapolis flight and moved to the luggage hold for the flight to Montana. Then it was taken off that flight and it arrived at the revolving carousel inside the Missoula airport after we landed. Then I picked it up and walked outside. And, right up to that relieved breath of cold November mountain air, I had expected to be stopped.

But now Kaori and I were back in Missoula, driving toward town. Kaori was in the front seat; the suitcase was on the back seat. Kaori said to me, "I like New York. I like rooftop. I forget other problem. Happy with you. I teach you a new Japanese word: yama." She pointed toward the dark mountains surrounding the Missoula valley in a ring, "Maybe you take me walking in mountains soon? Like rooftop up there."

Right then, I wanted to give the cash back to Tsai and erase the code I had changed. But every lie is a bent wheel, something that wobbles no matter how many attempts to straighten it and then keeps wobbling right up to its last hard turn.

Chapter 5 - Bearings

Half a million dollars. In my closet in Missoula. I was in bed with an artist. She was not sleeping well. In her sleep, she was talking loudly in Japanese. When I turned on the light, she sat up and stared through me.

I said, "You are having a bad dream. Wake up."

Kaori slapped my hand away, and still in Japanese, started yelling and kicked the covers away. Then she looked about my room and said, in English, "Take me home. This not my place. You not Jim. You not boyfriend."

She would not tell me what she had been dreaming. She would not explain why she was upset. A few hours before, we had come back to Missoula from New York. I had unlocked my front door, put the suitcase full of cash into the hallway closet, turned on the lights, and invited Kaori inside. It was the first time she had been in my place. She walked around, running her hands along the books, and looking at pictures on the walls. Then, she went into my kitchen and opened the fridge. She laughed because of how empty it was.

Then she went into my bedroom and saw her painting, which she had slashed, the one that I had taken from the dumpster behind her apartment. She said, "You put on wall." Then she looked down and saw the sketch that she had drawn for me in the restaurant and said, "This no good," and before I could stop her, she grabbed it and had torn it lengthwise, crumpled, and dropped it. "This not for you," she said. I picked up the ruined sketch from the floor and told her that I had liked it and that she had given it to me. "Why do you do these things?" I asked her. She didn't answer. Instead, she asked me where the bathroom was and said, "I sleep here. Then you take me home."

But now, she was panting, her face damp with cold sweat. She began pulling on her clothes, then pointed up at the slashed painting and said, "I give this to Jim," and she started to take it down from the wall. I asked her to leave it, saying that she had given it to me, and she repeated, "You are not Jim. You are not 'One Love.'"

I tried to talk to her, to calm her. I told her that she had given the painting to me, I asked her to put it down, but she shook her head wildly and yelled, "No. I trash painting. It trash." She kept yelling, and she told me that I knew nothing, that I had nothing in common with her. She said, "I give heart to Jim. I give nothing for you." Then she slumped against the wall, holding the slashed painting in her lap, and said, "I go home. You take me to apartment now. I go home. I go. I never love you."

I drove Kaori to her apartment.

In front of her place, she said, "This no home. This only place to paint." But she got out of the car, took the painting, her travel bag, and portfolio case from the back seat, and walked away.

I drove back to my house.

Instead of trying to go back to sleep, I put on a heavy coat and sat in the backyard. I looked up and thought about driving back to Kaori's apartment. Maybe I could knock on her door and say, "Hey. Let me in." Through her hands, with paper and ink, she had drawn emotion that I could see - so real - but she had not done it for me. I lifted my right arm and pointed at Jupiter and Saturn, close together, low in the Southeast above the lights of town. I moved my hand and traced the outline of the hunter, Orion. The familiar stars, the constant blanket through the years, and as distant as light and time can be. No warmth that my hands could hold.

I stayed in the backyard until the stars began to fade.

It was then Thursday morning, one day before I was scheduled to go to Seattle to meet with Dave Cheat, the manager of SLAM's transport coders.

There wasn't time to even begin figuring out how to convert paper to coins - as Tsai had suggested - but I did not want a half-million illegal dollars in my house. So I drove to a grocery store and bought a dozen quart-sized plastic storage boxes. Then I went back to my house, took the suitcase out of the closet, and emptied it.

I put one of the socks, stuffed with ten thousand dollars, into my dirty clothes hamper. Then I took the rest of the cash out of the socks and packed it into the storage boxes. It all fit neatly in eight boxes, and those fit into my backpack, which I put in the trunk of the car. Next, I checked that the entrenching tool - a folding shovel, the type sold in Army-Navy stores - was also still in the trunk. I then drove up the Rattlesnake Valley to the trailhead.

I walked fast for two hours. I didn't walk on the trail. Instead, I went up the open ridge, on the edge of the lodgepole forest. The November day was warm, with a hint of snow in the air and a feeling that winter would arrive soon. When I got high enough, I looked around. I was absolutely by myself and at least two miles from the nearest road or trail. I checked that the ground was not yet frozen. There was a tall, solitary, spruce tree. I walked to that tree. There was a clear view from near the tree down and across the Missoula valley. I took off the pack. In the front pocket were a few things that were always there: matches, a notebook and pencil, a small first aid kit, a red nylon poncho, and a Brunton - an old-school geologist's pocket transit. I took out the notebook, pencil, and transit. With the transit, I made a compass sighting across the valley to the top of Mount Sentinel, and I wrote down the bearing number in the notebook.

I took two more transit sightings of mountaintops and noted these as well. The first was of Mount Sentinel, the mountain with the large white "M." Then University Peak, with its beacons and radio towers. Then, finally, the third sighting, almost due south, to Bass Peak, with its glass-windowed lookout tower, where I had once hiked to with Helen.

Mid-summer, the one summer Helen and I were together, the summer before she went back to Detroit. She and I got to the top of Bass Peak, to the lookout tower, and climbed the steps. The door to the lookout was unlocked. We went inside. No one was there, but someone was staying there. Dishes were on a counter. A kettle of water on the propane stove was slightly warm. The logbook was open with a notation from earlier in the day. There was also a bed with a sleeping bag. Helen pulled my hand; she sat on the bed. She kissed me. She took her shirt off. "You are nuts," I said," The lookout could come back any moment."

"We will see him before he sees us," Helen said, pointing out the windows that lined all the walls in the lookout. The mountaintop was all stone, wind, and cloud, but no trees. The trail, which we had hiked up, zigzagged on the open ridge for half a mile before it became lost down beneath the curve of the mountainside. "We have to remember to keep looking," she said. Then she took off the rest of her clothes.

We dressed again. Helen took out a drawing tablet and a box of pastels from the daypack. Then she told me that I should do something for her while she was sketching.

"Do something?" I asked, with laughter, "Do you want me to light this stove and cook you lunch with this guy's food since we've used his bed?"

She said, "No, write something for me. This drawing I am starting is for you. I am drawing for you. Write something for me." She tore a blank sheet of paper from her drawing pad and handed it and a pen to me. She said, "Put some words down."

I asked her, "You want me to write to you?" Helen said, and these words I remember more clearly than anything she ever said to me, "Write me a love letter."

Equations and math. Tumbling from observing to saying to doing. I had never written a love letter. Since my mother had died, I never had anyone to share my thoughts with. "I can't write," I said. "I don't know how," I said.

"You can talk," Helen answered, "So you can write."

I looked one more time, down at the rocks, down through the wisps of cloud. Then I looked at the paper.

"Next to me." I wrote. I did not know grammar. And my spelling was phonic, a dropout's. However, I filled the page, and I turned it over and continued. I traced the outline of my left hand. Inside that, I drew a profile of the mountain we had hiked up, Bass Peak, with lines showing a triangle to where we had started hiking. "The steps we have taken," I wrote. Then underneath this, I drew another line, with the word, "Time." I wrote, "Winter. Eastern Montana. Nothing. Then you. Then Spring. Then everything." Under those words, I then wrote a formula for the derivative of an equation with imaginary numbers - the equations that used an impossible answer to the math riddle of 'what is the square root of negative one.' Then I wrote a formula for the slope of a rising curve and another formula for the intersection of those two equations. Then, along the bottom of the outline of my hand, I wrote more words with my dropout's grammar, fragmenting the sentences, like the brevity of math, like the beating of my heart.

I wrote, "The wind. The openness of together."

I wrote, "Helen, you are here."

I wrote, "Your shoulders, your arms moving as you draw."

I wrote, "I am with you. You are with me. The wind knows this."

I wrote, "You are the reason for words. I lean on this word, love."

I wrote, "True."

Helen gave me her drawing, and I then gave Helen my words. She said, "Enzi, you must always carry a notebook with you."

We left the tower as we had found it, leaving before the lookout person returned. Then we hiked back down with no worries of any future.

But I was worrying now, hurrying while still being practical. I took the poncho out of my pack and ripped a long, three-inch-wide strip from it. I reached as high as I could and tied the strip around the spruce tree. I used the transit again, taking a sighting back toward the spot I had walked from. I wrote down that bearing. Then I walked straight along that line, counting my paces. I stopped arbitrarily at seventy-three paces. I was using old technology. I was thinking of the sea and of stars.

I wrote five numbers in my notebook. Each number separated from the other with a period and the last number listed after a colon. "128.119.186.93:73"

The tree with the red ribbon was at the triangulation point of three good memories. The buried cash was seventy-three paces away at a bearing of 93 degrees from the tree. Because I work with technology, someone trying to understand what I had written would probably guess that the numbers were an IP address, a computer number. Even if they knew that the numbers were in some way a direction to hidden cash, they would probably search for a computer that did not exist. Or they might think of GPS numbers. But who would think, "Compass bearings? Paces?"

Memories are the most difficult codes to break.

I started digging. It took me an hour to make a hole large and deep enough for all eight plastic containers. When I was finished, I covered everything up and scattered the remaining dirt and stones. I was content that someone walking directly over the buried containers would not suspect anything. I took one long, careful look back at the spruce tree, seventy-three paces away, with the red ribbon tied to it. Any hiker seeing the tree and the ribbon would think it was nothing more than an old marker left by a hunter. I memorized the tree as well; its shape; its fractal outline against the sky. Even if someone pulled down the ribbon, I would remember this tree.

I swung on my pack, walked back down to the car, drove home, and put everything away. It was then almost five in the afternoon and growing dark. I sent Dave Cheat an email informing him that I would be at his meeting at SLAM the following day.

I went into my bedroom and looked at the wall where Kaori's painting had been hanging. Empty space. I looked at the bed. Empty space.

I closed the blinds and went to my desk. Blank paper. I stared at my phone. I didn't know Kaori's number. The only time she had called me was when she had called from inside the Missoula jail. I went back out and drove to her apartment and rang the doorbell. She opened the door. Her face had no expression. She asked, "What you want?"

"I am going to Seattle tomorrow morning. Business. Come with me? We were in New York yesterday. Come with me to Seattle tomorrow?"

"Why?" She asked. "I fight you. I yell. I take back everything. Why?"

"You are the only true thing I know right now. In Seattle, maybe I will see you draw. I want to watch you draw."

"Seattle," she said, "Good stores in Seattle." Then she said, abruptly, "Yes, I come."

"Great," I said. "I'll buy your ticket, and I'll be here to pick you up at six. Early."

I turned to leave, but she took hold of my sleeve, said, "You come here," and pulled at me.

"I am tired," I said, "I didn't sleep well last night."

"You sleep now," she said. "You sleep with me, now."

"Talk to me," I said, laying down on her narrow bed, "Talk to me in your language."

"Silly man, you not know my language."

I closed my eyes and repeated, "Talk to me." And she did. She spoke quietly with words that I could not understand, the sounds rising and falling, with a rhythm and a pattern that felt right. I fell asleep, again in her bed, again with her.

Then I dreamt of confusion. I was going backward, trying to resolve the past with a chronology that always moved forward. In my dream, I was listening to Helen asking me to find a way to make more money, and in my dream, I was saying that we did not need more. Then Helen was gone, and I was in an empty room saying, over and over again, that I had found money. My dream words became repeated and quieter until I was in the darkness of a sleep which had no time at all.

I woke up in the middle of the night. Dim light was coming in from the alley streetlight outside the window. It was the first time that I had woken up with Kaori still sleeping next to me. The sound of her breathing was slow. Her face, lit in the dimness, was calm, and she was beautiful.

I was tormented with why I wanted to be with Kaori, who was calm one moment and raging the next. But I gave in, my skin against hers, and she murmured and pulled me closer, and nothing else mattered.

Kaori and I had fallen asleep in the early evening, and we both woke up at about five in the morning. I went out to my car and used the phone to get her a ticket. When I came back into her apartment, she was dressed. She had her portfolio case and the same travel bag that she had packed a few days before. Then we drove to my house. She waited while I went inside and got some clothes, which I put in a duffel bag. When I got back into the car, she asked where my "big" luggage was. I told her that I was ready for simpler things. She said, "I make up for you. You dress like student, I dress this way." She was wearing black pants, a loose, white lace blouse, and a long black wool coat. "I dress like business for you," she said.

On the flight, Kaori told me she stayed in the downtown youth hostel called the Green Tortoise when she had been to Seattle before. She said that she liked it because people from all over the world stayed there. She also told me that there were "many fun stores close." She told me this like a young child describing the anticipation of eating cotton candy at a fair.

We were flying over the Cascades, and she asked if Tsai would be in Seattle. I explained that the people I would be meeting in Seattle did not know Tsai and that after the morning meeting, I would have the rest of the day free. She told me then that she would shop "while you work." She said, "You give me money. We pretend love."

Clean clothes. Gentle talk. Someone to wake up with. Maybe relationships would work if they were based on present-tense actions that never looked for a future beyond the next day.

I used to study the night, the stars, while camping next to my car. I learned names from an old star chart that I carried along with my highway maps. Mintaka, in Orion's Belt, the bright left eye of the Bull. Sirius. Vega. Trying for a direction beyond anywhere possible, I looked at distant points of bright light. I wished that I could find out where I was going by navigating by the light that had traveled forever.

On the flight to Seattle, I looked at Kaori and wondered what could happen if I tried to go on with her. She had said to me, "we pretend love," but we were again traveling with each other. The second trip in one week. And she was excited, happy, about being in a city that she knew, and about something so easy as shopping.

I looked at her and tried to forget that she was out on bail with four felony charges and that she had no legal permission to be traveling anywhere. And I tried to forget that the day before, I had buried eleven pounds of hundred-dollar bills in the Rattlesnake Mountains.

"I did it," I said quietly, looking out the window, so quietly that Kaori did not hear me. I said this as Kaori will soon say, "I did. I did it."

And I did take the cash, and I did bury it. So, I must say, true and clear as starlight, "I did it. I stole." And I caused death by doing so.

But this writing, this tense changing back and forth - past and future - hurts and cramps my hand, which holds this pencil. Difficult stories have more tense changes and points of view than the bright stars in a studied night sky. But those truest of points have no shame and no regrets.

In my real tense, at this moment as I'm writing, I wonder if these words will become the coordinates, and the bearings, to a history of what went wrong.

I would like to forget about my part in what has already happened and what, in these words, will soon be told. Death, shame, and regret. Like the entertainment of a wreck on a sharp curve - that wheel which finally wobbled off its axle - the flashing lights say, "slow down and look at what went wrong."

If you have come this far with me, touch what is near to you now, as I touch this paper.

Because of the time change, we had left Missoula at 6:00 am but arrived at 6:05 am. "Five-minute flight," Kaori said. It was so early that I did not think anyone from SLAM would be at the gate. However, when we stepped into the airport, there was Dave Cheat, and he was upset. He didn't say hello. Instead, he said, "I called you several times last night and this morning."

I shrugged and told him that I often left the ringer turned off on my phone.

He asked, "You ever check your messages?"

I said, "My assistant checks all my messages for me."

It was a bad start, but I was a director at the company while he was a manager. If I didn't become confrontational, there was nothing that he could complain about. So I said politely, "I've been busy, Dave, I am sorry that I haven't had time to check with Suzzy, but I am here now, so let's get to work. What did you need to talk about with me last night?"

We were walking down the airport's concourse toward the parking lots. Dave Cheat did not walk fast. He panted, and he sweated. I realized that he had not noticed that Kaori was traveling with me. Instead of stopping to introduce her, I waited until he started to tell me why he had been trying to get in touch with me the night before. Dave had been saying, "There's some odd stuff in your new functions. I told your assistant that you needed to bring hard and electronic copies." But then he stopped talking. I looked over my shoulder, and I said, "Dave, have you met my friend, Kaori? She's going to show me some parts of Seattle that I haven't seen before."

Kaori was wearing her dark glasses. She was carrying her portfolio case, as well as her travel bag, over her right shoulder. She stopped walking and turned to look at Dave. She held out her hand and said, "Pleased to meet you." When she did this, both of her bags slipped off her shoulder, the straps sliding down her arm and pulling the loose blouse she was wearing so that the neck opening exposed a lot of skin. Her bags fell on the ground, and as she stooped to pick them up, Dave said, "Let me get those for you," and Kaori smiled at Dave. His concentration, and anger, were broken.

While Kaori was getting her bags back over her shoulder, I said to Dave, "I have the documentation."

Dave said, "Let's figure things out after we get to the office." As we continued to walk toward his car, he asked Kaori about herself. Kaori explained that she "is artist." Dave Cheat said, "Maybe my company will buy paintings from you for our lobby," and Kaori asked, "You have company?" To which Dave Cheat answered, "I was employee number nine. We have over thirty-five thousand now."

It bothered me that this seemed to impress her. Then it bothered me that I was bothered by what seemed to impress her. So I stopped listening to the two of them talk. Instead, I focused on my plan to hide from a group of software security engineers the software backdoor I had hidden in their global financial network.

Driving downtown to SLAM's office building, Dave asked Kaori where we were staying. She was sitting up front with him, and I was in the back seat. She turned to me with a questioning look. I said, "I think we are going to stay at the Green Tortoise."

Dave said, sarcastically, "Right! That flophouse?"

Kaori answered, "The place good! Many languages. Many adventure!" I watched Dave's shoulders as she said this, and I saw them tense, then sag. Dave had not asked Kaori anything about the Green Tortoise, but his shoulders had shown me that he was intimidated, thinking that he should have known more about a place that was a few blocks from SLAM's glass and steel office tower.

Suddenly I knew how to hide - to obfuscate, that big, Tsai word - what I had done. I knew this because I remembered other meetings and talks with Dave Cheat and his coders. I remembered how their egos made them not ask about what they thought that they should already understand.

The patterns in a person's movements, in their voice, can be as distinct as a tree's fractal outlines against a mountain's fractal slope.

Dave Cheat could not read people. He looked at Kaori and saw her shoulders and stole glances at her midriff. He probably imagined wild sex occurring in the places where she slept. He had jealously watched a company which he helped to build acquire a small company, and he had assumed that I only knew how to make deals and avoid phone calls.

Watching Dave's reaction when Kaori said that the Green Tortoise was "many adventure," had shown me a way that Dave Cheat and his group could be fooled. They would not look closely enough to see something which they had already missed.

Several months before, during one of our covert meetings in New York, Tsai had said to me, "Enzi, a key to the art of war is to be underestimated. It is a great advantage."

Then, as Dave talked to Kaori as he drove, I thought of a way to explain to him and the others what they did not understand. I would point out, almost in truth, what I had done. I would present ideas that they might feel they should already understand. Then, I hoped, their egos would stop further probing.

We turned off First Street onto Pike, went uphill two blocks, and pulled into SLAM's underground parking garage. Dave put his ID into the card reader and found a place to park. He asked Kaori if she would like a tour of the SLAM building before he and I started our meeting. Kaori asked, "Breakfast first?" Dave immediately apologized, saying he forgot how early it was. He said he assumed we had eaten before we left. He stammered. He told Kaori he needed to check with the other waiting people, but he would take the two of us out to breakfast before the meeting. I stayed quiet during all of this. I followed them into the building's elevator, which took us up to SLAM's ground floor. Dave got out there, saying he would meet us back in the lobby. Kaori and I continued up to the executive floor.

I was used to the place, but Kaori was not. Everything was green. The furniture. The floor tiles. On the wall behind the reception desk, there was a drawing of SLAM's logo. It was an open hand holding a green world globe.

We passed a few people, and they all said hello. Kaori said, "Everyone nice. Everyone dress like student." She touched the frame of a painting that was hung in the hallway and said, "Good art. Place not student place."

I nodded and thought to myself, "It is a money place and a place of lies." But I said to Kaori, "Here's my office. We can leave our bags."

Kaori kept her portfolio case slung over her shoulder. "I take this one. I sketch maybe."

We went back to the lobby, where Dave Cheat was waiting.

He said to Kaori, "It's all taken care of. We have an hour before we have to start." Then we went back outside and walked one block to a corner restaurant. We all ordered and ate large breakfasts. "American food," Kaori said. Eggs, pancakes, sausage, and potatoes.

Kaori was telling Dave about Tokyo, the two airports, and how the trains and busses went everywhere. Dave told Kaori that he used to live in Japan and had been stationed in Okinawa. He said to her that he had been in the Army.

I would never have guessed that Dave could have lived in Japan. I would never have thought that Dave could have been in the Army. He was trying out Japanese words with Kaori and said things like "Ohio Gozimous," then, holding a hand against the side of his head, he said, "Moshi mosh," and laughed. Kaori laughed too, and said, "American soldiers come to Tokyo to meet Tokyo girl. American soldiers learn 'Moshi-mosh' so they can call Tokyo girl on phone."

Dave said, "I did try to meet girls, but I was so busy that I never had any luck."

She asked how he was so busy, and he said, "I was a network security programmer. I was monitoring computer usage between our people in Japan and our people back stateside. Worked all hours. Didn't get time to get out much."

Back and forth between calmness and fear, I wondered if I had underestimated Dave and if he had not underestimated me. I became scared again. He had never let on to me that he had been trained in network surveillance by the military. I opened my notebook, and began to write to calm myself down.

Dave asked me, "What are you doing, taking notes?" I turned the notebook to him. I had been writing some pseudo-code, a shorthand notation that coders use to sketch out the framework of projects. My pseudo-code was a drawing. Several boxes with connecting lines. One box had written under it, "check IP paket," another, "DES encrypt," another, "SS Layar." It was a trivial bit of nothing, and it was a nudge to try to ensure that he underestimated me.

"What is that," Dave asked.

I said, "plans for something I have been thinking of." Then I added, using the truth to start moving in the direction of my plan, "I always get nervous before meetings with you and the others. Thinking about code relaxes me."

"He works too hard," Dave said, looking at Kaori. "He also can't spell," and he told me, "Packet has a 'c'. L-a-y-e-r for layer."

I relaxed again. Dave was still Dave. Maybe while in Okinawa he only stared at screens for alerts and thought mostly about his next R&R. I could have told Dave that for every correct spelling of any word, there are numerous incorrect spellings that would still carry the sound of the meaning. But as Sun Tzu had advised, if there is to be war, be underestimated whenever possible. So I didn't say anything.

We went back to SLAM. Kaori decided to walk outside by the Pike Place Market and said she would meet me later. I asked her if she could find the way back to SLAM.

"I find way," she said. She looked upset and added, "I not child. I do everything."

Dave and I walked back to SLAM, and he stopped in the lobby, saying he would wait for me while I went to my office to get the documentation that I had brought.

"Is there a computer in the conference room, one that is hooked up to the company's network?" I asked.

He said there was.

"And a projector?" I asked.

He said there is one of those too. "But you didn't bring anything, did you? You aren't prepared at all."

I knew several things I could say that would upset Dave and escalate his mood back to where it was before he noticed Kaori. But I stayed quiet for a moment and said, "I have done a lot of preparation work for you, and it is already on the SLAM servers. In the files that were checked in several weeks ago."

Dave shrugged and said, "Well, everyone is in there waiting for us. Let's go and get started."

Four hours later, I came out of the meeting with the engineers. We were friends then, Dave Cheat and me. People from the company cafeteria had wheeled up a buffet table. Most of the engineers, including Dave Cheat, headed toward it. I told Dave that I was going to the lobby to wait for Kaori, and he said, "Hey if you two are going out for lunch, can I invite myself along? I would still like to pick your brain a bit more about why you need that recursion." I was going to say to him that I would rather be alone with Kaori, but instead, I said, "Sure, why not?" He would ask me nothing in front of Kaori that would come close to what he had already spent the morning 'picking' at.

Dave and I went down to the lobby, and Kaori was already there sitting in one of the green bean-bag chairs on either end of all the couches. As we walked up to her, she said to us, "Strange business. Fun furniture." Her portfolio case was on the floor, along with a plastic shopping bag from a shop at the Pike Place Market. I reached out my hand to Kaori, and she took it, pulling herself up from the chair. She said, "Found shop that sell drawing pencils, shop that sell charcoal."

Dave had already taken his car keys out of his pocket, and he asked us where we wanted to go to eat. Kaori said that we should go to Uwajimaya, an Asian grocery store in the international district. Dave said, "Thing I like best about Uwajimaya is there is a large parking lot."

On the drive to Uwajimaya, Dave said to Kaori, who was now in the back seat, "Enzi showed us some things today. Smart dude, this Montanan."

Kaori put her hand on my shoulder and gave me a slight squeeze. She didn't realize that I was Dave's boss in the company scheme of things, but I was happy. A feeling beyond content, a safe feeling. I rolled down the window. I put my right hand up onto the roof and tapped along with the music streaming through the car stereo. Dave Cheat's car. A slick, new electronic one. Complete with collision avoidance technology and autopilot control.

Let me be a janitor and a laborer again. Let me be happy poor. The times when it was enough to have any working car, cash for a tank of gas, with enough left over for a bag of groceries. Then driving on a Western highway, the mountains in the distance, and thinking, "That is where I will sleep tonight." Freedom from ambition with the sky opening ahead. True wealth.

But I was not there. I was in Seattle. Dave Cheat was driving, trying to answer Kaori's questions about what I had shown him that was "smart." Dave had started liking me and was now championing my ideas and was trying to describe checksums and data integrity to Kaori. He had repeated one of my meaningless phrases, "Fletcher cyclic redundancy works on data streams," which I had used to convince him and the others that my code had been added for efficiency. I had shown them what my code did, and no one in the room realized that I had been nearly describing the exact way the backdoor worked. Because, in that conference room, Dave and his engineers had been most worried about their egos and not their jobs.

They had found the backdoor that I had added to their network, but they did not understand it, and so they had called me to Seattle to explain. But they had not been thinking that what was confusing them was a security breach. Instead, they thought my changes were mistakes in how I was integrating the new Montana interface code. An interface that they had never wanted to be added to their existing code. In the conference room, I had started by describing the good things that existed in their protocol - code that I had to figure out and understand before adding my backdoor. I talked and drew diagrams to show them that I understood how their code worked and functioned. Dave Cheat and his engineers had started smiling. They saw that I had taken the time to learn and appreciate what they had invented. Invention that SLAM's owners had used to build a company, invention that no other company executives had ever tried to appreciate. And when I got to the code that they could not understand, the code which was my hack, the backdoor to the crime, the only "smart" thing I did was lie.

On the whiteboard, I wrote equations using standard algorithms found in thick books. I demonstrated that I had not done anything unique. Instead, I explained that I only added some basic data recursion checksums to make their network even more robust and to help make sure that the newly added Montana code would not cause new errors. The engineers nodded. Dave said that he had the same books on his shelf.

I knew that my 'obfuscation' could fall apart at any moment. It would have been easy to have shown that the polynomial expansion that I had described was not an error trapping checksum, but instead, it was where I had hidden pointers to tables, which led to other pointers and to the code that I had hidden in graphic files. The hijacking I had architected was partially possible because SLAM's engineers had not learned and thus had not recognized the modern use of pointers to reference abstracted functions. And partly because those same engineers had also turned up their noses at 'cute' graphic interfaces. But the hijacking mainly had been possible because it had been done at the company's weakest point: the place where employees counted their values as small integers - employee number 9, 10, 14, 21 - and were resentful that the larger numbers had stopped paying attention to them when money had begun to flow.

I complimented the engineers and complimented Dave Cheat the most. After a handful of hours, I wasn't worried anymore about anyone from SLAM looking at the backdoor code again. The code I had added would now be accepted as an "efficiency engine." In the meeting, we had also discussed an idea of Dave Cheat's for improving one of SLAM's user interfaces. Something that had nothing to do with why I had been asked to come to Seattle early that morning. I spoke up and agreed with Dave's ideas, offering to let the Montana coders work under the guidance of Seattle management.

What is weak, emphasize as strong. Not sure how to pronounce a word? Then say it loudly with confidence. If technology is outdated, the company board of directors will spend fortunes advertising that their products are the newest and best. To finance the lies, the board will fire a third of the employees, making stock prices go up. Then, before customers disconnect and go to competitors, the company will have made enough money on its lies to buy a startup company with new technology. But, of course, the new technology should not be a backdoor for thieves.

I was in Seattle, and Dave Cheat was driving to Uwajimaya's. My hand was out the window, tapping on the roof in time to the music streaming through the car while financial data streamed through the SLAM network. And British Telglomerate was now using SLAM's network to connect the two largest stock exchanges in the world. Dave Cheat bragged about this and told me that he had heard that SLAM's marketing department was working on another partnership. A deal with Golden Jacks, the brokerage house. Dave Cheat said, "Perspectives and Red Herrings are going to move through what we have done. Cool, right?"

Dave Cheat, employee nine, was so close to what I had done that he was touching it, but he did not feel anything other than ego and pride. "I was impressed," I was saying to Dave. "The way you packetized the standard IP headers and preserved their hierarchy, I think you did that in a way that is unique enough to apply for a patent."

"Close that window," Dave Cheat said, "I can hardly hear you." Then, in the quieter, windless environment, he asked, "You think so?"

As Dave pulled into the parking lot of Uwajimaya, I said, "Absolutely. But of course, patenting secrets gives away the secret." And he and I both laughed.

Dave Cheat, Kaori, and I were about to have a wonderful afternoon. However, in the evening, everything started to collapse.

Chapter 6 - A Green Place

The three of us, Dave Cheat, Kaori, and I, went into Uwajimaya, a grocery store in the international district of Seattle. Kaori had brought her portfolio case with her.

There were long, narrow aisles of packaged food from Japan, Thailand, and China. There was a seafood counter that sold fresh squid and sea urchins. Kaori had picked up a handbasket and was selecting items from the shelves. Kaori said she was going to shop for some "fun snacks" and then we should go to the deli for lunch. I picked up a large bottle of sake. A stairway led upstairs, and I asked Kaori what was there, and she said, "Books." So I told her I would be up there.

The bookstore had nearly as much floor space as the grocery section. There were thousands of books arranged by language. Japanese, Mandarin, Cantonese, Korean. I took books off the shelves and opened them. The words were in a language of pictures, of shapes. I had no idea about any of the meanings, but I liked my feelings when I looked at the characters. I found a book that had no English anywhere on or in it, a book that did not have a bar code. I decided to buy it. I went to the cashier, and I waited in line. On the counter, there was a glass bowl with two-inch square embroidered pillows. I picked one up. It was filled with sand and was meant as a book weight, something to hold the book's pages flat open on a table. It fit well in the palm of my open hand. I tossed it about a foot in the air and let it fall back into my hand. Then I threw it higher and caught it again. The book weights were covered with fabric, and each had different embroidery. Some had words written in Kanji. Some had images of Mount Fuji. Some had birds flying between trees. I picked up another one, tossed, and caught it. When it was my turn at the cashier, I paid for the bottle of sake, the book, and five of the sand-filled book weights. Then I went back downstairs.

I was walking through the isles at Uwajimaya looking for Kaori. The store was crowded with a city mixture of people, old and young. Most were shopping alone. I passed a couple who looked to be in their seventies. The man had one hand on the shopping cart, and his other was at the woman's waist, lightly holding the hem of her blouse. She was reading the label on a tin that she was holding. As I walked past them, she turned to the man and showed him the tin, and they both smiled. She put it into the cart. Moods surged like fast water, like rain with wind, and time twisted as my memories rushed over me again.

I was back with Helen, remembering shopping with her in Missoula at the market on the corner of Broadway and Madison. A market owned by an Italian soldier who was wounded at the start of World War II. He was put on a ship as a prisoner of war and sent across the world from Rome to a POW camp in Missoula. In mid-war, Italy became an ally of the U.S., and he was released. He and the Montana nurse who took care of him got married, and he stayed in Missoula. They opened their store. It was a story explained in a newspaper article, framed and yellowed on the shop's wall.

Helen and I would go into that shop and find cooking oils, cheeses, and bottles of wine. The Italian shop owner would talk with us as we filled our baskets. The owner talked about bread. He explained that the best bread was not from any store. He said we should make our bread by baking it on a flat stone put into the oven and heated hot. Helen picked up a can of anchovies and looked closely at it. She then held it in front of me and put the tin in our basket. The shop owner was saying, "It is simple. You put the dough on the stone. When it is done, you put the olive oil. You put those anchovies. You open that wine. You have a good meal. You have each other."

I did not need cash buried in a hole. "You open that wine. You have a good meal. You have each other." That is what I had. That is what I lost.

In Uwajimaya, I was walking past the couple and their cart. Even though I was still in the store, I opened the bottle of sake that I paid for when I bought the book weights. I took a long drink. Then I screwed the cap back on. After that, I found Kaori and Dave and joined them in line at the deli counter.

We got food from the deli and sat at a table inside and ate. Kaori was eating something she told me was called natto and said, "Stinky beans. I like. You no like."

I unscrewed the sake bottle again and took another hit. Dave and Kaori both looked at me, questioning. I held the bottle out to them and said, "You want some?"

I thought that Dave would warn me about getting kicked out of the place, but he surprised me by reaching out and drinking from the bottle. Then he said, "Your turn," to Kaori. She said, "No legal here," but then changed her mind and said, "So what. Nothing matters," she took the sake, drank, and put the open bottle in the middle of the table.

Kaori saw my bag and asked what I had bought. I showed her. "Book Chinese," she said, "No idea what it says." I told her I liked the way it looked. She nodded and said, "I like book. Small." She was turning the book over in her hands, running her fingertips over the binding. Dave said, with a good mood and smiling, that it was probably an accounting book.

Kaori asked me what else I had bought, and I poured the five book weights onto the table. "Why you buy?" She asked, but before I could answer, Dave Cheat said, "Those be for juggling!" and he scooped all of them off the table, lifted his three-hundred-pound self out of his chair, and was juggling all five weights. Five. Inside Uwajimaya.

I was impressed. Five, not three, five. People in line at the deli counter turned and watched. And while Dave was juggling, he glanced at me and said, "You do know the relationship between juggling and programming, don't you?"

I said I didn't, and he said, "Whatever number you can do, someone watching will always ask, 'Can you do more?' If I am doing three, they will ask, 'can you do four?' And if I do four, they will ask me to do five, then six. On and on." He dropped one of the balls, and all of them fell around him on the floor. He was breathing hard and sat down. I got up and picked up the bags.

"And," I asked, "the relationship to programming?"

Dave said, "Write code that solves a problem. Immediately you are asked to write more. More features. Make it faster. Juggle eleven balls even though eleven is impossible. I guess it can be fun trying."

I looked at Dave Cheat. I knew exactly what he meant. Then, almost to prove it, Kaori said to Dave, "Can you do six?" But he explained that it is easier to juggle seven than six. She said, "Huh?" and he answered her, "Odd, even. Even patterns keep balls in the same hand. Odd numbers pass back and forth." She did not know what he meant, and she reached over and took another drink from the sake bottle. As she was drinking, someone from behind the counter, who had been watching Dave juggle, shouted at us "No! No!" and waved his hand, pointing outside, "Take it there. Please!"

"We have been evicted," Dave said with a genuine smile. The three of us went outside. It was a glorious blue day. I smelled the closeness of the saltwater from the bay. I drank more sake, then handed the bottle to Dave, who also drank before handing the bottle to Kaori. She said, "I will be drunk in daytime," but she drank too. Finally, she asked me, "Can you do? You throw balls in air and catch?"

"Juggle," I said, "Yes, but not so well."

"Juggling should be a requirement of all coders," Dave said, "It should be the first line on a coder's resume. 'I juggle.'"

I suggested that we leave Dave's car in the parking lot and go to the waterfront. So we went over and stood on Fifth Avenue and called an Uber. In fifteen minutes, we were back downtown, near the boats and ferries. We walked to the end of a wooden pier, where there were benches built into the guardrails.

Dave and I tried to teach Kaori how to juggle, but after a few tries, she said, "Too confusing now. Nothing matters now." She picked up her portfolio case and walked over to the railings near the water. She leaned over the railings. I followed her and asked what she was looking at. "Down," she said, "But not far enough." She sat on a bench, unzipped the portfolio case, and took out a large sketchpad. "I will draw," she said. "You juggle."

Dave had walked near the bench, carrying the book weights. He tossed me one and asked, "Pass?" and we started throwing the five weights between each other. He asked me when I had learned to juggle, and I told him that my business partner, O'Neill, taught me. O'Neill said that being able to relax your hands and shoulders was important if you were going to sit hours at a time in front of a computer. Dave nodded in agreement. He told me that he learned to juggle in the Army. He said that he still juggles every day and had gotten good at juggling without getting out of his chair.

I was getting drunk, and the sun was shining, and I laughed out loud, still happy. Dave thought I was laughing at him and said, "In the Army, I also used to run. Hurt my knee, though. Then I gained all this weight."

As we were tossing the book-weights between each other, a man in his early twenties rode up to us on a bicycle. He had a bag slung over his shoulder, and he took it off and dumped a whole pile of juggling clubs by our feet. "You guys do clubs?" he asked.

Dave said, "Sure," so the two of them started passing the white plastic juggling clubs between each other. The guy had long, dreadlocked hair, tattered clothing, and attentive, bright eyes: probably another coder, another technically obsessed worker. "I juggle," at the top of his resume.

I was watching Dave and Dreadlocks juggle, and I sat down cross-legged on the boards, the bottle of sake next to me, Kaori behind me. I talked to Dave as he juggled. I asked him how long he had lived in Seattle. He kept his eyes on the clubs in the air, but he answered. He told me he grew up in Seattle. Again, I was surprised.

Then Dave asked me if I grew up in Montana. I told him that I did not. He asked me what I liked about Montana. I told him that the mountains were good for walking into, for getting away from everyone. He said, "I feel you there." He asked me how I ended up in Montana. I was going to tell him a lie and say I went to college there. Instead, I told him the truth. I said, "I was a run-a-way. Left home, worked all over, but stayed in Montana because of a girl I met there."

He said, still juggling, "I can respect that. But, man, you and I should have talked like this sooner. It would have made everything easier."

I had forgotten how close I was sitting to Kaori as I talked, and she suddenly asked, loudly and with anger, "You had girl before?"

I thought she was totally kidding, but I looked at her, and her face had that same look that I had first seen when she told me about "trashing" her painting. The same wild look I had seen when she woke from her bad dream in my house two nights before. I handed her the bottle of sake, but she didn't reach for it. Dave was not paying attention to us. Dave was busy having fun juggling with Dreadlocks. Kaori asked again, demanding, "You had other girl in Montana?"

"A long time ago," I said.

Kaori had been sketching, but then her hand stopped. She was staring past me, and she said, "Men should only have one. Women should only have one. I will not breath again." She turned her face down toward her sketchpad and furiously moved her hand across it.

I drank more sake, finished the bottle. I asked Kaori if I could see what she was sketching. She shook her head and said, "No."

I stood up and walked to the end of the pier, dropped the empty sake bottle into a trash bin, turned around, and leaned against the rail with my back to the water. Dreadlocks, the other juggler, was riding away on his bicycle. Dave was sitting down on the pier and was talking to Kaori. I was too far away from them to hear what they were saying.

"Other girl in Montana," yes, we should all have just one, we should all move gently from childhood into the arms of a true dream. We should all live in a world where there is no pressure, no failure, and no lies. I felt like walking back over to Kaori, sitting next to her, and watching her hands move on the paper. But, I also felt like being alone.

I turned my back on the city. I looked out over the water. The Olympic Mountains across the bay and in the clouds. The snow and the glaciers up high. There were sea birds in the air. There was wind. A ferry was coming in, perhaps a mile out, probably from Bremerton. I could make out the silhouettes of people standing on the bow. Bow this way. Stern the other. A boat that never made a turn as it went back and forth forever, but always in the right direction. I turned around again, and Dave Cheat was walking toward me. He came up to me and leaned on the railing. "That is one crazy girl there," he said.

"How so?" I asked.

"I asked her how the two of you met, and she told me that you got her out of jail. She said she was in jail because she knife-slashed another girl."

I leaned back, putting my elbows on the railing. I looked at Kaori sitting and sketching by herself. "Some of that sounds right," I said, "I did get her out of jail, but no knife. I don't know why she said that."

Dave nodded and said, "I am toasted. Good stuff. Sakaay. Stronger than it should be."

He was quiet a moment, then he went on, "She's shaking, you know, hands, feet, even her face. Twitching. I don't think she should drink. What is she drawing? She wouldn't let me see."

I told him that I didn't know and that she hadn't shown me either. And I said, "I have seen her when she is upset. I think she will be fine in a few minutes."

Dave said that he should be getting back to work, that he needed to check-in before the other engineers started to leave for the day. "I made everyone come in early," he said, "They were all angry at me for that."

"How come you didn't schedule the meeting for a bit later?" I asked.

He was looking out toward the Olympics. Then he said, "I always thought you and O'Neill were little snots. Something not right about you guys, something tricky. Marketing, hype, 'consulting services for the banking industry.' Selling smiley face crap." He was quiet, and I stayed silent too. Then he went on again, "Might still think that too. But it was good today, that math. And, hey, you are a juggler, right?"

I sighed and said, "Right, but not like you."

"Only because I have this bum knee," he said. "If I didn't, I would be walking around out there," and he pointed to the Olympics, "I would be walking more."

I, too, should have been walking more, spending more time outside, away from the lie. That I took straightforward mathematics and packaged it as 'something new,' and fooled Dave Cheat, fooled the other engineers, was wrong. It was "smiley face crap." Tsai told me that I could do it and take advantage of SLAM's weak understanding of programming. And Tsai had been right, but it was not feeling good.

Dave and I walked over to where Kaori was sitting. She saw us coming and zipped her sketchpad back into the portfolio case. She was no longer shaking. She no longer looked upset. I said that we should go back to SLAM, that Dave needed to go back to work, and that she and I needed to get our bags and find a place to spend the night. From where we were on the pier, It was only a few blocks walk to SLAM, but I remembered Dave's bad knee, and I called another Uber. I asked about Dave's car, and he said he would get a ride back to Uwajimaya. Then Dave told me, "Hope what I said back there was alright to hear." I told him the truth. I said, "it was perfect to hear."

"Hey," Dave asked, "you guys want to meet up later for dinner?"

I should have said 'sure', but instead, I said that Kaori and I had an early flight to catch in the morning. Dave said, "next time then."

After we got our bags from SLAM, we walked down to the corner of Pike and Second and went into the Green Tortoise. She had been silent ever since we left the pier, holding her face in a hard way that I had not seen before. We went into the building and up the stairs to the hostel. As we were coming up to the check-in desk, Kaori said to me, "Separate rooms. I pay mine. You pay yours." Before I could answer her, we were at the counter, and the desk clerk was saying hello to us. Kaori had taken out her passport and said, "I need room. Own room." The clerk glanced at her passport and said, "Konichiwa. Only Japanese I know." Then he told her that a private room is sixty dollars and turned an old-fashioned registration book toward her to fill out and sign.

Then I told him that I needed a room as well, and he asked where I was from, and I said "Montana." He asked me if I had a student ID, and I told him that I didn't. He explained to me that the rooms were only for students or people traveling from other countries. As he told me this, Kaori was walking away from me, heading toward her room with her key.

I told the clerk I understood. I caught up with Kaori, and I asked her, "What is going on?"

She stopped walking, turned to me, and said, "What you mean? I go to my room. You drunk. You go somewhere else. You go find first girl. You stay with her."

I shook my head. I didn't understand anything, but I asked Kaori what room number she was in, and I told her that I would come back later in the evening to see if she wanted to go out for food. She asked me what time the flight departed back to Montana, and I told her that our tickets had us leaving the next afternoon, at two, and that we would get a ride to the airport at noon. She said to me, "You told Dave we leave in morning. You liar. No respect. You come here tomorrow at noon then," and she turned and walked away from me.

I was on the street again. Midafternoon. Drunk. Kaori was a child. I was thinking this as I started to walk up Pike Street. I was going to walk the few miles to Capitol Hill. I would pretend that the traffic noises around me were the wind and the rain and pretend that the concrete and asphalt were the rocks and trees. I would pretend that I was back in Montana, walking up a ridge. She's a child. I walked. She said, 'Other girl, first girl.' I walked, and the sake started to wear off. I began to pay attention, and there were patterns on the sidewalk, patterns to the traffic congestion, patterns between my breathing and the swinging of my arms.

There were patterns to everything, even patterns to chaos.

I walked past the Marriott. I went in and got a room. Then I came back out. I was going to keep walking, but because it was an expensive hotel, there were taxis out front waiting to give rides to the people who hadn't figured out smartphones and Uber. A driver was leaning against his cab, talking excitedly into his phone. He was speaking in a language that I did not think I had heard before, and he nodded to me as I looked at him, and he pointed, questioning, to the back seat of his cab. I got in. He stayed outside talking on his phone for about a minute more. Finally, he got in and said, in a thick accent, "Where to, my friend?"

I asked him if he knew where a good place to get coffee and read was, and he said he did and started driving. I asked him what language he was speaking, and he said, "Somali, the language of my home."

I asked him if he knew other languages too. I could see his face in the rear-view mirror. He said, "Of course. I am alive because I know other languages. I know Somali, Arabic, English, and French. But, of course, I know others too, but not so well."

"You are alive because of your languages?" I asked.

He then told me that he escaped mass killings because he spoke Arabic to border guards and spoke English to Americans. He asked, "You know this book that I am reading now?" And he held up a book so that I could read its cover. "This author says it best. He writes, 'You survive by telling stories.' You, my friend, should read this book." The book he was holding was called "The Reawakening" by an author named Primo Levi.

He put the book back on the front seat and said, "Too long a story how I got here." We had stopped at a red light, and he turned around and looked at me through the cab's open partition window. He was maybe 25 years old, his face bright, his eyes optimistic and brilliant, and he said, "I want to understand the dreams of my girlfriend. She is a wonderful girl. She talks in her sleep, but when she wakes up, she says only little things. She says we must learn each other's language to share dreams. So I am learning Spanish, and she is learning Somali."

The light turned green, and we made it one more block and then were stopped again. He said, into the mirror, to me, "I think it is true, my friend. You live best if you share stories."

We were driving again. He asked me what languages I knew. I told him only English, and the driver said, "Hmmmm." Then I told him that although they were not the same, I knew some computer languages. The cab had stopped in front of a café up near the corner of Olive and Broadway.

I paid the driver through the open partition, and he looked directly at me again and said, "Computers are not people, my friend. You must learn real languages to hear real stories. Computers are machines."

"Listen," I said, leaning forward, "Can I ask you something? Something about a girl?"

He smiled broadly, and he said, "My friend, don't you know that is my most favorite subject. Best talk. Forget all the wars, all the other problems," and he turned the engine of the cab off.

So, I told him about what had happened. My mentioning a girlfriend from years ago upset Kaori and how she had checked into the Green Tortoise by herself. I told him about bailing her out of jail, about going to New York, and how she said that she was 'not with me' but how she slept with me anyway. Finally, I told him about how, earlier in the day, as she was sketching, she was trembling.

The Somalian cab driver - the man of stories and languages - reached through the cab's partition and pushed at my shoulder and said, "My friend, you must not leave this person alone no more. I will drive you back to her now!" Then, without saying anything else and without waiting for me to answer, he turned back to the wheel, started the cab, and drove to the Green Tortoise.

In front of the hostel, he said, "Something, I feel, is wrong."

As I told him about Kaori, he had stopped me often for details, and the story had taken a long time to tell. With the walking I had done earlier, then checking into the Marriot, and then talking, it had been about two hours since I had left Kaori alone. I thanked the cab driver again, handed him some more cash, and went into the hostel.

I went upstairs, walking past the check-in counter without anyone noticing. I went down the hallway to a stairway that I had seen Kaori go up, then went up another flight of steps and into another hallway. It looked like a college dormitory. There were a few people in the hallway talking. Several doors were open, and music was coming from the open doors. I said brief hellos to the people I passed, and I walked to the door with the number Kaori told me was hers. I knocked lightly on her door.

She opened it almost immediately as if she had been standing by the door waiting. She said, looking down at her feet, "Come in." Her voice was thick, lower-pitched than I had heard before. I thought she was doing this to keep quiet so that no one knew that she was sneaking me into the room. So I went in quickly, and she closed the door before I had done more than glanced at her or the room. It was dark. There was no window, and the only light was from two lit candles on the floor.

I told her that I was no longer drunk and that I was sorry I got drunk. She said, "Don't care. Nothing matter."

She was standing by the door, still with her face turned down. I said to her that I'd checked into a hotel up the street, and I asked if she was hungry.

She said, "I never eat again."

My eyes were getting used to the dim light, and I looked around the small room. She had torn about a dozen sheets of paper from the sketchbook, and they were spread out on the floor and the bed. I recognized Kaori's rapid-hand style, the wide, smudged lines of the charcoal mixed with fine details from a pen. The entire floor was covered with sketches.

"You've been working," I said, and I knelt by the closest drawing.

There were three people in the sketch, two were standing, and one was on the ground near them. I thought the sketch was of Dave Cheat and Dreadlocks, with me sitting next to them on the pier. Then I looked closely. One of the standing people was waving an arm upright - there were lines of rapid motion - and in the hand was a knife.

It was a smudged, charcoal drawing of a fight, fine detail frozen in fine, red ink. The person on the floor was in a heap. Red lines trailed along the body and around the feet of the two standing fighters. I recognized that the person holding the knife was Kaori. I pulled another sketch closer to me, into the candlelight. It also showed Kaori holding a knife. A long, broad blade, like the one I had seen in her apartment the time I washed her dishes. In this drawing, she was slashing at the neck of a girl sitting on a bed. One hand held the knife, while the other hand pulled the girl's long hair. The third person, a naked man, knelt on the bed. He was falling toward Kaori and the knife. The drawing showed movement. In the flickering candlelight, I saw that it was Kaori rushing into a room where Jim and Elizabeth had been in bed. In the drawings, I saw her cutting Elizabeth's throat.

"You like?" Kaori asked, her voice thick and strange, "You like what I do to girl who is not first girl, to girl who is not me?"

"No, I do not like," I said, "I do not like these at all."

As I was kneeling, Kaori stepped directly on top of the sketch that I was partially holding, her barefoot tearing the paper. Then, she walked across the other sketches, picked up the furthest from me, and held it up.

"This one. You like?"

It was too dark for me to see the drawing. I said, "I can't see it. Too dark."

She took one step toward me, stood still, and again demanded, "You like?"

"I still can't see it," I said.

Kaori made kind of a crying sound, sort of a quiet scream, and rushed up at me, holding the large sheet of paper in front of her until she pushed into me, knocking me over. She still pushed at me as we were both now on the floor. She was saying, "Look. You look, you see." Then she sat up, and even though I was upset, I sat up too, and took the wrinkled and torn drawing and put it on top of the other ones that I had already seen.

That drawing was of two people - Jim and Elizabeth - having sex. Jim was on his back, and Elizabeth was sitting partially on top of him. The drawing was done entirely in green ink. There was no charcoal, no indication of motion, just fine-lined clarity. Their two faces, though, were both blurred and distorted and were cross-hatched and ugly.

"I don't need to see this," I said and pushed the drawings away.

"This one," Kaori said, getting up and picking up another drawing. I stood up, not wanting to let her run at me again. Instead, she came up to me and held another sketch in front of her, and said again, "Look. This art is me."

The sketch was of the couple, Jim and Elizabeth, lying crumpled on the floor and Kaori about to cut herself. In the sketch, she was holding the knife against her middle.

"You should not be doing this," I said. "This is wrong This is crazy."

"You know wrong? You know crazy?" She demanded.

I didn't know what to do. I said, "Kaori, sit down. Please," and she sat down suddenly and heavily on the floor. Then she started pulling the sketches together into a single pile in front of her.

"I thought today you were drawing us as we juggled," I said. "I thought you were happy today."

"What you know happiness?" She asked. She started tearing at the pile of sketches, ripping corners off, then folding the torn corners into dense triangles.

There was loud music coming through the wall from the next-door room. There was talking from outside in the hallway as several people walked past. I was watching Kaori's hands fold scraps from the drawings, which had become a pile of folded triangles. I could hear her breathing. It had gone from gasping to normal. I could feel my own heartbeat. I could hear the paper as she folded it. I had been standing, not moving, ever since she asked me what I knew of happiness.

Then I said to her, "You can't do this. You can't imagine killing them or yourself."

She didn't look up, but she said, "Only one love."

I felt that she was right, but I knew that she was wrong. So then I said to her, "Come on, forget about them," and I knelt next to her and started to put my arm around her shoulders.

There was a snapping flash, green with pain, and I was instantly nauseous. I thought that she had stabbed me in the face with something. I touched my face, but I didn't feel a wound. Like she did to the cop on the night that she was arrested, she had punched me hard, but I was not built as strongly as that cop. My nose was bleeding heavily. My jaw clenched, my eyes squinted shut, and I couldn't see. I thought that she was going to keep hitting me, maybe actually stab me. I pushed away from her on the floor, rolling over the piles of paper that had been her sketches. I shuffled myself backward until I came against a wall. Then I sat up, both hands covering my face. I tried again to open my eyes, and I was able to, and I was looking at her, and she was sitting, not moving, face down, her arms hugging herself.

I stood up. There wasn't a bathroom, but there was a sink. I walked toward it, keeping my face turned down so that the blood dripped into my hands and not onto my shirt. I turned on the faucet and let the blood drip. My ears were ringing. I pinched my nostrils and turned toward her, not sure what I was going to say or what I would do. She had picked up a candle, moved across the floor, and was sitting by a sketch she had not torn up. I was scared of her, but she was not moving any closer to me. Instead, she was studying the paper, holding the candle above it. There was a drop of my blood near the center of the sketch.

"Sensual," she said. She touched the drop with her finger and picked up a brush that was on the floor. Using my blood, she drew a large character across the charcoal, across the ink. "This means 'Happiness,'" she said, "Kanji."

I was upset. I was afraid. I stayed standing and upset, but something was pulling at me from the sadness of the sketches, which made me want to try to hold Kaori again. I was still pinching my nostrils, and I felt blood pooling inside my sinuses. "I think you broke my nose," I said. "This is not good."

She slid closer to me, against my legs, and she bowed her head down until her face was against the floor. She reached up to me. She touched my hand. Then I was sitting next to her. She lifted her face from the floor and said, "So, so sorry." She cried, and I saw, in the candlelight, her tears dripping down her face. She pushed her face against mine, and there were new flashes of intense pain, but I didn't pull back. Then I was tasting her tears. I let go of my nose, and the blood poured out and dripped onto our lips. She had put both of her hands on my face, and the blood was smearing, and I didn't care. I was lost. And without stories.

"I hit Jim. I no hit you." She said. "I hit Jim, I hit Elizabeth. Stomach is broken. Heart not break. Stomach breaks. Hunger is gone. Sad."

I was crying then for both of us. My face hurt. I got up and went back to the sink. I took off my shirt. I turned the faucet back on. I splashed hot water over my face, on my chest, on my arms. I leaned there, near the running water, until the bleeding stopped.

I stood up straight and turned around. Kaori was still sitting on the floor. In the candlelight, I saw white tracks from her tears through the blood, my blood, on her face.

"You understand?" She asked, "You understand looking at art? You see I kill? You see I will kill me?"

I didn't answer. I was thinking of things like emergency rooms and therapists and trying to figure out what it meant that a girl, who I had been falling in love with had just broken my nose.

Then she asked, "Why you not yell at me for hurting you?" She stood up. She walked to me. We were the same height. It was her eyes again. Maybe mine as well. Falling into each other. But it didn't last. Instead, there was the sound of head-banging music coming from the next room.

"Ugly music next door," I said.

"Green music," she said, "In green place."

"Don't kill yourself," I said. "Don't kill anyone."

"Too late," she said. "I did it. I killed. I did yesterday. Before we slept," and she knelt again, leaning forward so that her face was against the floor, her arms around my feet.

"What?" I asked. "What do you mean?"

She repeated, "I killed. I did it yesterday." She gestured toward the remaining drawings, and she pushed at the pile of the torn ones.

"I did," she said.

I did not understand at all. "When?" I asked.

"Yesterday," she said, "Before you come. Before you ask to go to Seattle. Yesterday. After we back from New York."

I said, "Stop holding onto my feet." I kicked at her. I moved away. I sat down on the bed. She remained kneeling, her face hidden by her dark hair, which was touching the floor. I asked her again because I still did not understand, "When?"

She said, "I say already. Afternoon. I think of Jim all time in New York. I think of him when I was with you." She sat up and said, slowly and clearly, "I no love you. I only love Jim. Only one love."

I didn't say anything, and she continued, "Afternoon. I go to his house. I kept key. I open door. I go in. I go in bedroom. I do what I draw." She waved her arm toward the drawings and the torn paper. Then, still kneeling, she again lowered her face against the floor.

I asked her, "Kaori, why did you go to his house?"

She sat up and looked at me. She turned her head and smiled and said, "Bad music those people listen to. Should tell them turn off." She stood up. She walked over to the sink. She touched her face, looking in the mirror at her reflection, with my blood on her skin. She turned on the water and washed her face, the same as I had done half an hour before. Splashing the water upwards, cupping it, moving her hands.

But nothing was refreshing in what she was doing. Nothing was good about watching her. My face hurt.

She looked at me again. She said, "I want talk to him. I want to tell him about New York. I want to tell him you 'nothing.' I took knife. To show him. Knife from apartment to house. Not to kill. To trash. I go to Jim's house to trash other paintings of mine. I go there to trash what was mine. To trash. To start again."

Then she giggled. Her mouth opened like a yawn, but with laughter coming out. She collapsed on the floor. Her laughter turned to wailing but abruptly stopped. Then she said, "I forget that he no have painting. I forget he gave all back already. I open door with key. I go in. I see wall where painting had been. I see nothing. I walk in house more. I hear good music. It was my music. I go in bedroom. It was my bedroom. Then fast. I trash her because she there. I trash Jim next. He with her again. Then I shower there. It was my shower. Then I go back to apartment, to my paint place.

Then you knock on door. I open. You say we go Seattle. I forget everything. Happy with you. Pretend with you."

I needed to call someone. Or to go somewhere and curl up by myself and find a pattern, some sense. Find some equation out of the awful noise. But, instead, I said, "My face hurts. I need ice." She answered, "I find," and then she left the room.

I blew the candles out. The only light then was from the narrow slit under the door. I found the bed again, and I lay down. The bed was not right to curl up on. It was like a stretcher in a morgue, in a place where there was no window, no sky, no stars, not even any clouds.

A few minutes later, Kaori came back into the room. She held the door open for a moment, looking into the dark room. Then she closed the door and came over to me. "Here," she said, "ice." She was holding a towel that she had filled with ice cubes. "I find machine," she said, "I find towel. All good now."

I held the wrapped ice across the bridge of my nose and against my closed eyes. She pushed at me and said, "move," and I slid over until I was against the wall. She lay down next to me. She pulled the bed's covers over us. I knew I should not have been there. I worried that she would hurt me more, that she might even kill me. I also thought that she might kill herself if I slept. From what she had shown me, the sketches, and what she had said, those were real worries. Then she said to me, whispering, "Be with me now. I will be 'other girl,' you will be 'other boy.' We close our eyes in this green place. We pretend."

Crazy is crazy, but lonely is lonely. I do not know which is the saddest.

I wanted to be anywhere else. I did not want to be with Kaori. I did not want to be in the room with her. It hurt to talk. It hurt to breathe. And with the swelling or the coldness from the ice, there was a sudden twitch, a tic, that went up each of my cheekbones to the corners of my eyes. I wanted to walk or run, sleep, and wake up somewhere else. But instead, in the darkness, we found each other again. So I said, to the darkness, not to Kaori, "Everything now is a lie."

The ice melted, and the water ran through the towel and soaked the pillow under my head. The next-door music finally stopped. Kaori was sleeping against me.

Then it was morning. I could tell because I had been sleeping. I could tell because conversations coming from out in the hallway had woken me.

I got off the bed and went to the sink. I turned the light on. Both of my eyes were blackened, and the bridge of my nose was swollen. The dead blood under my skin was already turning an ugly tinge of green.

Kaori woke up and walked over to me. We looked at each other's reflections in the mirror. She said, "No more crying. No more hit. No more kill."

I asked her reflection, "Nothing else bad? No killing 'self?'" She didn't say anything.

We left the Green Tortoise and went outside. It was dawn. We walked to the Marriott, where I had checked in the evening before. When we went in, the doorman looked at my face and the dried blood on my shirt and asked if we were guests. I showed him my keycard. Then Kaori and I went up the elevators to my room. Inside the room, I took off my clothes, went into the bathroom, turned on the shower, and sat down in the tub, leaving the drain plug in. The bath started to fill with hot water, and the room filled with steam. Kaori came in and pulled the shower curtain back, and climbed into the tub with me. She said, "We take bus now."

I said to her, "No, we can still fly. We can get on the afternoon flight."

She said, "I no understand."

I said, "We don't need to take a bus."

She giggled. "No," and she moved and strained her mouth and said, "I say bath. You hear 'bus.'"

She splashed water on me. No paint on her hands now. No reason to understand more than there was. She had touched me by how well she showed her feelings - the rapid clarity of emotional talent - but what I was seeing now was dreadful. In the bath, she poured shampoo in her hands and washed her hair. Some of her red hair tinting stained the soap with the faintest of colors. She rinsed her hair, and she opened her eyes, giggled again, and said, "You like bus with me?" She held one of her legs up above the bathwater, lightly pushing me in the chest with her foot. Both of her arms were wrapped around her other leg, pulling her knee close to her face. She said, "We forget everything. Play now in bus. Forget."

I wanted to forget. I hoped that Kaori had made up her story, that she had imagined, nightmared, then drawn. I started to reach to her but stopped before touching her. I was thinking that, in Missoula, she could not have killed two people and then, an hour later, pulled me into her apartment and to her bed. I was also thinking that she could not have broken my nose and then been trying to tease me with her accent and her body. But that is what she did, and that is what she was trying to do.

I got out of the bath, got a clean shirt from my duffle, then dressed.

There was no eating, no talking. I checked out of the Marriott. She carried her bag and her portfolio of sorrows. I carried my duffle. I remember the nylon strap that was over my shoulder and walking up Pike Street. I remember looking at the traffic lights, noticing how they switched from yellow to red in a timed order. I remember people on the sidewalk, their shoes especially. I remember the laces too, and the way they were tied with bows or with ragged knots. But I do not remember getting into a car, though I do remember being in one. I was looking down at my shoelaces, and I remember thinking about the night before, about Kaori's hands moving rapidly, and the tearing and the folding. I remember each of the drawings, the solid lines, and the blurred ones. In the drawings, the girl who was slashed, her eyes were open, and her look was of terror, but the boy's eyes looked dreamy and calm. The space between the ink showed the knife steel. The darkness became the wooden handle in Kaori's hand. I can remember all of this, but I could not remember when I tied my shoes. I cannot remember asking the Uber driver to take us to the airport. I cannot remember Kaori there beside me. And I cannot remember arriving back in Missoula. But the events that happened after we got off the flight, the events accelerating my words into the immediate tense of now, I remember perfectly.

Chapter 7 - Pascal

Kaori told me that she had killed her ex-boyfriend as well as his new girlfriend. She said she slashed them both with a kitchen knife as they were having sex. She drew sketches, which she showed me the previous night in The Green Tortoise hostel. When I told her that I did not want to look at the drawings, she hit me in the face. I think that she broke my nose. If she told me the truth, then as she was murdering her ex-boyfriend and his new girlfriend, I was burying the stolen cash. Right after that, I had gone to Kaori's apartment and had sex with her without knowing what she had done.

Our flight from Seattle landed in Missoula. Kaori and I walked out of the airport and got into my car. Kaori said to me, "You so silent."

I didn't answer her.

I drove back toward town. It was late in the afternoon, and the air was cold. Winter was knocking on the sky. I got to Kaori's apartment and parked, but left the engine running. She asked me, "What you do now? What I do?"

I looked at her. The portfolio case that she was holding in her lap was huge. I touched Kaori's hand. I said, "Go inside. Cook yourself some food. Eat. I need to have someone look at my nose. See if there is something they can give me, some drugs or something."

"I hurt you," she said, her head bowing down, her long hair covering her face.

I wanted to yell at her, but instead, I quietly asked, "Kaori, did you kill Jim and Elizabeth?"

She looked up at me. There was no flinch, no rapid eye blinks, no tremble in her hand. Instead, she calmly said, "Yes. He mine. She wrong to be there."

As she said this to me, I remembered how the last sketch she showed me, which she forced me to look at by pushing it at my face while my nose was bleeding heavily, was a sketch of her killing herself.

I turned the car engine off. I said, "Ask me to come in with you, and I'll get you started on cooking some food."

She smiled then, nodded her head, and said, "Yes," and we got out of the car and went inside.

I put rice in the rice cooker. Then, I filled the tea kettle with water and put that on the stove.

Her painting easel in the center of the room was empty. So I asked her, "Do you have any blank canvases? Can I watch you start a new painting? I have seen you sketch, but I have never seen you paint."

She nodded and got a blank canvas stretched on a wooden frame and put it on the easel. Then, she asked, "What I paint for you?"

I said, "Paint how you feel now."

She took a tube of black oil paint and squeezed some of it directly onto the center of the canvas. She picked up a long-handled brush and touched its hairs lightly into the paint, then moved the brush diagonally up the canvas, leaving a thin, black line that faded into wisps of gray. She took another tube and squeezed a dab of orange paint near where the first line ended. She put a dab of red paint next to that. She used the same brush, mixing the two colors into the black paint that remained on the brush into a deep, golden red.

I had expected blood and pain. Instead, the canvas where her hand had moved became an evening sky.

She poured some turpentine into a container on the easel's tray. She rinsed the brush. She picked up a wooden palette and another tube of paint. She put paint onto the palette. Then she put another dab of paint from another tube on the palette. She used the brush to stir a new color. Then, her hand went to the canvas, where she touched and smoothed the black paint with a fingertip. Then she touched the brush, then touched the canvas again. She put her hand in the turpentine. She wiped her hand on her shirt. She moved the brush again, and there was a tree, then another tree, then a grove of trees.

She made a new color. She wiped her hand on her shirt again. The white, lace shirt that she was wearing in Seattle. I saw that the oil paint had gone through the fabric and was staining her skin.

She was still painting. The trees became leafed, the foliage became bright green and yellow. She put an azure stripe of sky underneath the sunset. Then she painted, with fingertip and brushstroke, two moving figures. Two people danced under the trees in blurred motion. Their arms were outstretched. One had a foot off the ground. She painted the grass beneath them as a swipe of color.

The teakettle started whistling. I got up, found the tea, and poured the boiling water into a cup. The rice was still cooking. I brought Kaori the tea and put it down on the table next to her easel. The painting was perfect, and I wanted to tell her to move away from it, but instead, I said, "I have to go. My face. I'll come back soon. You drink this. When the rice is done, you eat. I'll be back soon."

She nodded and said, "I finish painting for you. Then you come back."

I went back to my car. I started to dial 911, but I stopped. What was I going to say? That someone I bailed out of jail the week before had shown me some drawings? I touched the bridge of my nose. Tight and painful. Would I say that she broke my face because I would not look at what she had drawn? Would I then say that as I bled, I stroked her hair, that I breathed close to her, that I felt her shudder?

I put the phone down and drove downtown. I parked in front of Worden's market. There was a payphone, one of the last anywhere in town. I used it to call the bondsman, the gun-carrying person who had helped me get Kaori out of jail.

He answered, and he remembered me. I told him that I had a problem and that I wanted to talk with someone. So I asked him what he was doing.

He asked, "She skip on us? Is she gone?"

"No," I said, "She's inside her apartment. But I think she saw her ex. She says she killed him. Killed the guy's new girlfriend too."

I heard the bondsman sort of 'snort' on the phone. He said, "Why talk to me? Call the cops."

"I'm not sure of anything," I said, "not sure if she is making things up. Not sure if she is telling the truth..."

The bondsman interrupted me and said, "Everyone lies."

We were both quiet for a moment. Finally, I asked if I could meet him someplace.

"That girl couldn't kill anyone," he said. "I can tell a Fella that 'cause anyone who talks about killing is always the worst kind of liar."

"She didn't talk much," I said. "She mostly showed."

"Showed a Fella? How?"

I said that I didn't want to talk about it on the phone. Again, I asked if I could see him.

"A Fella's persistent. That's a truth," he said. "OK then." He told me that he was in his truck. "In my office," he said and told me that he was parked at the jail and had been waiting about an hour for someone. However, he emphasized that if I hurried over, he could talk with me for a bit.

I hung up, and I was at the jail in less than seven minutes. There was a white pickup truck with a camper shell parked by itself in the lot, and I saw the bondsman in the front seat. I pulled up next to him so that our driver-side doors were next to each other. I rolled down my window, and he rolled down his.

He asked, "What happened to a Fella's face?"

I didn't mention my face, but I briefly told him about going to Seattle, about Kaori's drawings. I told him how graphic and detailed they were and how the last one I looked at was a self-portrait of her killing herself.

"That samurai ritual? Where they gut themselves? Is that what she drew?"

I nodded yes.

He said, pronouncing it slowly, "Sepp-uku." Then he asked, "She grow up in Tokyo?"

Again I nodded.

The bondsman declared, "Suicide capital of the world. That's Tokyo."

I told him that before going to Seattle, she and I had been to New York. I told him that I was worried about calling the police to check on her story because I would have had to explain the out-of-town travel.

He said, "Those were her restrictions. Not a fella's. And if the girl is in hand, if she shows up at the hearing, and if she has stayed away from those people she attacked, it should be okay. A fella should be okay."

"But if she has killed those people?" I asked.

"She ain't killed no one," he said.

I felt better, but then I was still worried about her killing herself. I told him this.

Instead of answering, though, he said, "A Fella never did say what happened to his face."

I touched my nose. I winced. "You wouldn't happen to have any aspirin on you?" I asked.

"Always have something," he said. He reached into a coat pocket and handed me a plastic bottle.

As I swallowed the pills, he said, "A Fella still hasn't said about his face."

"She punched me," I said.

He started to laugh. Loud. Then he stopped and said, "Sorry. Can't help laughing at how things work out. Help someone and a Fella gets his lights knocked out. Story of our sad lives, ain't it?" He continued, "Worst beating I ever did get was from a girl. She came up behind me on the sidewalk. Daytime. People all over. Knocks me on the head with something hard, knocks me flat. Stars and lights. Starts kicking me. Thought I was going to be dead. And I still miss her."

I could tell that he was waiting for me to ask more, but I was thinking about Kaori back in the apartment. "Then you think it will be all right if I call the police and have them check on her story?" I said, as I started my car.

He looked at his watch. He said, "Tell a Fella what. Let's go over to the boyfriend's place and take a look. Knock on the door. Then a Fella will have a better notion of how to handle things. Might help to know what a Fella is dealing with, then dump her fast and hard."

He turned around and rummaged in the back seat of the truck's extended cab. He brought a plastic box into the front seat with him. I couldn't see what he was doing, but he finally said, "Here it is, got it."

"Got what?" I asked.

"Copy of restraining order they gave us when we bonded her out," he said. "One order against one Kaori something or 'nother to stay away from one specific, pissed off, ex. The address is 216 Grain Street. You know where that be?"

I told him it was near where she lived and that I could find the place. He told me to drive and said he would follow. Then we both drove off the jail's parking lot.

He parked his truck behind me in front of the house. A blue house with shrubs in front and tall trees showing from the back yard. There was a car parked in the driveway.

The bondsman got out of his truck, holding the copy of the restraining order. He said, "Think I'll knock on that door. Say I'm a checkin' to make sure that the girl hasn't been violating her bail terms, make sure that she hasn't been un-restrained." Then he walked up to the front door and rang the bell.

I saw him ringing the bell again. And again. I could see his face become concerned. He waited a bit and came back. "There is some music playing in there," he said, "but no one's coming. I think a Fella and I might look around a bit."

"I don't want to go in there," I said, "I don't think we should go in there."

"Never said nothing about going into a place. Me and a Fella are going to walk in the yard. Check out the windows. Take a look from outside the place."

I got out of my car, and the two of us walked up to the house. I heard the music then. Radio music. Loud. We knocked hard on the door, but again there was no answer. We walked behind some shrubs along the east side of the house. There were no windows there at all, so we kept going to the back of the house. The back yard had a tall, wooden fence and juniper and lilacs, their dry leaves scattered on the lawn. There was a white, metal lawn table back there, and walking up to it I saw that it was covered with stains from oil paint, stains from the many colors that Kaori used on her brushes, the brushes that she would have put down as she stood and painted.

I want to make these words run on here. I want to keep scratching with this pencil and fill this page, turn it, and fill another. I want to describe the other lawn furniture and the colors of the leaves and the autumn trees. I want to describe the backyard more and find gentle words to lean on. I want to slow down and describe how, looking at that yard, I could imagine it in the spring and in the summer. A spot beautifully opposite to her lasting memories of her crowded, concrete childhood. Memories she had shown me through her sketches on the first night I was with her in her apartment.

I want to keep writing to show you that I am not wanting to turn around and look. I don't want to describe what comes next. But you must already know, as I knew, that the truth was moving up on us, fast. The bondsman was saying, "This sure is the window that she sure busted," and he was touching my arm, saying, "A Fella needs to look at this."

There was a sheet of plywood held by its top edge against a broken glass window with a strip of duct tape. "This wood is in the yard," the bondsman said, "We are not inside, so no harm moving it a bit." He took a folding knife from his pocket. He was now wearing leather gloves that I hadn't notice him put on. He used the knife to peel the edge of the duct tape, which he then pulled the rest of the way from the window. He folded the knife blade back and returned it to a pocket of his jacket. Then he pulled the sheet of plywood back, and it fell on the lawn.

Music poured out of a jagged hole from the center of the picture window. The window Kaori broke with her bare fists the night she was arrested. It was dark in the room. There was no movement. The bondsman, still standing a few feet back from the window, yelled, "Hey. Y'all in there? Y'all about?" There was no answer. From the same pocket where he had taken the knife, he took out a small flashlight. He stepped close to the window, moved his face near the broken hole, and snapped on the flashlight.

I was about to say that we should be going, that there was nothing to see, that Kaori had a wild imagination, and that I was sorry for having wasted his time. I was about to say this when the bondsman jumped back, spun toward me, and said, "No one should ever see that." He knelt and picked up the sheet of plywood. He lifted it back up, putting it against the window as he found it. He rubbed the strip of duct tape, pushing it back to where it had been, sticking it to the glass. Then he looked around where the plywood had fallen on the lawn and ruffed over the grass with his boots. Then he walked rapidly out of the backyard and to his truck. I followed him.

Then I asked, "What was it? What did you see?"

He was upset. He was still holding the flashlight, which he was tapping against his leg. Finally, he opened the truck's door and said, "Follow me."

I said, "We need to go to her apartment. I don't want her to kill herself."

He answered, "That could be the best thing that would happen now," but when he saw that I was upset by what he had said, "Ok, a Fella should drive to her place. I'll follow."

I got in my car and drove the three blocks to Kaori's apartment on Arthur. I parked, and the bondsman pulled up behind me. I got out of the car and went to his truck, to the passenger side, and I opened the door, and I got in.

"Tell me what you saw. Tell me what I should know," I said.

"I need to think," he said. "We need to be careful here."

I said again, "Tell me what you saw."

"A Fella knows what I saw," he said, "Already told me what was there. I didn't believe a Fella. Didn't believe that she could do that. But she did. A girl is on the bed. A guy is on the floor. Lots of blood. I think a Fella needs to call the police now."

He had both of his hands on the steering wheel. And he kept talking and said, "No sir, never should have seen that. No sir." Then he sighed loudly. "Didn't do nothing wrong. Looked in the window. That's all. Could have seen what was there without touching that board. But I am forever plain stupid."

He asked, "What does a Fella think we should do here?"

I didn't answer. There was no game now. No impression of someone ripping off another, no feeling that anything was hidden. A shared raw sense that we were both without anyone and should at least get our stories straight.

I said, "I didn't see you do anything wrong. You just looked in the window. Right?"

He held his hand out toward me to shake my hand, and he said, "Pascal. Pascal Ameto."

I looked at him, and he said, "It's my name. I don't tell many people. It's not on the ads or my card. But a Fella should know." It was a real handshake this time. No flashes of guns, no sense of threat.

"I need to go in and be with her," I said. "I need to make sure that she is not..."

"Yes, go in there. Yes. Go in and get the girl. Don't tell her that I am here. Go in there and bring her out. Drive her to the station, bring her to the police. I'll drive behind you. Then tell them what you told me. That's all."

"Alight," I said, "Then I went into the building and knocked on Kaori's door.

It was quiet at the door. There was no answer, no sounds from inside. So I knocked again. And again, nothing. But then I heard Kaori say, "A moment. Please." And the door opened.

She was smiling. She asked me, "You find medicine for face? You better now?"

I walked past her as she closed the door. She said, "I almost finish," and she pointed her brush at the painting. That painting had no solitude in it, no violence. The combination of the colors, the way they lay next to each other, the deepness of the sky, the deepness of the ground, and the motion of the two people dancing, it all showed that they were not alone.

"I think this painting is finished," I said, "It is lovely." And I sat down in the chair near the painting.

"I become famous soon?" She giggled. She sat on my lap. I felt her hands going around the back of my head. I felt the wooden handle of the brush that she was holding rubbing against the nape of my neck. She said, "I paint happiness. Everything good now." She moved her face toward mine. She tried to kiss me. I turned away. I pushed at her. She pulled my head toward her, pulling me hard. She said, "We pretend. You my love. You tell me why you like my art. Tell me."

I stood up so that she had to stand too. She kept both of her hands around my neck. She dropped the paintbrush, and I heard it clatter on the floor. I reached back and put my hands around her wrists. I moved her hands down to my side. I looked at her eyes.

I asked her, "Kaori, why did you kill them?"

She stared at me. Then she said, "I forget," and she turned and tried to walk back to the easel, but I didn't let go of her hands. I turned her toward me, and I asked again, "Why?"

She relaxed a bit. Then she said, "Jim. He say I waste time. He say I should get other job. He say art no good." She pushed at my chest, "But you saw. Why not he see?"

Then she said, "Oh, rice done. I check." I let go of her wrists, and she walked into her kitchen nook. But, instead of filling a bowl with rice, she picked up a knife from the sink. She touched its point, blade up, against the exposed skin of her midriff above her belly button. I saw the skin around the knifepoint depress slightly. She was holding the knife with both her hands, one hand over the other, thumbs pointing down.

"Kaori," I said softly.

I took a few steps toward her and reached for the knife. She stepped back and turned the blade away from her so that the heels of her fists were pressing against herself. The knife was pointed up at an angle.

She insisted, "You only look. You no touch. This not for you." Then she walked past me, to her painting and stopped in front of it. She said, without turning around, "Please, sit again. Tell me when you understand art."

I did what she asked, I sat down, even though I wanted to run out the door and call for help.

She took the knife and, using its point started scratching thin lines through the wet oil paint. She held the blade like a brush, moving it with a scraping motion across the canvas, with enough pressure to slightly tear the canvas, bringing the fibers up through the surface of the wet paint. After each stroke, she wiped the knife tip on her hand and then wiped her hand on her shirt. "Paint should be more dry," she said, "But this okay. This will show."

Across the painting, there was now a new drawing emerging, gossamer-like, something that was almost not there. The outline of a face. Like the face in the painting that I had taken from the trash dumpster on the night after I had driven her home from the party. Closed eyes, full lips, hair that sprawled. It was Kaori's face.

I touched my nose and winced. "Kaori," I said, "I left ice in my car. I need to go outside for a moment. I will be right back."

She said, "Yes, you come back. I be here." She said this without turning, she said this as she was still moving the knife over the canvas, scratching lines for individual strands of hair.

I walked out of the apartment, and I left the door slightly ajar so that it did not latch. I walked out to Pascal, waiting in his truck.

"I can't do it," I said, "I can't bring her out here. I can't be the one who does it. I can't be the one to bring her back to jail."

Pascal nodded. He said, "Guess a Fella can't bust his own girl, no matter how bad she is." Then he said, "Makes the most sense that I do the telling. Since I saw the bodies. Been thinking about it. I figure that a Fella don't have to be part of this at all. Figure that I was checking up on the girl, making sure she hadn't been around the ex. The only crime is hers. That's what I figure." He shrugged and said, "Why not wait inside with her. Don't think it will be long before someone will be back here." Then he started the truck and drove away without looking at me.

I went back inside. I opened the apartment door without knocking. She was standing at the painting, holding the knife in front of her face. She turned her head and looked at me. Then she turned her face back toward the knife.

I walked over and reached toward her hand, toward the handle of the knife. I put both of my hands around her hand and the knife's handle. She hardly moved as I took the knife slowly from her. Then I said, "Kaori, let's sit down now," and she nodded.

We were sitting on her bed. I put the knife on the floor. Then, with my foot, I slid it under the bed.

She was looking at the painting, at the easel. She said, "I could not do. I could not kill." I didn't say anything. Then she said, "Self. Not kill self." And she turned her face toward me and there were tears on her face, and she asked, "What wrong with me? Why I so sad? What I should do now?"

Crazy and wrong. A room filled with paintings and emptiness. Three blocks away, two dead strangers. Next to me was a girl who killed her "One Love" and then wrapped herself about me, closed her eyes in the dark, and said, "You."

The impossible wish, to change the past.

Greed and loss. Dirty hundred-dollar bills that I had buried in clean mountain earth, which was now winter freezing. Cash that I wished could speak for me and say that I was no longer a janitor. Money that I impossibly wanted to show that I could have been anything.

A week ago, on the rooftop, up above Manhattan, Kaori whispered into my ear that I must love her "One time only." And I heard what I wanted to. I touched what felt good.

But now I was lost. She had smashed a window, bit her ex-boyfriend, pulled her rival from a bed, and punched a cop. Then I bailed her out of jail and fallen in love with her and her drawings. And now I saw that I was part of her escalation from the smashed window to murder. I had pretended, with her, "One Love." But there was no undoing cold, parted flesh. No math, no skill, no magic, that had yet learned how to restart dead or broken hearts.

There was knocking on the apartment door. Kaori opened it without asking who it was. Two police were there. She did not seem surprised. They asked her to step into the hallway. She did. I came with her, but one of the officers told me to step away. But I was still close by when the other officer asked her if she knew anything about the two dead people, about Jim and Elizabeth. She didn't hesitate. She said, "Yes, I did it. He was mine. He not hers."

They arrested her. They put handcuffs on her. They took her outside. They put her into a car. I was not arrested, but I was told to get into another squad car, and I did.

We went to the station. I didn't see where Kaori went. I was taken into a brightly lit room with overhead fluorescent lights. I expected to have to wait there for a long time. Instead, a detective came in and explained that I didn't have to say anything and that I was not under arrest.

The detective was runner thin. He looked like he never tired. He reached into an inside pocket of his coat and brought out a pack of cigarettes, and offered them to me. When I told him that I didn't smoke, he put the pack back in his pocket. I noticed that the pack was new, that it hadn't been opened. I asked him if he smoked, and he said, "No. Want to make sure that you are comfortable. But we don't really allow smoking in here anyway. Glad you said no."

Staring at my face, he asked me what happened, and I was about to tell him that Kaori punched me, but instead, I said, "I'd rather not talk about it," and he said, "Fine."

He suggested that I call a lawyer. I told him that I didn't respect lawyers. He agreed with me, but he said, "Double homicide is double-dead serious. I'll be straight with you. Until we know what happened, you are suspect. You could be arrested right now. You could be in jail now."

I answered, "I'll say the same things with or without a lawyer, so let's get this over as fast as possible."

The detective placed a microphone in the middle of the table and pointed up at a corner where there was a wall-mounted video camera. He turned on a switch on the side of the microphone and explained to me that everything I was saying would be recorded and videotaped. Next, he requested I acknowledge that I was given a chance to have a lawyer present. After I said that I understood, he began asking me questions. He asked me to explain what I had been doing with Kaori, how I knew her, and where we had been together.

I explained about her calling me when she had been in jail. I stated we had gone to New York to buy artwork and that we stayed in the Green Tortoise and stayed in the Marriot when we had been in Seattle.

He asked me about my face again. "Who broke your nose?" I didn't answer. He asked, "Did you have any contact with this Jim and Elizabeth that your friend keeps talking about?"

I answered, "No. I have had no contact with those people other than listening to Kaori talk about them. So I have no idea who they are."

He inquired again about my face, "Did someone hit you?"

Again I didn't speak. The detective looked at his watch and switched off the taping equipment. He told me to stay in town, to be available. He wrote down my cell and my work phone number and address. He told me that I could go. He didn't offer to get anyone to drive me back to Kaori's apartment, where my car was parked.

It was one in the morning and snowing outside. The first snow, after the first knocking of winter. The beautiful, soft time before the wood smoke and frozen fog started mixing into a dull dome over Missoula.

Instead of calling a car, I walked the four blocks from the police station to Maloney's bar. Other than the bartender, I was the only person there. I ordered a shot, then called Pascal. He answered right away. I told him that I had just left the police station, and I explained that, other than not saying anything about removing the sheet of plywood, I had told the cops the truth.

He responded, "I figured a Fella might do that. I did it too. We didn't do anything wrong."

I asked him how long they had questioned him, and he said, "About an hour."

I told him that I was at Maloney's and that they were still open.

"Know the place well." Then Pascal said, "I like people who do stupid things for women. But a Fella should have left this one alone. Should not have called me, that's for sure."

I told him I was sorry, and I was about to hang up when he said, "Hold on. I'm parked two blocks away. Drink would be good on a night like this."

Two minutes later, he parked in front of the bar. When Pascal walked in, the bartender nodded a familiar 'hello.'

I asked Pascal, "You sleep in your 'office' too?"

"Everything except piss and shit and shower. Got tired of losing houses and can't stand landlords."

I paid for drinks. The bartender moved away from us, sat on a stool, and read a newspaper.

Pascal asked, "Did you see her?"

I told him no and described the questions I had been asked.

He said they asked him the same sort. He also stated that he assumed that we wouldn't be in any trouble, "Except for maybe having to stick around and answer the same questions another dozen times." He added, "This will be big news in town. 'Jilted foreign student murders two.'"

I told Pascal that Kaori wasn't a student. He asked me how she made her living, and I said I didn't know but guessed that she had received money from her parents.

Pascal asked me what I did for a living. I told him that I was a computer coder. He asked if the pay was good. I told him it was. "Good job?" he asked.

"It used to be," I said. "But it's not about computers anymore. Instead, it's about cheating and lies."

"That's what ruins everything," he said. We both looked at our shot glasses.

I was drinking Stoly, Russian vodka. Pascal noted, "There's benzene in that. Gives it that 'industrial' flavor." He told me that he had once had a girlfriend from Norway. She had been a student at the university, and she liked Stoly. He said, "The 'Nordsky' was a dance student. Legs went up to here," and he held his hand up by his chin. He said, "She and I came in here. Got drunk together." Then he was quiet.

I said, "I met a girl in this place. A long time ago. We walked out that door," and I pointed toward the back, "we went dancing." I didn't say anything else.

Pascal then said, "Let's get out of here. It's not right to sit near ghosts." He got the bartender's attention and asked for a bottle of Irish.

"What flavor?" the bartender asked and gestured to the package liquor shelves where there were five different brands of Irish whiskey lined up.

"The best stuff," Pascal said, "the cheapest." And the bartender put a fifth into a paper bag.

We went outside, and I told Pascal that my car was parked by Kaori's apartment. He said he would give me a ride, and I got in the passenger side of his truck. It was snowing harder. There was no traffic on the streets. As we started to drive down Broadway toward Kaori's, Pascal said, "I have an idea of what to do now. It's two in the morning. I assume there's no hurry to get home. Want to go do some night shooting?"

"What?" I asked.

"Paper and cans," he said. "Make some loud noise and some small holes. Always seems to help."

"Sure," I said.

Pascal drove down Broadway, drove through East Missoula, and turned up Route 200 along the Blackfoot

River. After about fifteen minutes, I asked him where we were going, and he said, "Jonsrud Road. Twenty miles or so. A place to think. A place to make noise. No one around."

When we got to the Jonsrud turnoff, he put the truck into four-wheel drive. There were about three new inches of snow covering the gravel road surface. Then, less than a mile up the road past the campground, a barricade blocked the way. We stopped in front of it, our headlights reflecting off the sign "Road Closed for Season." Pascal said, "Give me a hand moving this," and the two of us pulled the barricade, which was mostly a support for a highway sign, to the side. I waited while Pascal drove the truck past it, then the two of us moved the sign back to where it had been.

I asked him how much trouble we could get in by driving on the closed road. Pascal replied, "I've got a fishing license. In Montana, if you are near a river and have a fishing license, you can do anything." We both laughed, and he said, "Crack open that bottle. I think I can drink and drive here. Only ones I am going to run off the road now will be us two sorry fools."

I opened the bottle, and Pascal stopped the truck again, rummaged in the back seat, 'the kitchen,' he said, and found a package of paper coffee cups. He stepped out and scooped up a handful of snow.

"Want to cut it with a bit of fresh ice?" he asked. I nodded, holding my cup toward him, and he dumped some snow into my whiskey.

As we started to drive again, he said, "Check out the darkness on this side. That's a black way down. Fifty feet to rocks and water. We will take our time."

I agreed that we should go slow. I refilled our paper cups and looked out into the swirling snow, bright and confusing in the headlight beams, and I let Pascal pay attention to the darkness that mattered.

Ten miles past the "Road Closed" barricade, up the Jonsrud Road in a snowstorm, Pascal pulled the truck to an embankment above the river and parked. He left the truck's headlights on. They lit up the forest near us, and there, about fifty feet away, was a fallen log. Pascal said, "This be the place."

He got out and rummaged in the camper on the back of the truck. He returned with a duffel bag. From that, he took out paper targets and a staple gun. He walked over to the log and stapled a row of targets onto it. Then he came back to where I was standing, leaning against the front of the truck with the headlights on either side of me.

Pascal taught me how to fire a semi-automatic forty-five. In the bright light from the headlights, he showed me how to stand and instructed me how to breathe right up until the gun went off. He said, "Pull that trigger slow and steady so that it surprises you. Don't be yanking it."

"This is a 1911," he said, "it has a kick. A Fella has to remember to keep his thumb down 'cause when it fires the slider flies back and a thumb that's left up there will be a bummed-out thumb." He also pointed out, "Remember that with each shot another one is ready to go. Level the sights again, grab that breath, and pull that trigger again." He also added, "Three number one things to remember about guns are, 'one', they are always loaded even if they ain't. 'One,' keep the finger off that trigger until a Fella be killing the target. And, 'one,' they are loud. And a bunch more number one stuff, like don't shoot at night or when a Fella is drunk."

He was right about the noise: even while wearing earplugs, it was loud.

We spent half an hour taking turns shooting at the targets. Each time I fired the gun, all I saw was a white flash of flame. I liked the heaviness of the metal in my hand. I liked the way my hand felt after each shot, like having connected with a baseball bat against a fast-moving pitch. But it was much easier than swinging any bat. It took almost no skill, other than not flinching, to pull the trigger. The power was too easy.

I picked up the bottle of whiskey, took another drink, and said, "I am drunk. I can't do this anymore."

Pascal answered, "After this afternoon, one of us had to get shit-faced, and it has to be you since I am the one who will have to drive the rig back to town. Even a Montana fishing license don't give no one no right to kill no body." Then he reached into the truck and turned off the headlights. And like that, the darkness was total.

I still felt the snow falling on my head, but I could not see anything. Pascal said, "Nothing like being out here. No worries," and I heard him sit down near the left front wheel. So I sat down too, in the snow, by the other front wheel. I leaned back against the truck's bumper. I was still holding the bottle of whiskey in my hand, and I drank more from the bottle.

Pascal said, "I came right to this place before. Different season. Spring then. A few years ago, with Nordsky."

I was quiet, and he continued.

"I met her when I tried taking classes for a bit. She was here because in Norway they have so much money --- that whole country is oil-rich --- that they have this free college for everyone thing, 'cept there aren't enough colleges there. The King, a real King, pays college kids to go study wherever they want. And Nordsky wanted to come here to Montana. I don't feel old now, but I was 20 years older than her then, and when she found out she said, 'No way I would get involved with you.' That hurt. But I dogged her, she didn't seem to mind. I told her she had the best attitude of anyone I had met, and she did. She had a good attitude toward things. She took chances.

"I brought her here. I wanted to listen to her talk outside. I wanted to keep from being interrupted by the boys who followed her around in all the bars. That's what I said to her, I said, 'You always have boys around you. What can I do to talk to you without boys around you.' I said to her, 'I ain't pretending nothing. I like the way you look. I like your voice. I want to drive with you and hear what you have to say.'

"That's when she asked me how old I was, and when she told me I was too old. But she still took a drive with me. Right here. To this spot. Exactly. Except the truck was over there," and he snapped on the flashlight he must have taken from his pocket, stood up, and pointed it back to the snow-covered dirt road. "The truck got stuck up to the axles in a drift. Right there."

Pascal sat down again, looked out over the river, and snapped off the flashlight. Then he continued talking.

"The road was closed, same barricade, but it was end of winter closed for a reason. Snow drifts in the shadows. I told her we might get stuck. And, like I said, we got stuck right here, evening time."

He waited a bit, and when he didn't say any more, I held out the bottle, reaching with my left arm across the darkness until the bottle nudged against him, and I said, "I think you'll be fine driving. Have another sip."

"A taste," Pascal said, and he took the bottle, and I heard him drink, then he continued.

"She weren't worried. She bragged about how tough she was, how she was from above the Arctic Circle, a 'Lap Lander.' And she brags that she was used to the dark, and how she could stay warm. And how she could go days without eating. She was teasing me because she already knew that there was all kinds of food in the truck and blankets and everything. It was a Friday night, and there was no place either of us had to be for a while. I made a fire, down there," Pascal snapped on the flashlight again, and pointed the beam down toward the water. "A fire by the riverbank."

"Want more of this?" he asked, and he handed me back the whiskey bottle.

I asked, "You still have blankets in the truck?"

"Yep," he said, "Sleeping bags too."

"OK," I said, "Keep going with this story, but I think we need to spend the night here. I think both of us need to drink and not drive anywhere."

Pascal answered, "I judged a Fella right. Fella isokay, even if you don't do real work. Computers. That is bull crap."

"I tot-a-lee agree," I said and drank more whiskey.

Pascal snapped off the flashlight and continued.

"We have this fire going. I go and get some food and cook it, and we eat. I have a bottle of wine too, and I get that, and we drink. Now it is getting dark, but there is still some light, and I say, 'The best time to shoot guns is when you are drunk,' and I go up to the truck, stuck there in the snowdrift, and come back with the same 1911 you were shooting now. I show her the gun, and she tells me in her country they are illegal, but I explain about the fishing license -- how almost anything is legal if you have a fishing license -- and she starts laughing. She wants to shoot the empty wine bottle, but I won't let her. We shot at the stumps across the river there, safe as can be. No broken glass to ruin no good spot. Then she starts bragging more about how tough she is, all worked up because of shooting, and I don't know why, but I take all my clothes off, and I swim across the river. Right there," and Pascal snapped the light on again and aimed it into the falling snow down toward the Blackfoot, an inky black moving reflection of memories.

"Swimming. Always was good at it," Pascal said. "And I got to the other side. But there's no bank to climb up, no rocks. The hard kind of snow, that kind that is mostly end of winter ice. But I'm still able to get up there. Then I yelled that she should come across too. She yelled back that she thought that I wanted to see her without her clothes on. So I yelled that she was damn-straight-right. And she started laughing so hard that she fell. Laughed herself silly, drunk, and laying there on the ground. But all her clothes are on. And she's warm by the fire, and she's staying there. Me, I'm standing naked on an ice bank on the other side of a river. I am freezing. Teeth start chattering. Now it doesn't matter my age, I'm numb, dumb, and stupid. And drunk. I'm not thinking about the girl anymore, I only want to get to where it is warm and not to die. And I sure as shit didn't want to go back in the water but there's no other way." He turned on the light and pointed toward the far bank again. It was steep and rocky, and I could imagine it as a bank of ice in April.

Pascal continued, "I did it, though. I done swam back. Got up next to that fire, crouched over it close as could be, hugged that heat, singed my private parts, almost. And a Fella knows what? A Fella knows what that laughing Nordsky does?"

I responded that I had no idea.

"Nordsky comes over, still laughing, but says, accent like maple syrup on a pile of biscuits," he drank more whiskey, "She says, 'I was wrong about you. You are exactly my age.'"

Pascal was silent for a long time. I listened to the low sound of the river mixing with the sound of the snow falling around us. Then Pascal continued, "Nearly managed to keep that one. Lasted almost two years. She liked how I danced with her, liked how I tossed her in the air and caught her. Boys couldn't do that." He let out a long sigh and yelled, "Cover your ears!" I did cover my ears, and he fired another gun, one with a deeper roar of noise, that long-barreled revolver he was wearing on his belt the first time I met him. Six slow times into a straight-up, hundred-proof, drunken sky.

After the echoing of the revolver shots had faded, Pascal said, "Nothing works out forever. If a Fella knows what I mean, it can be right while it's happening. Way I enjoyed those legs. Seeing them next to my face, dancing, holding her, her smiling down at me. The best was laughing with her. Liked that part best of all.

"In Norwegian, Nordsky told me, the worst cussing a Fella can say is, 'draw till helvete.' It means, 'go to hell.' Say that in Tromso and you have a serious fight on the spot. But say, 'Go fuck yourself,' and you get a smile, a slap on the back, and the Norwegian Fellas there will buy you a beer. I went there. Tromso, but I couldn't take the winter. Legs or no legs. No sun at all. Came back here. She didn't. She told me to go to hell when I left. I told her to fuck herself. She smiled and kissed me goodbye. Nothing works out forever." Then he said, "But what you had happen with your crazy one is not right. That will follow your tracks far into forever. To that I say, helvete.' "

A broken nose throbbing through the whiskey. Ears ringing from gunshots. No fire to huddle over after coming back from swimming across an ice-cold river. No one to impress.

The sky was dumping snow. A foot was now on the ground. I was shivering in my wet clothes. I told Pascal that I needed to sleep. He got a sleeping bag for me. He also handed me a tarp, which I spread out in the snow, and then folded over myself like a collapsed tent. Pascal climbed into the back of the truck, into the camper shell where he slept. I tried looking up into the storm, but I could not see anything. Not even a hint of direction. I pulled my head under the sleeping bag there on the ground and felt closer to where I belonged than I had in a long time. Draw till helvete. Draw to hell.

Chapter 8 – The Weight of Snow

I woke up. The sky was starting to show light, and I felt a weight pushing on me. The storm was over, but there was a foot and a half of snow on the ground, covering everything. The spruces and the ponderosas looked like Christmas cards. I broke off dry branches from underneath some of the spruces, and I dragged them back near the truck. I found matches on the dashboard, and by the time Pascal woke up, I had a fire going, the smoke rising straight in the calm air.

"Kind of expected a Fella would know how to warm himself," Pascal said as he stood next to the fire, his palms out toward it, "Even a Fella with money."

I asked, "Why do you say that?"

Pascal answered, "I deal with those who pretend to have what they ain't never going to get. Shows in everything they can't afford. Especially in their attitude." He squatted down, picked up a stick, and stirred the fire. The sun had come up over the ridge to the southeast, and the flames had disappeared in the sunlight. Pascal continued, "People I deal with mostly have always been taken care of. Ones who started out when they were nineteen saying, 'I don't need money,' because they had never been without it. Then they hit twenty-five. They have a job that sucks, and they lose that. Their parents boot them out. The circus nets by then are torn to crap from falling on them so many times." He threw the stick into the fire. "Some get angry, like someone owes them something. I end up with those, the angry ones, the ones who get busted for selling meth, and other stupid things like shoplifting garbage from k-mart, writing bogus checks to pay for quarters for the gambling machines.

"But someone who has been busted broke, if they can take care of themselves from that point, they act different. They build their own fires."

I asked Pascal if he was ever 'busted broke,' and he said, "When I first came here. Bought a house right off and lost it the next year. Poorest state in the country, Montana. Used to be Mississippi, but we whooped them when the Butte mines closed."

He stood up, he stretched, "Could have gone somewhere else then, that would have been the easy way. But I figured it out 'cause I like it here. Place where we can drive thirty miles and get snowed in," he smiled into the morning sun. "Fella ready for me to fix up a pot of coffee? Might as well relax a bit before we find out if we're going to be able to negotiate our way back." He turned and walked back to the truck, the snow coming to his knees, and he said, without facing me, laughingly, "Looks like the 'Closed for Season' might be for real."

Pascal had a spare radiator hose, three metal toolboxes, two buckets of spare parts, and a hundred-foot spool of half-inch steel cable. He had a shovel. He had a hand winch. He had an ax. He had a black plastic gun case that contained a Russian SKS, "Cheap, accurate, and legal," he said. I saw all this because he kept handing me things to get out of his way as he dug through the back of his truck. Then he crawled out, dragging a heavy bundle that clanked. "Here we be," and it was a complete set of tire chains wrapped in a canvas tarp. He said, "I've had these for years, never used them."

We shoveled away snow from behind the wheels. Then we spread the chains out behind all four tires and backed the truck onto them. As I was helping him with the chains, I asked, "Had these for years, but you didn't use them that time you got stuck with the Norway girl?"

He winked and said, "There are times when getting stuck is a good thing."

We made it to the highway. Pascal said, "Chains and a four-wheel drive can do." Then we took the chains off and continued toward town, where there were only a few inches of snow on the roads.

Pascal dropped me off at my car in front of Kaori's. He said, "A Fella and I need to stay in touch." Then he drove away.

I drove back to my house, showered, changed, and then went to the office. Things were routine. Suzzy looked at me and said, "What happened to you?" and touched her face. I told her I slipped in the hotel and hit my face on the shower fixture.

"Slick move," she said. She asked about the trip to Seattle and the visit with Dave Cheat. She also handed me a stack of phone messages and told me there were several voice messages I should listen to on the main office number. So I went into my office, closed the door, threw all the phone messages in the trash, and deleted the phone mail without listening. Then I turned on my computer and erased all my emails without reading any of them.

"Kaori is gone," I said to myself. I counted how many days I was near her. Almost nothing. My face hurt, and I couldn't breathe through my swollen nose. I needed patterns and abstraction that would not push, punch, or hurt.

From a shelf, I took down a math book published in nineteen thirty-five. The binding was split leather. The author's introduction described ten years spent working on the manuscript and the difficulty in conveying his ideas with the limited font and character typography of the time. It was a book I bought when I was eighteen for a dollar. I had worked through the book several times. My notes lined the pages. Yet, there was nothing in the book that was confusing anymore, everything was comfortable, and it was a place where I was safe.

Differential equations --- predictive math that was needed before computers to calculate problems. The real-world problems of multiple variables with no exact solution. Like the wiggly lines on a sheet of paper that do not all cross at one single point. Where would the lines become closest to each other? Where is the center of gravity of weightless confusion? With computers, it only takes a few lines of iterative code --- instructions that repeat themselves again and again, into the millions and billions --- nibbling away at the confusion to get the most balanced solution in milliseconds. But in 1935, it took something better: it took slow peace.

I turned off the computer by yanking its power plug from the wall. I turned off my phone. I found a blank notebook and a pencil. I sharpened the pencil with a penknife. Then my hand moved, and my thoughts stopped racing.

When I came out of my office, there were more messages taped on my door. I left them there. I went home. I ate, I washed, I slept. The next day the weather had turned colder, and it was snowing again. On the way to the office, I stopped at Worden's market and bought a Missoulian. The front-page story was about Kaori and the two murders. I started to read the article, but then I threw the entire newspaper away. There was nothing there that I wanted to read. I got to work, and Suzzy handed me more messages.

O'Neill also stopped me before I got to my office and wanted to know what happened in Seattle. He told me that he had a call from one of Dave Cheat's engineers offering to help us set up any new hardware that we might want in Missoula. O'Neill said, "They've never offered us anything before. Now they are offering to send us fast machines. Ones with multiple GPUs. What gives?" I explained that they were pleased with the work we had been doing. I told O'Neill that Dave Cheat said, "the Seattle group wants to develop a closer working relationship with Missoula." I summarized for O'Neill how we would be working more closely with Seattle.

O'Neill likes fast computers with multiple monitors. He smiled and said, "Whatever you did, keep it up. This is great."

Several days went by. I didn't look at the newspaper. I didn't look at any news, and I didn't talk with anyone. I went to the office each day, closed my door, and studied old math. I also went to the university library and found a book that had Plank's and Heisenberg's original papers, which were dense with math. I checked the book out and started working through the calculations. Their way of imagining the distance and speeds of energy inside atoms and between stars and planets converged toward a truth that had no connection with control, money, or ambition. The irony was that their work became the foundation for the greatest of all controls: atomic bombs and power.

Then, a week after the murders, Suzzy knocked on my office door. She said, "There's someone here. Says he is a detective. Says you haven't been returning his calls." Then she smiled and added, "I told him you haven't been returning anyone's calls."

I asked Suzzy to let him in. It was the thin detective. We shook hands, he sat down, and I closed the door. He asked me if I had been following the news, and I told him I hadn't. He then told me that Kaori had confessed but that there still might be a trial. From his briefcase, he took some stapled pages and handed them to me.

Thin said, "I want you to look at this, see if it jogs any memories." It was a printed transcript of what I had told him the night Pascal saw the bodies, a transcript of what was recorded. "You told me that you and she went to New York after you bailed her out of jail. Did you meet with anyone else there?"

I said, "No. I just talked with several gallery and shop owners."

Thin took a reporter's notebook from his jacket pocket, paged through it, and said, "This is what she said, 'Had drinks with Enzi's friend from Texas.'"

I shrugged and said, "Someone we shared a deli table with. He had a strong accent that she was curious about. I told Kaori that he was probably from Texas. She might have thought I knew the person."

Thin asked, "Texas tell you his name?"

"I don't remember if he did," I answered.

Thin read from his notebook again, "Here it is. Tommy Tsai. That was his name." Then the detective took a business card from the briefcase and handed it to me.

It was Tsai's card, embossed paper, raised ink. The Logo. The title, "Vice President of Broadband Networking." I looked at it and handed the card back, and shrugged again.

The detective said, "Curious he would have given her his card. Seems close to the sort of work you do," and he looked toward the row of monitors on my desk. Neither of us said anything else. Thin stood up, and he started to leave, but he turned and asked, "What was in the 'case' that he gave you?"

I didn't say anything, and Thin sat back down in the chair, opened his notebook again, and read, "'He gave Enzi a case. We went to bar in the top of a tall building.' Why do you think she said that?"

I said, "I have no idea. Call the name on that card and ask."

"Did that," Thin said. "Mr. Tommy Tsai said he gives out business cards all the time, especially to women, and he told me the same story you did. That he happened to share a table with you two. Said he remembered her, but not you. Says he does not know who you are." Thin looked at me and touched the bridge of his nose, tapped it twice, and said, "Looks like you're healing." When I didn't respond, he went on, "Thing about this one is that everything she says is in the open, and parts are illustrated. Like those sketches you said she showed you in Seattle."

I nodded. He continued, "She's been sitting in her cell, and she asked for a pen and a notebook, which we gave her, and she keeps filling pages with new drawings. Exact drawings. Drawings that match the crime scene. Accurate. But there are other drawings which she says are from the two trips you took together. You want to see?"

I asked, "See what?"

"The drawings." He opened his briefcase again and brought out a cardboard-bound school notebook. The cheap kind with the speckled black and white cover. He thumbed through the pages. It had letter-sized lined paper, and each page was covered with detailed sketches made with a blue felt-tip pen.

"Here we go," he said, and he held the notebook open so I could see.

It was a drawing of Tsai and me in Katz's. We were standing, facing each other, and it showed Tsai handing me the briefcase, with both of our hands holding it. There was a window behind us, and Kaori had sketched what was out there, parked cars with men in oversized pants slouching against them. She had also drawn the street sign, making it larger than the perspective, and she had penned in the sound of the street name, in English, 'Hue Son.' She had also drawn three Kanji characters underneath the briefcase.

Thin closed the notebook and put it back with his other papers, then snapped shut his case, stood up, and looked at me. His two eyes were different shades of color, one dark green, the other light blue. Both of his eyes seemed to be made of glass; he never blinked. He said, "I went over to the university before coming here. Japanese language professor. 'He takes the money.' That is what she wrote."

I didn't answer.

"She has other drawings of you," he said, "with more Japanese." Then Thin left my office without waiting to see if I would respond.

I waited a few minutes, then left, telling Suzzy that I was going to get some lunch on the way out.

I drove to the payphone in front of Worden's market and called Tsai on his burner. There was a loud click, the phone had been answered, but all I heard were honking horns. I asked, "You driving?"

Tsai, after he heard my voice said, "London. It's like New York here." Then he asked if I was ready to have a 'face-to-face' again. He said he had 'more' for me. He said, "We can discuss methods that are less physical and more modern." He said I should be able to set up a crypto wallet with a few presses of keys. "That stuff you do," said with a sing-song Texas accent that made me remember foremen on the oil rigs, who yelled, "Get moving!" They all had Texas accents too.

I asked, "Why did you give her your card?"

He didn't answer, and I continued, "Did you hand it to her when I was spilling drinks in the Rainbow Room?"

He paused for a bit, and then he said, "A bit of a mistake. But I've already had a short, pleasant talk about this. As you seem to know."

I said, "She killed two people. She told the police that she was in New York with me. They asked what she and I were doing there --- unrelated to her crimes --- they asked because she was out on bail and was supposed to have stayed in Missoula. She told them about meeting you, and they found your business card, and now they know you, and I met."

His voice turned hard. "Enzi, Enzi," he said, "You're the one who started it by meeting her. We'll talk again soon," and he hung up on me.

I was standing in front of Worden's market. I looked across the street to Charlie's bar. I was thinking about going in to see if there might be a mid-day drunk sitting on a barstool to talk with to help me feel like I was back on the honest side of life. Maybe one who would tell stories about working in the woods or highway crews. Someone I could swap some truths with. But perhaps what would have helped me the most would have been a drug dealer. Someone I could have secretly observed working his trade, watched how the exchange of palmed cash for little baggies of heroin transpired. Maybe that would have given me clues about how the more experienced criminals moved and breathed and managed to spend their non-sleeping hours without collapsing.

Instead, I went back to my office and tried to work, which meant going through the backlog of voicemails and messages.

Most were quickly scanned and deleted. A few I responded to with brief calls or emails. Approving purchases of software updates. Confirming that I had read monthly reports about several new hires. Calling back a coder in Seattle who wanted to put in a transfer to move to the Missoula office. All the details that rolled together to create the demands of the job. Work that was not work but was bureaucracy and waste.

But then there was a voicemail from the day before, which got me to sit up straight and made my heart race. It was from Dave Cheat. He started by asking about the hardware that his engineers had configured and sent to Missoula. Then he asked me to let him know if I needed more. In the voicemail, he said, "Hey. I looked more at the transport checksum you set up for us. I sped it up about one ten thousandths of one percent faster now." He said this with pride in his voice, not gloating. He went on, "Found a mistake. You had a de-referenced pointer that was causing a memory overrun once every thousand-twenty-four packets. It wasn't causing damage, but I changed the code so that the overrun doesn't happen anymore." He paused. Then the message continued, "I've checked in the changes. No biggy, but look at the fix, and I'll install it across the network. And give me a call. I want to talk about you coming back here for some more juggling." I felt a shiver of dread.

I logged into and ran the version control software and looked at the changes that Dave Cheat had described. It was my hacked backdoor, and he had changed it so that it would no longer run. He had also added several lines of comments in the code, detailing his change so that I could not delete what he had done without bringing blatant attention back to my hack. I logged out of the version control system and called Dave Cheat. He answered.

I told him that I had looked at the changed code, and I said it was "cool" that he found a mistake and fixed it.

He said, "I almost didn't notice it. It is so minor. I almost left it the way it was, but it was an easy fix. As soon as we hang up, I'll check in the changes and get it live everywhere." Then Dave suggested that I should come out to Seattle in the next week. Said that he would schedule a full day off site, and that maybe he and I could drive over to the Olympics, "Spend the day talking, you know, away from SLAM."

I told him that sounded like a good idea.

Then he asked about Kaori, "How is that girlfriend of yours?"

This meant he didn't know about the murders and had not read the Montana papers. I replied, "I haven't seen her in a while. So it was kind of a transitory thing."

He said, "Well, if you do chance into her, she is more than welcome here too."

I told him that was not likely, but I would check my schedule and probably come out on Monday. I said I would get back to him that evening, and we ended the call.

The Thin detective had indicated that he was watching and wondering about me. Then, on the same day, Dave Cheat had let me know that he turned off the hack that I had managed to install. The backdoor for which Tsai had given me half a million dollars.

As I was driving home, I was thinking about how to tell Tsai what Dave Cheat had done. I thought that I would tell Tsai that he could have back everything he had given me. For a few moments, I was thinking that he would enjoy following my treasure instructions. But I was also thinking how he would have to wait until the late spring for the snow to melt to be able to dig up the money, and that his own buried cache down in Texas --- the coins he had bragged to me about hiding almost as a hobby --- was an easy desert-treasure, not the snowed-in type that I buried. But I already knew that he wouldn't want it back. I already knew what he would want.

I tried to sleep, fighting to find a few hours where there were dreams that had no mistakes.

It was morning. I started to make coffee, but then my phone rang. I answered, and Tsai said, "Turn on that other phone." Then he hung up.

I turned on the burner that I had gotten from Tsai when I was in New York. I was finishing making coffee when it rang.

"Your code stopped working last night."

I started to tell him what Dave Cheat had told me the day before, but Tsai interrupted.

"We know he found it. We know he turned it off. He doesn't have a clue what it was for, though. So, you figure something out and get something new in there. Fix it."

"You in Seattle?" I asked, "How did you know that Cheat found and fixed the hack? You have someone else helping you there?"

Tsai answered, "It doesn't matter where I am. Or who else I work with. You need to fix things." There was a threat in his voice. A sound I had not heard from him before.

I moved the phone from my ear and held it down by my knee. I looked out the window of my kitchen, up to the close by north hills. There was a trail there that zigzagged on the slope, and I could see two people walking up, taking an early morning hike. I imagined these were happy people who would never have to answer mysterious calls ordering them to do illegal things. But I also now had more cash buried in the nearby mountains than most people will ever have in their lifetime. I heard Tsai speaking from down by my knees, and I looked at the phone and thought about hanging up. Instead, I brought the phone back to my ear and said, "Sorry, didn't hear what you were saying."

He said, "Let me make this clear. We lose a fortune each day that the system stays down."

I explained that it was complicated to reintroduce any discovered backdoor. I told Tsai that I didn't think Dave had suspected anything improper. But I also said that he had spent enough time studying the code I had added so that additional changes to the system would now be apparent to him, and that he would then realize what the code was really for.

Tsai said, "You won't have a problem. That will be taken care of. Start planning on getting things fixed."

I responded, "You are not listening to me. You don't understand that this is not easy, that a new change is not possible now unless you want it to be discovered and recognized as a backdoor and…"

Tsai interrupted, "No, you haven't been listening to me. You do not have a choice in this matter now."

Then Tsai said, "We have history. You and I. But it is like the history I have with the counter man at Katz's. He and I talk. He gives me samples and asks about how my day is going. But I know he's the counterman, and there is a counter between us. He might be looking at me, thinking, 'I hate selling this schlep matzo balls.' Enzi, this has never been about you and I liking each other, and you do not want to hear my thoughts right now. You do not want to remove the counter between us. Go to Seattle. Get in again. Go push some buttons or whatever it is that you people do."

Then I heard the click of Tsai hanging up on me for the second time in two days.

Chapter 9 – Luke's

Tsai ordered me to Seattle and hung up on me. I was tired of the wires, the networks, and the phones. I wanted to see her again.

I drove to the jail, parked, and went to the front door. There was no window, only a locked door in a brick wall. I pressed the buzzer button, and a voice from the speaker in the wall above me asked me what I wanted. I talked to the speaker, gave them Kaori's name, and said I wanted to see her. The voice told me that visiting hours were only on the weekends unless I had a court order to visit with her now or unless her lawyer accompanied me.

I went back to my car and drove downtown. I turned off Front Street and drove into the parking lot by the river, where I had seen Pascal's truck several times. It was there, and I saw Pascal sitting in the front seat, reading a book. He smiled and nodded when he saw me. He got out of his truck and said, "Haven't heard from a Fella in a while. Wondered about him."

I told him that I was looking for him and guessed he would be parked down here.

"Only leased lot downtown," he said, "land that no one wants, yet. Probably be a hotel soon."

I asked him what he was reading, and he held up the book. "If Not Now, When?" by Primo Levi.

"Good?" I asked.

He shrugged, and tossed the book into the cab's back seat, and asked, "What is a Fella thinking about now?"

I asked him if he knew anything about Kaori, about what was going to happen next.

He said he didn't know anything other than what he had read in the paper.

I told him that I had stopped reading the news.

He said the newspaper hadn't written anything that we didn't already know.

I told Pascal that I wanted to talk with her, and had been to the jail, but I would have to wait until Saturday to see her, or go in with her lawyer. So I asked him if he knew who her lawyer was, and Pascal told me he assumed that it was one of the public defenders, and he told me where their offices were.

We were both standing and leaning against Pascal's truck, looking toward the back of the buildings on Front Street. Pascal pointed to a new building close to us, the back of a restaurant. He said, "That used to be Luke's bar. Before it was burnt. A Fella remember the place?"

I told him no.

He said, "Luke's. There was a pizza place in the back. The newspapers said that a grease fire started in an oven." Then he asked, "A Fella want to hear something never told before? A Fella want to share a secret?"

I answered, "Sure. I'm already holding a few of them, one more won't hurt."

Pascal nodded, then said, "It wasn't no pizza fire. It was someone hiding in the back closet. He piled up cardboard pizza boxes and empty beer cases in a corner, and he lit it.

"I found out 'cause last year he got busted for a repeat DUI. A family member called me from someplace, my number in google search, and wired me money. Had me bail him. Sad case. At the hearing, they sent him to Warm Springs for 60 days of treatment, and he hung himself there. I figure I can tell a Fella what he told me."

Pascal pointed back to where Luke's had been, and he went on, "I used to go there all the time. Live music most nights of the week. You sure you were never in there?"

I told him no.

"A Fella missed the best part of Missoula. Anyway, Luke's looked like a tough place. Harleys in a row outside. Barmaids with tattoos. Spit on the floor, that kind of place. But it wasn't bad, it was music and great dancing. Ace Wheeler's talent showcase. Banjo Bill Wylie. Eric Forrest. Jay Rummel. Good dance place."

I asked him if he brought the Norway girl there, and he said, "Luke's was way before Nordsky's time."

"Anyway," he said, "College girls would come with their boyfriends. And all these old-time, broke-down cases, they would mostly stand by the bar watching the girls. Quiet, hard-drinking. You'd see memories drowning in their eyes."

He continued, "Client who killed himself, he tells me that he was at Luke's every night drinking until he couldn't hardly walk. Then he would get in his car and drive and get his DUI's. He tells me, though, that he didn't use to drink at all. He tells me that the first time he walked into Luke's, nearly twenty years ago, a girl asks him to dance. He said she was, as he put it, 'a perfect beauty.' You must understand that my client is what I would call 'a perfect ugly.' Twisted, pitted, face. No 'sim-it-tree.'

"And this 'perfect beauty,' was a blind-drunk-drinker he tells me. He tells me a story. Tells me that she was fired from some big-city ballet that was doing a performance at the 'U'. Fired for being drunk. Fired, then she goes straight downtown and picks up my client. She even tells him that she wanted to know what someone with a 'rough face' was like. Tells him that she was tired of 'pretty people.' She tells him that. But he doesn't care, 'cause now he is in love.

"He had a job, and a rented place, and she stayed with him for a while. Each night the two would go to Luke's. Dance, and drink. He said she loved dancing almost as much as she liked her drink. But then, no explanation, she dumped him. Then he finds out that she was shacked up with someone else. Then a while later, someone else again. She stayed in Missoula, though, and she kept going to Luke's. She kept dancing and drinking. My client said he also kept going there, to Luke's, sitting at the bar, and would stare at her and whoever it was she was dancing with. Said he was waiting for her to come back to him. He said he even kept an unopened fifth on the bathroom counter and a full ice cube tray in the freezer -- said she liked drinking whiskey with ice in the bath." Pascal shook his head, and continued, "Then, my client said, she stopped coming into Luke's, and that he never saw her again.

"Anyway, she was gone 'bout twenty years, but my client kept drinking every night up there," Pascal waved his arm toward where Luke's used to be, "said he kept going into Luke's each night, sitting, and watching the girls. Said he if he drank enough, he would see her face in all their faces. See the strangers become his 'Beauty.'

"Then he burnt the place down. And he didn't get caught. Told me that he had to do it to save his life. But it didn't help, he kept drinking and told me he kept seeing her face even when he slept. Probably saw her face too clearly when he was taking treatment at Warm Springs. Finally, ended it all with torn bedsheets and a light fixture."

Pascal sighed, "I figured he gave me his life story. Gave it to me alone. Now I've shared it with you."

Then Pascal added, "Guy walks into Luke's his first time, and a friggen ballerina falls into his arms. His first mistake was meeting her, and his second was thinking it would happen again."

Pascal asked, "Is that going to be your story? Gotta say, a Fella has the same look. Haunted. Looking for more of the same bad...." but before I could answer, he smacked the side of his truck and said, "Hell. I see the same look in my eyes when I shave. Same look in most everyone's eyes. Looking for lost chances." Then he pointed at me, his finger lightly touching my chest, and said, "A Fella happens to have his one locked in the slammer for keeps. That must hurt. Come on, let's go find out which one of the lazy snakes is hers. Your turn to drive."

Pascal got in my car and gave me directions to the public defender's offices which were nearby. We went inside. The guy at the front desk knew Pascal, and the two talked about the weather for a while and how cold the coming winter would be. Then Pascal asked the receptionist if he knew who was handling the 'artist murderer.' The receptionist answered, "Clint Eulichol, for now. You want to talk with him? I think he was about to go visit with clients, but you might be able to catch him if you hurry," and he pointed upstairs.

We went up a flight of stairs to an office with an open door. Inside was an albino man. His hair was typing-paper-white, and his eyes were red. He looked up at us as we knocked on his door, recognized Pascal, and said hello to him. He glanced at me and spoke to Pascal, "Don't be asking for specialized exceptions. I am booked solid in an extravagant manner." He said this with pauses as if he was crudely fishing with worms for big words in a stagnant pond.

Pascal answered, "Aw, Clint, this is a friend," and he introduced me and said, "This Fella is the sorry-assed fool who bailed out 'Kaori Y', double murder, the first time. He was hoping you could spend some of your valuable time with him."

The lawyer looked at me and then at Pascal. He shuffled folders on his desk, then looked up at a clock and said, "There isn't truly a purpose, a point. She doesn't want representation. She has presented no defense in any manner. However, being that we live in a death-penalty state, she must have councel." He sighed and continued, "I am as yet temporary. There will be someone from Helena taking her files from me soon. Besides," and he looked up at the clock again, "My entire day is orchestrated by obligations. No time at all for unscheduled encounters."

I explained that I wanted to talk briefly with Kaori and had been told I would have to wait until the weekend unless her lawyer accompanied me. So I asked him if there was any way to get me in that afternoon. "Any chance at all?" I asked.

Eulichol again looked at the clock. Then he looked at Pascal and said, "In private practice I would be able to charge for breaking my schedule."

Pascal asked, "What would a 'private practice' lawyer be able to charge for such a thing?"

Albino answers, "It would be a three-hour disruption --- and lawyers who handle capital cases get at least three-hundred an hour." He sighed again, shuffled more folders on his desk, and said, looking at me, "But then, I am simply a ward --- if you will --- of the state. Much the same as all our clients become. I must be off."

Eulichol stood up, put on a heavy coat, and turned the collar up to go above his ears. He also took a white felt cowboy hat from the coatrack and put that on too.

We left his office and went downstairs with him. He paused by the steps and put on a pair of dark sunglasses, and said, "I'm heading out toward the jail..." and he paused.

Pascal looked at me, then back to the lawyer, and said, "This Fella here might be heading out that way too. Tell you what, wait for him a tad before you buzz yourself in. Fella might be interested in talking with you then."

The lawyer nodded, then said, "I have realized that I have forgotten something of need. I will be about ten minutes delayed," then he turned and went back inside.

Pascal touched my shoulder and said, "Come on," and we walked back and got in my car. "Is it worth nine hundred bucks for you to see her today?" Pascal asked, "Mr. Sleaze is giving a Fella the chance to get to the bank. I know. He does things like this. It's the reason he still works for the city. He makes money doing almost nothing at all."

I told Pascal that I didn't need to go to the bank, that I had enough cash, and yes, it was worth it. Pascal nodded, then said that I should give the money to him and drive to the jail and wait. Pascal told me that he would give the nine hundred dollars to the lawyer.

I took ten one-hundred-dollar bills from the wad of cash in my coat pocket and gave them to Pascal. I said, "Keep one."

Pascal removed one bill from what I had handed him and put the rest into his coat pocket. Then he handed back the extra hundred and said, "I never take this sort of dirt. Reason I am broke all the time. I might facilitate it a bit, but I don't want to profit from any of Eulichol's sleaze. He would be hiding from the sun even if he did have pigment. The freak show shines right out those eyes. Bleak." Pascal got out of my car and said, "I'll walk back to my 'office.' A Fella can drop by later." Then he headed back into the public defender's building.

I drove to the jail. Second time in one day. The road was spotted with ice, and the sky was the color of depression. At the jail, I went and waited by the door with the buzzer, and after a few minutes, the lawyer's car pulled into the lot. He got out and walked up to me, whistling. I nodded at him, and he said, "I examined my schedule and found I am actually supposed to visit one 'Kay-or-i Y' today."

"Imagine that," I replied. Then I said, fast, "I want to be alone with her. You understand that, right?"

He shrugged, and said, "I shall ask the jailor in private to determine the appropriateness of your private request. I shall pass on the information that you have indicated, that you have personal affairs to discuss." Then he pressed the buzzer, and we stepped inside in an air-lock room that stunk of unwashed feet and guilty sweat. Then we were buzzed into a long hallway that was blocked by a security checkpoint. The albino talked briefly and quietly with a jailor and filled out some form. Then we both emptied our pockets. Keys and wallets and phones went into envelopes.

We walked through a metal detector and, escorted by the jailor Eulichol had spoken with, were led through another electronically locked door into a hallway lined with metal doorways. I assumed that the jailer would have us wait in some kind of meeting room and would have seen if Kaori had wanted to see me, but instead, we were brought straight to her. While we were walking, the lawyer explained that he would wait out in the hallway while I visited with Kaori. The jailor said, to Eulichol, "While she is in this place, you make most of the rules, I'm an escort. I'll be outside the door." Then he added, "She's on suicide watch anyway. Camera sees and hears everything. The desk will be watching and recording."

We stopped at a numbered door, and the jailor used a pass card key, something that looked like a hotel keycard, and opened the door. He didn't knock. He didn't ask permission.

Kaori was alone in the cell. It was about five feet wide by ten feet long with a high, ten-foot ceiling. There was a bed, a sink, and a toilet built into the wall at the end. Kaori sat on the bed, cross-legged, hair in front of her face, sketching in a notebook. She didn't look up. The jailor motioned me in and said, "Mash this button if you need attention. Otherwise, I will be back in fifteen," and he pointed to a black button near the door. Then I was locked in, alone, with Kaori.

For about half a minute, I stood quietly and didn't say anything. She was wearing a jail uniform that looked vaguely like bright pajamas. She was also wearing slippers like the ones she had on the night I bailed her out. I could hear her uneven breathing, a quiet gasping which was in time with the motions of her arm. She was crosshatching and filling in an area in her sketchbook with a rubbery-looking felt tip pen. Finally, I said, "Hello, Kaori."

She stopped drawing and looked up. I had expected her to be angry or indifferent, but instead, she happily exclaimed, "You!" and dropped the pen and pushed the notebook away. She jumped off the bed and came and hugged me. She said,

"You visit me!" She stepped back and asked, questioningly, "You take me out? You bail me?"

I shook my head no. I said that she could not be bailed out. I explained that I was there to see her and that we didn't have much time.

She nodded and pointed up to a recessed video camera that was mounted in the ceiling's corner and said, "They watch all time. I know. So shamed. Light never goes off."

I touched her hand and said we should talk. I stepped around her and sat on the bed, but she stayed standing. She saw the discoloration that was still across my face, the bruising from where she broke my nose, and she asked, "Face hurt? So sorry. Not you I hit. Not you."

I answered, "I'm fine." Then I said, "No, I am not fine. I am, how did you say it once, 'I am so sad.'"

She said, "You remember everything. But must not be sad for me. I be sad for me. Me my own lonely. Me my own time." Then she clapped her hands together and said, "I have idea. Play game. I tell you happy word. You tell me happy word."

I asked her what she meant, and she replied with, "Plum. So good. Dark plum." She closed her eyes, she moved her tongue slightly out of her mouth, over her lips, she said, "So --- how you say --- dee-lee-us." Then she opened her eyes, and said, "Now you. Give me happy word."

"Delicious," I said, "Yes, plums are delicious." She was looking at me, honestly waiting for me to say a 'word,' a single word. Again, like the first time I had seen her, I had no idea what to do or say. I was not even sure why I was there. I wanted to confess to her about the cash I had buried. I wanted to tell her about Tsai. Or I wanted to ask Kaori about herself, about everything that I would otherwise never know about her. Sweet drink. Plum. A game. A child. No good word. No single word. I picked up the sketchbook, another school notebook with lined paper, and I asked, looking at her, "Do you need other notebooks, ones without lines?"

"No!" she answered, "Those not happy words. Game is happy word! Then I talk." She came over and took the notebook from me and held it. "Say happy word now. Give me happy word."

I was quiet for a few moments. I said, "Moon." She smiled, and I said, "Full moon on a clear night." I looked at Kaori, and she was still smiling, so I went on, "Stars. No city lights. A clear sky."

"And day will be clear too?" She asked, nodding, "Day good like night?"

"Yes," I answered, "Sleep in the day," I pointed at the narrow slit of a window up by the ceiling at the far end of the cell, "With sun from the window to make your dreams bright."

She said, "You not so good with one word, but you good with more. I say my next good words. Game sister and I played. Two words. Watermelon. Round."

As I looked at the folds of her prison clothing, no happiness came to me. I was remembering her feet and her hands and remembering her breath on my face. I asked, "Kaori, do you need me to help you understand anything? I saw your checkbook once. Your money, does it come from your family? Does anyone in Tokyo know you are here? You should let someone hire you a good lawyer."

She said, with panic, "This not good words! Bad words!" But she went on, she said, "Tell no one. My shame." She bowed her head, then she said, "You look." She opened the notebook in her hands. She showed me drawings, turning the pages one at a time, not saying anything. All were beautiful. None were violent. I asked again about the lined paper, and she shook her head no. She said, "No bars here," she motioned to the walls and to the door which had no doorknob, to the slit of a window, "They tell me this jail not real one. Other jail will have bars. Paper has bars. Bars are right. Lines are bars," and she moved her hand along the lined paper in the notebook.

I tried to explain that she had not had a trial yet, but that after the trial unless she were innocent, she would be moved to the state prison.

She said, "I know. I had my trial with knife. I failed." She looked up at the video monitor and said, "You tell them I no kill self. You tell them nothing to see. You tell them I failed."

I started to talk again, but she interrupted me and said, "No. Now you look."

I find moments without looking. Memories. Like books on a shelf, there is a scattered chronology, a disjointed stratum. Storms followed by windless gray. But then there are the peaks – a soft evening rain in a bright sunset sky with a rainbow arching over the darkening east. Then the rainbow doubles, the new colors reverse, and the center of the partial circle becomes connected with a perfect and invisible line from the sun behind my head. Does it matter that she was a chance moment? Do the thickness of the spines on the cluttered shelf matter? Do the physics of light explain the beauty of color?

We have no choice other than to become veterans of time, but is it wrong to hold onto the sparks even if they still burn?

I can say, "On this day, I woke up, worked, ate, and slept." I can say, "During this month, it was the same as the last." But can I ask, can I say, "I want more?"

Kaori said, "One love." Did she sleep with me to burn her memories? Her "one love," who I never met and who is now dead. She used me. I knew. I know. I didn't care. I don't care. I want more.

"You look. You no touch." I remember her saying this to me in New York. I was kneeling next to the hotel bed, and she was lying on top of the covers. She had turned crosswise so that she faced the wall of glass and the cityscape night.

Then, in the jail cell, I was paging through the notebook that she handed me. In the drawings, her hands were always touching him. His shoulder. His arm. His face. And she was always looking at him. In those drawings, though, he was never looking at her. He was looking away. He looked down, or he looked past the steam rising from a cup of tea.

She had killed her 'one love' when he no longer would touch her, and she had also killed the person he had been touching. And she used a jailhouse felt-tipped pen and on ruled paper --- with lines that were the bars that her cell did not have --- showed me images that were already becoming the sparks that would keep burning.

I pointed to a sketch with a teacup, which had a Kanji character underneath it, and I asked, "What does this say?"

And in the jail cell, while Kaori knelt on the floor next to where I was sitting on the bunk, she put her hand on mine. Then fast, she took it away. She looked up into me --- right into me --- and said, "Spring."

Then she told me, "Met in Spring. I seventeen. He soldier. He visit Tokyo. We Karaoke. I go visit in Okinawa. Train all night. Morning I make tea for him. He tell story about home in Montana. Says come to Montana."

I closed the notebook and tried to give it back to her. But she said, "No. You take. You look. You understand art."

Then the door to the cell opened, and the jailor was there telling me I must leave. I stood up and tried to hug her, but she turned and faced the back wall of the cell. She said, "No touch. Ever again. Everything gone. You go now. Forever."

Walking through the hallway lined with the numbered doors, out of jail, Eulichol, the albino lawyer, nodded toward the notebook I was carrying and asked, "You get your money's worth?"

I said, "Shut up," and he smiled like he was used to hearing people say this to him all the time.

Chapter 10 - XX

Days and nights went by. The fresh snow had been trodden into dirty ice, but I had not noticed much else. I went to my office in Missoula each day, closed the door, read old math books, and answered occasional messages. There had been no other news regarding Kaori and no other contact from the thin detective.

And nothing from Tsai. I was hoping that Tsai had decided that the backdoor code had run long enough on the SLAM network to have been worth his briefcase full of cash. I thought that maybe I wouldn't hear from him again.

Then, on a Thursday morning, Suzzy knocked on my office door and said, "You hear about what is happening at SLAM?"

"No," I said.

She said, "Dave Cheat was in a car wreck. It's awful. He's dead." She paused and then continued, "Fritter called. You are supposed to call him now."

Dave Cheat is dead. Dead!?

I remembered him juggling. I was leaning on the railing, looking out over the water with him. He was telling me about a bad knee. Had I gotten him killed for five thousand hundred-dollar bills buried in the mountains?

Suzzy was looking at me, waiting for me to say anything.

"What!?" I asked.

Suzzy said that it happened yesterday evening. She said, "It's sad when someone you know dies."

I picked up the phone and called Tsai. Called him directly. Not caring about his fear of phones. I wanted to ask him, "Did you have Dave Cheat killed so I wouldn't 'have a problem.'" There was no answer.

I started to dial the corporate number for BTG, but then I stopped. I thought that even if Tsai had killed Dave Cheat, what would confronting him accomplish?

Instead, I called Seattle and asked for Fritter's office, SLAM's CEO. Fritter answered and said, "Bad about Cheat."

I asked him about the wreck, and Fritter told me that no one knew yet what had happened. He said Dave was driving in afternoon traffic. "Not much to explain. He veered off of I-5. Maybe overcorrected. Flipped. Caught fire. Bad," he repeated. Then he said, "Need your help now, Enzi."

"That new car of his, that Tesla," I said. "I thought it couldn't crash."

"Software," Fritter said, "you know about software. Always bugs."

Then Fritter said that he needed me to come to Seattle immediately "to help transition the coders who worked for Cheat." He said, "They're a smart group, shouldn't take more than a few days on site."

I asked Fritter why he wanted me, and he said, "Dave was saying great things about you. He used to complain about your Montana group's incorporation into the company. Turn-a-rounds are impressive. Hold on...." Then I heard Fritter talking with someone else in his office, and then he got back on the phone and said to me, "Straight talk, Enzi. Lot depending on our work with British Telglomerate. Must make sure that continues smoothly. Need you to jump. Be a rockstar. You need to be here now."

Again, I was quiet. Like the questions from the thin detective that I wouldn't answer. Because the only safe answer is no answer. "You have the right to remain silent." For a reason. Because if I spoke, I would yell. I would shout, "Your employee number nine died yesterday, and all you need now is the BTG deal to continue smoothly?" I held onto my right. I was silent.

Fritter asked, "Enzi? You there?"

I took a deep breath and told Fritter that I would catch the afternoon flight and be at SLAM early the next morning. I went home, packed a few clothes, and flew to Seattle. The five-minute flight took an hour.

When we landed, it was raining outside and crowded in the airport. As I was walking through the concourse, a man came up and started walking close to me. Our shoulders brushed together. I looked at him. He was short and solid. His hair was dark, about an eighth of an inch long, like his head had a five o'clock shadow. The back of his neck was tattooed with symbols that I couldn't understand, the letters jagged and of different sizes. He was wearing a worn leather jacket. He smelled strongly of stale cigarettes. Each time we were jostled together by the crowd, I tried to move further away from him, but he pushed against me until I was nearly walking against the wall. Finally, when we were near the men's restroom entry, he stepped in front of me, directly blocking me, and made me abruptly stop. Then he said, "Sorry about this, Mate."

He had a British accent. Before I could answer him, he grabbed hold of my shirt, pulled me off balance, and tripped me over his leg so that I fell hard. I was lying on the floor at the entrance to the restroom, with people walking past me. The short man who had done this to me was walking away, mixing with the crowd in the concourse. As I lay on the floor, I remembered his hands as he grabbed my shirt. They had identical tattoos, a purple X on each finger's knuckle. X's on the left. X's on the right.

People stepped around me. No one offered help. The floor was wet and soapy. When I stood up, I saw that I had been thrown down next to a warning sign that read, "Caution," and which had a drawing of someone falling.

I looked for my travel bag, thinking that I had been robbed, thinking that it had been the motive for the attack, but it was there on the floor. I picked it up. It was like nothing had happened. Except my shoulder was sore from falling. And the front of my shirt was ripped open with most of the buttons torn off. I went into the restroom to put on another shirt from my travel bag.

The restroom was crowded. I stood at a sink next to a man who was washing his hands and talking loudly. He was wearing a blue-tooth earpiece. He said, "We have been over this a hundred times. There's nothing more to talk about," but then he said, "Hold on, I have another call coming in, don't go away."

The rows of sinks and mirrors. The faucets that went on and off without being touched. Toilets that flushed and refilled automatically. Disordered lines of men. The endless loop of the airport security warnings playing from speakers in the ceiling. It was something worse than chaos. It was tiled loneliness.

I left my torn shirt in the restroom trash bin, went back to the concourse, stopping first to look left and right, then stepped back in with the crowd.

I got a ride downtown and checked into a motel near SLAM. I left my bag in my room and went across the street to a restaurant and had dinner.

When I came out of the restaurant, it was still raining.

Someone said, "Hey Mate." I looked, and leaning against the wall was the short man with the shaved head with the X's on his knuckles. I stepped back. I said, "Come near me, and I start yelling."

"No, you won't," he said, "sorry about that bit near the loo. Mutual friend told me to get your attention first and talk later."

"Tsai, are you here because of Tsai?"

"Names don't work, Mate. Let's walk." And he went past me, down the sidewalk, toward where the waterfront turns from tourist to grit. He didn't look around, but he knew that I was following him.

"You owe me a new shirt," I said.

He stopped walking. He had a child's school bag, a book-bag daypack, slung over one shoulder that looked like it had books in it. He said, "Mutual friend said to deliver this," then he took the bag off his shoulder, and from an arm's reach away, threw the bag hard at me. It hit my chest and fell onto the sidewalk.

"Pick it up, Mate, take a look," he said.

I did. It was heavy and lumpy. I unzipped the top of the bag and looked inside. It was filled with bundles of hundred-dollar bills, each with a paper band that read, "$10,000."

"There's your shirt, Mate," he said. "It should have been your bloody teeth too. Still could be."

I zipped the bag closed and held it loosely. Then I held it out to him, but he said, "Won't take it, Mate. Not worth it. And our mutual friend had this message for you. 'Do your job.' So toss that in the water if you don't want it."

Then XX walked into the traffic, forcing cars to swerve and brake. When he got to the other sidewalk, he was gone.

Back in my room, there was an envelope slid under the door with my name on it. I opened it. It was a sheet of thermal paper from a fax. The hotel must have kept one around to go with the taxi stands. The fax had one typed line, "Payphone. End of the lobby. Midnight."

Before midnight I took the elevator downstairs. Connecting with the hotel's lobby was a hallway, and at its end were a few payphone kiosks and chairs. I was the only person there. I sat down at the last phone and waited. Then the phone rang.

I picked it up and said, "A fax? More cash? A phone? Really?" Then I asked, "The Brit, was that necessary?"

Tsai didn't answer me directly. Instead, he said, "You count what he gave you?"

I told Tsai, "I don't want more money. I didn't ask for it. Not going to do anything for it."

Tsai said, "You are not done."

I said, "I'll leave this cash in some locker. I don't want it. And I'll give you back the rest too. But you'll have to wait until spring for that, after the ground thaws."

Tsai said, "So, you buried it. Good. Safest way."

I asked, "Did you hear anything I said? I am done. I don't even want to know what is going on. I am done. You can have all the money back."

Tsai said, "Too late. You proved you could make this work. Now it isn't about the money we gave you. Now it is about what we are losing every day, I have partners. They are your partners now too. And you are making them angry."

I wanted to be the one to hang up first, but I kept listening as Tsai said, "Turn it back on, Enzi." Then he hung up on me.

Back in the hotel room, I dumped the daypack's contents onto the bed. There were fifty bundles. Another half a million dollars.

I wondered how Tsai had paid Mr. XX, the Brit, to kill Dave Cheat. I doubted Tsai had paid him using bundles of old hundred-dollar bills. I bet that Mr. XX was the proper sort who preferred Krugerrands and Canadian Maple Leafs. Or maybe Mr. XX took his pay the easy way in crypto wallets on thumb drives. Tsai probably only used dangerous cash with me as an angry joke, like he was saying with it, "You people who push buttons, go and figure out what to do with paper." You people. You coders who think you are in control.

For enough money, cash, gold, or crypto, machines can be corrupted. Moving mass can be made to look like a momentous accident. The words of physics. "Momentum," that word which means a product of mass multiplied by velocity. "Direction," that word which is the vector of going. Then a rapid turn of a wheel or a fast hack of a microprocessor in a network-connected car. Then the final word would be "kinetic," as the direction brings the momentum to an abrupt halt, with all its mass times velocity squared.

I put the cash back into the daypack and put it up on the closet shelf.

Early the next morning, I called the front desk. I explained that I was working in my room for the day and that I wanted to be left alone. They told me to hang the "Do Not Disturb" sign outside my door but that they would also let housekeeping know not to clean my room. Then I left the hotel by a side door and walked the few blocks to SLAM.

I went straight to Fritter's office. He always looked like an indifferent Southern California surfer working on his tan while scanning the water for anyone who might dare to encroach on the next wave. But, his look said, "All the waves are mine."

Fritter and I shook hands, and we stayed standing, and he said again how unexpected and sudden Dave Cheat's death had been. Then he said, "Glad you are here now, Dude. Dave had taken a liking to you. That will go a long way working with his peeps. Need to make sure the British work is cool."

Fritter didn't say anything about any sort of memorial for Dave or say anything else about the accident.

I went downstairs with Fritter to where the coders had their cubicles. Cups of coffee and computer monitors. Printouts of code and thick software manuals. Whiteboards with database schemas and flowcharts. Office kitsch and fluorescent lights. The only windows were many cubicles away. It was the standard sort of location where companies put their coders. Like a parking garage, but with carpet and without cars.

I said hello to the coders I had talked with during the meeting two weeks back. Then I listened to their sincere sadness about Dave's death. He had been liked.

Fritter interrupted the talking about Dave and told the coders that I had taken over Dave's responsibilities until a new project manager could be hired. The coders nodded and didn't say anything. Fritter then said that I should be given time with anyone I needed to talk with. Next, Fritter, the company CEO, told the coders that I had been given full access to get into all the files and all the networks. He said, with emphasis, "A lot riding on this British deal." Then he said, "You guys rock," and headed back to his office.

As soon as Fritter was gone, the coders looked confused and told me that there were no problems, everything was working, and that the deadlines were not a worry. They said that the only active new work had been adding the Montana interface code, and that had been completed. A coder said, "I'm not sure what Fritter's worried about. All the other work for BGT was completed a month ago," and added, "Fritter never has a clue."

I told them then there wouldn't be much to do but that I still needed to spend some time looking through everything to satisfy Fritter's request.

The coders nodded, and they shared more anecdotes about Dave. They talked about how much he liked juggling and how he had told them he had juggled with me that day by the pier. They also told me about his favorite bar, a place where there were one hundred and fifty different types of microbrew on tap, and that Dave had been working on drinking a pint of each. "Place gives you a tee-shirt after you have drunk a pint of all hundred and fifty, but Dave also paid the bartender five dollars for each empty mug after each new beer. Said he wanted to keep track to make sure he would get the free tee eventually." The coder went on, "that shirt, if he had managed to drink his way into it, would have cost him seven-hundred-and-fifty dollars! Dave loved things like that. Tee-shirts and memorabilia," and the coder pointed into a cubicle and said, "This is Dave's."

I looked over the cubicle divider, and there were a set of juggling clubs, a shelf lined with beer mugs, and the five book-weights I had bought from Uwajimaya's. I had forgotten about them and realized that Dave must have taken them when he left the pier.

I went into Dave's cubicle and sat down. I turned on his computer. The six connected monitors lit up with SLAM's green logo. I used my company ID card, along with my thumbprint, to log into the SLAM network. A message box appeared stating that Fritter had upgraded my security clearance.

The coders had gone back to their cubicles, and I was left alone. I logged into the version control system and found the exact date and time when Dave had found, and removed, my backdoor. I read the notes that he had added. He had written that a memory overrun was removed. He also noted that the over-run did not appear to cause any problems other than causing a minor network slow-down when it occurred.

I looked at Dave's default version control settings and saw that they were set for maximum change tracking, logging dates, and times for every computer file he had opened. I scanned the list of file names, and I saw that even though he found where I had de-referenced a pointer to a function -- the memory over-run, which he had thought was a minor bug --- Dave had not opened the actual backdoor file, which was hidden in the graphic files for the interface.

I changed Dave's version control settings to stop logging file activity. Then I changed his system clock so that everything I was doing would appear to have been done the day before his car wreck. Finally, I created a temporary project and added a new de-referenced function pointer, hiding it one layer deeper than my earlier code had been. This deeper method of calling the backdoor would mean that that hijacking of SLAM's network would only degrade its performance by a fraction of a fraction of an already tiny amount. If I had done that the first time, Dave would never have noticed.

I looked at my new code changes. Then, I looked at the time. It had taken twenty-one minutes to reinstate the backdoor, the hack that Tsai – and his 'partners' – needed to continue to steal the financial data from the stream between New York and London.

Twenty-one minutes and one innocent person's death.

But it was not turned on yet. Before the new code could work, it would have to be installed everywhere on the SLAM network by being checked into the main code body. And that was then one mouse click away.

My hand lingered on the mouse.

I looked around. No one was standing nearby. I looked around Dave's cubicle again. I looked at the photos on Dave's shelves. I stood up and picked up the closest photo. It was a younger Dave. He was wearing a backpack and smiling. Behind him were mountains. In the photo, he was not alone; he held hands with a woman wearing a pack. I turned the frame over and took the photo out of its holder. "Leslie and me by Mount Olympus" were written on the back of the photo," and the date, about ten years earlier. I put the photo back in its frame and looked at another. Family photos, children, a Christmas morning by a tree, presents, and torn paper. I didn't take any more photos out of their frames. I looked at the books on his shelves. Mostly software books of dead computer languages. Perl. Awk. But there were poetry books too. Charles Bukowski. Linda Pastan. And some fiction. Michael Fitzgerald. Chandler. And there was a paper-back, yellow and blue, called "The Periodic Table," by Primo Levi, which I took off the shelf and thumbed through. It was a book by the same author the Somalian cab driver, and Pascal had also been reading. The author the cab driver told me had written, "You survive by telling stories." An author who, three weeks before, I had never heard of.

I sat back in front of Dave's computer with its six monitors. I put my hand on the mouse and moved the cursor over the "Check In" icon. One click and the backdoor would be active again. I could then go back to Montana and read old math books. There would be no XX coming for me again. The counter would remain between Tsai and me.

I hesitated and looked again at Dave's photos and books. And the shelf of beer mugs that had only made it about halfway to its hundred-fifty mug goal. Even if the military had trained him, Dave had not been a 'cloak and dagger' person, and he should not have died because of anyone else's greed.

I took one deep breath, and without checking it in, I deleted my temporary project. Then I reset the computer's time and date back to where it should have been, and I logged out of SLAM's network.

In a cubicle, several coders were talking together and laughing. I explained to them that I had finished reading Dave's project schedule and had looked at the current delivery status. I said, "You were right. Everything is solid and already done. You don't need any interference from me." They all smiled and went back to the stories they were sharing. And as I walked away, I said quietly, not sure if anyone could have heard, "I've added enough chaos already."

I left SLAM without talking to anyone else and without doing what Tsai had told me to do.

No one had been in my hotel room. The daypack was still in the closet. I took it and my travel bag and caught a car up to Capitol Hill, near where many students lived. In a corner grocery store, I looked on the bulletin board, the type with thumbtacked cards. There were a few cars for sale. I called from the burner and found someone about twenty years old who was selling their first car, an old Subaru. I offered him the amount that he was asking for, and he seemed surprised. I told him I would pay cash if he could get me the car right away, and he drove over.

The plates and tags were good, and I told him I needed to leave them on until I got down to the motor vehicle department. He started to say he needed to check to see if that was the right way to sell a car, but when I told him it was all legit for cash purchases under five thousand, the kid said sure. I paid him, and he signed the title, and I told him that I would have to wait to fill out the blank parts with my name until I got the new tags, confidently telling him that is the way it is done. He was counting the hundred-dollar bills which I had given him and said, "Sounds good." Then I had a car without my name connected to it. Another sort of burner.

I had been in Seattle for less than 24 hours. I wanted to get back to Montana before XX found out that I had gone and before Tsai realized that I was not working on turning on the backdoor again.

I stayed on I-90 and drove straight through, only stopping for gas and fast food. I went the speed limit and was in Missoula nine hours after leaving Seattle.

Back in Missoula. Nighttime. The hint of smoke in the winter air, people burning lodgepole and spruce in their woodstoves. People comfortable and safe. I parked the car two blocks from my house and left the daypack full of cash, covered with a blanket, in its back.

Chapter 11 – Empty Graves

When I checked my voicemail in the morning, I skipped through messages, erasing each after listening for a few seconds. But there was one from the thin detective that I listened to carefully. His message said that he saw that I had visited Kaori in jail and he wanted to meet with me again. He left a phone number.

I thought about ignoring him. But I wanted to know more about anything regarding Kaori. So instead of returning his call, I drove downtown in the Subaru with a daypack full of cash covered by a blanket. I went to the police desk in city hall. I asked to see Thin, who then came out to the reception desk to meet me.

"Didn't expect to see you," he said. He motioned me to follow.

I thought he was leading me to go into one of those interview rooms they show in the cop shows, the ones with nothing on the walls except a two-way mirror and a video camera, but instead, I followed him through a door with his name on it and into his office.

Thin sat down behind a wooden desk. Attached to one end of the desk was an old paper dispensing contraption, which looked like it had come out of an antique mall after having been on the counter of some butcher shop. But instead of wide butcher wrap, the contraption held a roll of bright white typing paper.

Tacked on all the walls of his office were the continuous paper scrolls that must have come from the dispenser on his desk. Some were short, a foot or two long, but others wrapped completely around the office's four walls. Drawn carefully on the scrolls were parallel, colored lines, which varied in width from fine to thick. Above and below all the lines were carefully written notes.

Thin watched me, waved his hand, and said, "Take a look."

The scrolls were timelines. The sort of long charts that history teachers tack up on the walls of classrooms.

Most of Thin's scrolls had multiple colored lines. Some lines were a few inches long. Others ran the entire length of the scrolls. Lines stopped, crossed each other, or moved apart. Most lines ended abruptly.

I glanced at Thin, and he said, "Look around as much as you want." He leaned back in his chair. "But what you want to see is not up there. It's here," and he tapped at the scroll of paper that was currently stretching out across his desk.

The scroll in front of Thin reached about mid-point on the long desk. Kaori's name was at the start of a fine, red line that began at the beginning of the length of paper and then grew wider. After her name, the first annotation read, "Tokyo," with a date. Near that date was another orange line, labeled "Boyfriend/Jim," which started above Kaori's. At a label that read, "Missoula," Jim's line moved onto Kaori's line. Then, a few inches past that convergence, a green line labeled "Elizabeth" began. Elizabeth's line curved down from the top of the paper, met Jim's and Kaori's lines, and caused Kaori's to bend abruptly downward.

My name was on Kaori's scroll, by a purple line that started a foot from where Kaori's began. My line widened at the point where I bailed her from jail. Then it widened more where Tsai, Kaori, and I had met. That was also the start of another line, labeled "Tsai," which began at another annotation reading, "NYC."

Kaori's line veered up on the scroll, away from mine. It ended Jim and Elizabeth's lines where it intersected them. At that point, there were many annotations with the date of the murders. Then Kaori's line leveled and continued, with its last annotation being a date and, "Arrested/Jailed."

I was looking at this when Thin asked, "Do I have things right about you?"

He did have things right. They were perfect. He had what I had told him. Almost nothing.

"Does it look correct?" Thin pressed again.

I didn't answer. I kept my silent right.

But I asked him a question, pointing to the scrolls on the walls, "Are all these crimes that you've solved?"

He moved his hand off Kaori's scroll, picked up a pen, and started flipping it between his fingers and over his knuckles. The way some people do with quarters. The detective nodded, yes. Then he asked, "You grow up here?"

I didn't answer.

He leaned toward me and said, "Well, I was born here. Went East for a while. Studied to be an architect. Bored. Came back."

He watched me, seeing if his confession would elicit some dialog. It did. I asked, "You curious about Kaori because of her drawings?"

He nodded. "That. And that she's a murderer." He paused, then said, "And because of you."

I knew he was pressing me to talk too much, but I asked the detective another question. "Why did you come back to Montana? You could have been," and this time, I waved at his walls, "a cop who draws lines anywhere."

He smiled. He didn't answer me. That was his right. Instead, he opened a drawer in his desk and brought out the notebook of Kaori's drawings that he had shown me the last time he and I had met. Thin said, "This case is simple. We know who did the killing. But I want your opinion." He turned to a bookmarked page and reached across the desk and handed me the notebook.

It was another sketch showing our trip to New York. It showed Kaori and me on the rooftop of the New York

Palace. Even though it had been drawn with a jail-issued felt tip, the sketch was detailed. The perspective was from above, as if she had climbed one of the radio masts and drawn what she had seen while looking down. The sketch showed the street with traffic. It showed the machinery and cables on the roof. She drew the low, narrow ledge. All of it had been drawn accurately. But she had also drawn something that had not happened. She had drawn herself naked and standing on the ledge, arms outstretched, balanced like a high-wire walker.

In the drawing, there was also a naked man sitting alone on the gravel. Me. It was a drawing of me, with a lot of Kanji characters on the bottom of the page.

"I had the writing translated." Thin said. He took a sheet of paper out from a folder and read, "Man takes me from jail and touches me. Man shows me place to jump. Man helps me kill my love. Together we do what I cannot do alone." Then the detective asked, "What does she mean?"

Between concrete and sky. My hands were under her shirt. Her hands on my shoulders. Her mouth against mine, the hum of air compressors, the roar of traffic from five hundred feet beneath us. That was where she had been, but then she had moved her right hand, her drawing hand, and drawn the truth that showed that she had been alone, even though I had been with her. Her arms and legs had been wrapped around me, but her thoughts had been elsewhere. And her thoughts walked her along the ledge, on the verge of a jump, on the edge of a fall.

I looked quietly at Thin and thought to myself: "She meant I killed the importance of her boyfriend, broke his touch, made her be a 'Nasty girl' who had sex with a drunk stranger on a rooftop." But to him, I said, "No idea what she meant. No idea at all."

"You do whatever you want," Thin said. "Don't you?"

I did not answer him.

He said, "You own that software company, the one in the Central Square building?"

I answered that question. I said, "I'm an employee there. It is a public company that has a Missoula office."

He asked, "You come and go? Right? You do as you please? That's what I hear. That's what I see. That sounds like ownership to me. That or you're a 'preem-a-donna'."

I didn't say anything, and he went on, "I checked with your company, SLAM, right? No one knew that you were in New York. I also checked with British Telglomerate," then he rummaged in a file and found Tsai's card again and read from it, "BTG. Tommy Tsai. Vice President of Broadband Networking." Then Thin said, "No one knew he was in New York either. I checked. Someone told me that they thought he was in London at the time when Kaori says she met him."

The detective leaned over his desk, holding out his hand, and asked me for the notebook, which I gave back to him. He then flipped through it and found the sketch that he had shown me during our earlier meeting. The sketch Kaori had drawn of Tsai handing me the case filled with money, on which she had written underneath, in Kanji, "He takes the money."

Kaori probably had guessed what it held while we were in the cab driving toward the NBC building. She had glanced at me while I had taken the first envelope of cash out of the briefcase. Then she probably noticed that I always had hundred-dollar bills after that.

"Know what I think?" Thin asked, "I think there is a connection between this Tommy Tsai, you, and her family back in Japan. I think you were part of something that didn't go as it was supposed to. I know that she killed these kids." He tossed several glossy photographs onto his desk, crime photos of Jim and Elizabeth as they were found, which I didn't look at or touch. "But I think you were supposed to be part of it too. I think you got the money from Tsai, and you were supposed to do something for it. Maybe you were supposed to have done it for her."

I suddenly felt the same as when Dave Cheat had found my backdoor hack but had only thought it was an overrun bug.

Thin was close, but he was wrong.

"Not Japanese," I said.

"What?" Thin asked.

"That person, with that card," I answered, "we chanced into each other in New York, that's all, but I think 'Tsai' is a Chinese surname. Not a Japanese name. From his accent, I guessed he grew up in Texas. You are wrong to think he is anything other than a Texan, or anything other than what is on his card."

Thin waited for me to say more. But I was quiet again. I had already said too much.

"I've been checking on you," Thin said, "Gaps in the work history. People you work with don't know much about you. I don't think you have friends. I don't think people like you."

Again, I didn't respond, and he continued, "I think maybe you were only supposed to have messed with the kids' records. That's what tech people do, right? Mess with files, get people in trouble, right? Were you supposed to mess with them? Maybe break them up? She wrote," and he hits the notebook loudly with his fist and repeats from memory, "man helps me kill my love."

He stared at me. Then he asked, "Were you the 'man,' or was it Tsai?"

Neither of us said anything. I could hear talking from the next-door offices. I heard a mechanical clock ticking. Then Thin leaned back in his chair again and said, "I also just don't like you."

And I shouldn't have, but I said, "But you like her? You like what you feel when you look at her drawings? You see her drawings and they touch you, right?"

He glared at me.

"I liked her, and I liked her drawings," I said, "But I don't know why she killed her ex. I don't know why she killed the other girl. I wasn't any part of it."

Thin put Kaori's notebook back in the desk drawer, stood up, pointed at his door, and said, "Get out of here. I'm not going to threaten you because you already know that I have."

I left the police station but didn't want to be anywhere inside. So I drove up the Pattee Canyon Road, behind Mount Sentinel. I parked at the Crazy Canyon trailhead and walked a few miles up an old fire road until I was above the polluted air.

There were tall Ponderosas on the open hill slopes. I stopped under one of them, leaned against it, and put an arm partially around the tree. The bark was broken in natural patterns. I looked up at the branches and those spiraled around the trunk. A Fibonacci sequence, a growing spiral.

As my sweat cooled on the back of my shirt, I began to get cold. In my coat pocket, there were matches. I started a fire. A raven glided past and landed in the nearby tree. He croaked loudly and was answered by another raven from across the canyon. I put more sticks on the fire. Thin had been right in that I didn't have friends. What I had were people who needed what I could do for them. I had rocks and trees. I had fire and ravens. And I had patterns.

I kicked at the snow, and the crystals that were thrown into the sunlight sparkled. I did not see the "infinite" that schoolbooks use to describe snow, saying that each snowflake is unique. What I saw instead were repeating fractal sequences. The branches that were on the tree above me repeated. The patterns in the bark of its trunk repeated. The snow that I kicked sparkled with repetition.

Tsai had said, "Go push some buttons or whatever it is that you people do." Tsai didn't want explanations, no matter how brief. He wanted results and money. The same as most people. But Tsai's infectious greed demanded more.

I saw my future in the patterns of my past. Like a fractal cycle, in the sparkle of memories that are never the same. I kicked at the snow again.

I saw myself having friends. Then losing friends. I saw my best friend, Helen, having sex with another man, who I had thought of as my friend too.

I was working with the v-v-vacuum, and working at losing my stutter. Working on being at peace, living with my 'one love.' She was in college, and I had a job – I told you this, but I still must remind myself often, through telling you, of where I had been.

She had a family. A father, a mother, and sisters that she called and talked with often. About social events, about a cat, a dog, and about dorms and apartments, about jobs, about cars that their friends were buying, about good, normal stuff.

In the evenings coming back to the house that we shared was the closest I ever came to normal. Sometimes there would be friends from her classes visiting. The windows in that north-side Missoula house did not have curtains, and I would pause outside for a few moments and look in.

Then I would open the door and come inside to the warmth and the comfort. Those of us who have lived on the streets and the road know how much this means: a place to go into where no one will ask you to leave. And then, if you are also welcomed, you have a home.

And with Helen, it was a home. Sometimes with friends. Those evenings, all of us drinking and talking, but me mostly listening. Listening to the talking about what was wanted. Talking from people who had never been without, but who always wanted more.

Sometimes, when I was part of the conversations, my words did not have enough wanting to fit in. But there was nothing more I wanted, and I often didn't know what to say.

If I talked about the work I did, my janitor work, or about fixing old cars, I fit in a bit. But if I tried to talk about my mathematics, my patterns, then all the lightness left. So mostly, I tried to just listen.

When it was Helen and I alone, it was different. When it was her and I...

... The stitches had come out of her hand and wrist. I am tracing her thick scars with my fingertips. Candlelight, laying together on the bed. She tells me that she owes me her life. I say the same. We are both right.

There is a garden. "These are the best tomatoes ever," Helen says, coming inside, holding the hem of her skirt so that it has become a basket. "Come and try one." I go to where she is standing. I sit on the floor. I lean against her bare legs. She says, "You're tickling me." She hands me a tomato, and I bite into it like an apple. It is delicious. I push my face against her thigh. She lets go of her skirt, and the tomatoes bounce across the floor. She laughs. She lays down on the floor. She says, "You always know exactly what I want you to do. So how come you can't talk with my friends?"

One of those friends, another art student, brought her flowers and bottles of expensive wine. He also left drawings for her. One time a drawing of a hornet crawling on an open hand, on the wall next to the front door. He had drawn it with ink directly on the wall and written next to it, "Love you, Stewart." When I asked Helen why he would do this, she got angry at me and said, "Don't insult me. It's you I love."

The same evening that I had asked about the drawing on the wall, Helen asked me, "What do you want to do with your life? This not having money thing is getting old."

Instead of saying some easy lie like, "I'll try to get into college and become an engineer," I told her the truth, "I have no idea. I'm here with you. That's enough amazement for now."

Then, a few weeks later, I came home early with good news. I had gotten a new job, which meant more pay.

Because I kept fixing things, the place where I was working had promoted me from a janitor to their repairman. I had left work early with this news. It was mid-morning, the sun streamed through the windows, and I walked through the unlocked door.

They were there in the middle of the floor. She was on top of him, facing me, and she and I looked at each other.

I'm trapped with the details, but I won't share them with you.

I stepped backward. I closed the door. I got in my car, which I knew how to fix. I left.

It was death, except no one bled, no one died. Books left behind, clothing, candles, the garden, and the trinkets that money had bought but which were not enough.

Runaway, runaway, runaway. Much more than a word...

Then, two years later, after she was gone, I came back to Missoula. For a while, her ghost haunted me, especially near the places where we had been together. But when I avoided those spots, when I kept to the edges of the memories, they faded, and I stayed in Missoula.

The night we had found the bodies, that night in Maloney's, Pascal had said, "It's not right to sit near ghosts." He was right. I kicked snow over the fire, and the smoke turned to sooty steam, and its cold dampness covered me. The fractals stopped sparkling.

I was in Crazy Canyon. The sun was setting, and a cold wind whistled down the darkening canyon. There was another half-million in hundred-dollar bills in the back of the Subaru. Cash that I had not asked for and cash that I did not want. Cash that I knew Tsai was using to show me the insignificance of every part of my life. But that bag of cash also told me that neither Tsai nor his partners had anyone else they could get to do what they needed.

I walked out of Crazy Canyon and drove away from town, and headed east.

After an hour of driving, the interstate curved into the valley of tortured towns. Deer Lodge, Galen, Warm Springs.

Signs near the prison in Deer Lodge warned travelers not to stop for hitchhikers.

Then, at Galen, where the exit sign read, "No Services," I got off the highway, because I wanted to slow down, and drove south to the frontage road and past a bar with fifteen-foot-tall letters on its roof, a sign big enough to be read from the interstate. The sign used to read, "DUGOUT," but the first two letters had blown down and were rusting in weeds behind the bar, so the sign read, "GOUT."

The "No Services" town of Galen had the alcohol treatment prison. And one bar. People who worked in the prison drank in Gout before driving back to their homes.

I continued east past Warm Springs and the state mental institute, then up and out of the valley. Then down again, into Butte.

I headed up what used to be called "the richest hill on earth" but was now a toxic cinder. I parked by the Dubliner, a ten-story brick hotel built a hundred years ago, which had become half derelict since the mines shut down. Now it was a place that rented rooms for cash by the week without asking for identification. I asked for a specific room number, and it was available. The room was on the highest floor that was still in operation. The room had no phone and no television. The room had a solid oak chair and an even more solid oak desk. On the desk, there was a lamp with a green shade. I turned the lamp on and turned off the overhead light. No traffic sounds. No sounds from people in the other rooms. The room was the same as it had been years before when I had first stayed there.

My first time in Butte: before Helen, before software, before networks, before Tsai, before Kaori. I had been drifting up from work in Wyoming when I stopped in Butte, Montana. A gas station attendant pointed up to the Dubliner and told me that it was a cheap place to stay. After I had checked into a room there, I went outside and walked on the streets named after slow dreams and fast poison. Gold. Silver. Mercury. When I passed the public library, I went in. In a collection of mining books, there were a few old math books. On that shelf, there was also a thin, new textbook.

It was on that textbook's cover that I first read the word "fractal." The math in that book did not have the complexity of differential equations or calculus. Instead, it was a math of simple equations which fed their easy results back into themselves, over and over again. I took a pencil and a sheet of folded paper from my coat pocket. I wrote down several of the book's examples.

There were drawings in the book of a lake shoreline, and explanations of how that shoreline could be measured in a way that made its length endless. The smaller the steps of measurement, the greater the final distance. This "fractal" math showed that the Greek paradox of Zeno had been foolish. Zeno had seen an arrow heading toward a target and said he could prove that the arrow would never hit. After leaving its bow, the arrow would come halfway to its target. Then it would continue and be a quarter of the way, then an eighth, then a sixteenth, then on and on. The ancient math showed that the arrow would forever be an endless, smaller, and smaller fraction away from hitting, and thus the math proved that it would never hit. But of course, that was wrong. Arrows pierced targets. Arrows changed the lines on the history charts.

I also read equations from that library book that described another word that I had never seen before, "recursion." Those fractal equations showed me a way to view the repetition of my stutter and my flip-flopping view of reading. For the first time, I saw math that described a world that I was part of. But I did not see that I was also about to start learning tools valuable enough to kill for.

I stayed until the library's closing time. Then, I brought the book to the librarian and told him that I didn't have a card but wanted to know if I could borrow the book for a few days. He asked where I lived. I told him that I worked all over and was driving through town, but I would stay in town while I studied what was in the book. The librarian nodded and said, "Well, in Butte, a person is as good as their word," and he let me take the "Fractal Geometry of Nature" back to the Dubliner with my word that I would return it before I left town.

I stayed in the Dubliner for three days and filled pages of paper with equations that recursively became the Julia and the Mandelbrot sets. I glimpsed what could be predicted if the results of simple equations were fed back into themselves millions, billions, trillions of times. I had learned what a computer could be used for without ever having pounded a line of code.

When I returned "The Fractal Geometry of Nature" to the librarian, I stopped and looked at a framed black and white photo on the library wall. It was an early aerial photo showing the richest hill cluttered with mining camps and mineshafts. I noticed hundreds of light-colored mounds along the photo's edge. The mounds spiraled slightly, with a neatness and a pattern that nothing else in the photograph had.

The librarian came up to me as I was looking at the photo and said, "Place was a mess even before they dug the pit."

I asked him about the organized mounds.

"Empty graves," he said. "Refugees from wars and famine. The slaves of the Anaconda company. These," and he softly touched the glass of the framed photo, "are empty graves of the Chinese, who died by the thousand. Go up there now, and you will see where the relatives came and dug up the bones to take back to San Francisco, Seattle, New York. To all the Chinatowns that connect with pain back to here. But first, next to the graves, they cleaned off every racist speck of Montana dirt with tweezers and bleach. Left that hatred on the hill," and he tapped the glass.

I looked at the librarian. I asked him if his relatives had worked in the mines in the photo. He nodded yes. He pointed on the photo to a sprawling mining camp, where you could see tent tops, clotheslines, and rubbish heaps. He said, "I'm part Chinese and part Irish. Two sad histories met, and my parents stayed." Then he said, "Step outside while I smoke, and I'll show you something."

I walked out with him. He sat down on the street curb and lit a cigarette. "Here," he said, and he nodded at the road surface, "Look at this."

I sat next to him and looked at the road. There was a pothole in the asphalt, which was exposing a buried layer of red brick cobblestones.

The librarian said, "These bricks came from kilns that were in China. Then the cargo ships that brought the refugees over, ships meant to be filled with lumber or coal, those ships couldn't draft right with their soft, human loads. Even packed with people, the ships were not heavy enough, so the owners stacked bricks down there with them." He kicked at the exposed cobblestones and said, "Imagine the misery. Then they sold the bricks to the Anaconda, and you can still find these cobblestones on the back railway streets from Seattle to here. Everywhere the Chinese worked building the railways, tamping black powder into spark holes, or digging for copper. Everywhere they died."

The librarian threw his half-smoked cigarette into the middle of the street, then stood up and walked back into the library, saying to me before he went in, "Ten years working here. No one ever noticed or asked about those graves. Come back and borrow books anytime you want."

Now I had returned to the Dubliner and to the same room where I had first started learning fractals. I bought a bottle of Jameson from the bar off the lobby and went up to the room. I sat by the window at the same desk. Outside were the lights of Butte. The place where copper for all the wires had come from. Edison and Westinghouse on the East coast had figured out the physics and the business of electricity. But the metal for their needs had to be dug from this hill. And the laborers who died by the thousands had come from across the world, from wars and famine.

Then their bones were dug out of the poisoned, racist dirt, scrubbed clean, and taken away. And now, the lucky bones were stored in heirloom boxes in top-story apartments and condos of the richest cities around the world.

I drank from the bottle.

I was drinking too much.

But I kept drinking more until I was watching Butte's lights blinking off with the approaching morning. I was going to sleep for a few hours. Then I was going to drive south. Down I-15 toward deserts and salt. I was going to run away again.

Then I started thinking about Tsai and his two grandfathers from China who came to Butte. I remembered the librarian who long ago tossed his cigarette into the middle of the street and told me about bricks piled around refugees.

I turned on my burner and called Tsai's burner. Secrets on secrets. I had no idea what time it was wherever he might have been. I didn't think he would answer, but he did.

"Where are you?" Tsai asked.

I said, "You told me your grandfathers both worked in Montana." Then I asked, "Did they also both die in Butte?"

He said, "You didn't do the job you were paid to do."

"I don't want your money," I said and added, "And usually when someone doesn't do a job, you fire them. You don't have a thug throw more money at them."

"This is bigger than you can imagine," Tsai said.

"Do you have their bones?" I asked. "Did your parents go and dig them up? Or was it you? Is that our 'Montana connection' you spoke of when you first stalked me? Are you getting some revenge against the wires and Montana by using me?"

Tsai ignored the questions and said, "You sound drunk. Finish your job. The debt to my business partners grows."

"Answer me about your grandparents' bones," I said.

Then Tsai snapped, "Do what you know how to do, or all the people you care about will end up in boxes like my grandparents' bones."

I thought he was going to hang up then, but he didn't. He was waiting to hear me respond. I drank more whiskey, keeping the phone near my mouth so that Tsai could hear me swallow. Then I said, "I'm a friendless freak. There is no way for you to pressure me."

He said, "They will start with your business partner. Then the one who answers your phones. They won't stop. Think hard about what is at stake for you."

Finally beating him to it, I hung up and turned off the phone.

I went down to the hallway bathroom and was sick. Then I went back to the room and passed out on the bed.

When I woke up, it was getting dark. Again. I had stayed up for an entire night and gotten so sickly drunk that I had managed to turn day and night upside down. I went outside and walked to the M&M. I sat at the bar near several men who looked like they hadn't known a steady job in forty years but were still being worked to death. No one was saying anything to each other, and I fit right in.

After I ate, instead of heading south, I drove the two hours back to Missoula.

Chapter 12 – Iteration

B ack from Butte. Back to Missoula.
Running away, then returning.
My present was feeding on my past, and my future was waiting for the recursive loop to complete.

Again, I parked several blocks from my house, which was lucky because as I walked up to my front door, someone was sitting in the dark on the steps. He said, "Hello, Mate." Then he lit a cigarette and said, "Kept myself busy waiting for you."

I had stopped several paces away from XX and expected him to do something fast and violent, but he didn't. Instead, he shook the match out, and in darkness, said, "Give me a bell tomorrow. Left you the number inside. With another present." Then he walked past me and was gone.

I went inside and flipped on the lights. Torn apart and scattered on the floor of my house was all I owned. Poured over everything were cans of house paint and motor oil from boxes out in the carport. There was also a gagging bite of insecticide fumes, and I kicked at an empty can of wasp spray. Books, papers, dishes, clothing. Everything in my house was in ruined confusion. I went from room to room, turning on the lights. Every wall had multiple holes bashed in between the wall studs. And I saw that XX had spent time individually ruining things. Clothes were dumped from my dresser drawers, and those drawers were then smashed. Legs were broken off chairs. Books were torn in half along their spines. Water was running out from the bathroom, where the sink and toilet had been smashed with a sledgehammer --- a sledgehammer I did not own, which was left lying on the bathroom floor.

The only things in the house that weren't destroyed were the ceiling lights, my computer, and the desk. And one chair. Everything not needed for me to "push some buttons" was ruined.

He had not broken the windows or the door, probably meaning that he did not want neighbors to hear, but other than that concern, it seemed that he hadn't cared if I walked in on him while he was doing his trashing.

It did not look like he was searching for anything. This became clear when I found, laying on top of the computer's keyboard, another school daypack like the one he had thrown at me in Seattle. I unzipped it, and there was another jumble of ten-thousand-dollar bundles of cash. And a note which read, "Mutual friend says your debt has grown." The note also had a phone number, followed by "NOON."

I turned on the computer, and using several private networks, each located in a different country, I connected to the version control server at SLAM. I could modify, replace, and check in my backdoor code in less than an hour, making it look like I had done it while in Seattle a few days before.

But Dave Cheat would still be dead.

Why?

Every three months, publicly traded companies release financial reports --- computer files from spreadsheets created by accountants. Information that was then placed on SLAM's network. A network that was trusted to be encrypted and absolutely private. Knowing the numbers in those quarterly reports while they are being worked on, even a few hours before they are released, makes it trivial for options and futures traders to place lucrative trades. Trades that make millions of dollars in moments.

How much had Tsai and his 'partners' --- partners who now seemed to include Fritter, the CEO of SLAM --- made in less than a month of siphoning secret data? Enough to make daypacks full of cash, and at least one life, insignificant.

I could still do what Tsai wanted me to do, which might get him and XX to leave me alone. But there would be other security audits. How long would it take for someone else to stumble across a new backdoor? It had taken Dave only four weeks. And now he was dead. Who else would die?

I had rolled out of a car once and walked away with nothing but my clothes. Did I still know how to do what was right?

I turned off the computer.

The fumes from the paint and wasp spray were making me dizzy. I grabbed the latest delivery of cash and went outside. I walked the dark neighborhood streets, making sure no one was watching me, for about half an hour, then I walked back to where I had parked the Subaru. I opened its back hatch and tossed in the new bag of cash. Its heft felt like another half million. That meant my insignificance to Tsai had accumulated to one and a half million dollars. The scale of what I had gotten involved with felt larger than a mountain of copper. It felt like a mountain of arsenic.

I walked back to my house and examined my legit car in the carport. I opened the hood and looked at the engine. I didn't know what I was looking for, but I wanted to find something tangible to take apart, disarm, and fix. But there was nothing. I closed the hood and drove downtown to the office.

Even though it was late, O'Neill was working. I saw him at his desk through the ground floor office window. When I went inside, he was surprised to see me.

"Nostalgic?" He asked, "Feel like you need to pound some late-night code before you can sleep?"

I said, "More than you will ever know."

O'Neill said he never saw me code anymore, "Not since you became establishment."

"Same salary and stock options as you," I said to him, "You are establishment now too."

"Remember when this wasn't about the money?" He asked, "Remember when it was fun?"

I looked at O'Neill, and I did remember. "You know what?" I said, "Dave Cheat, he was okay. He was a juggler too. I found that out when I met with him before his car wreck."

"You two get to juggle?" O'Neill asked.

I told him we did, that we were outside by the waterfront in Seattle and that a third person came up and had joined in, and Cheat and he passed clubs for a while. I said, "Watching the two of them reminded me of when you and I first met."

"Passing is where it's at," O'Neill said. Then he got up from his chair and picked up a cloth bag from the corner of the room.

"Now?" I asked, "Eleven at night?"

"Parking lot is empty," he said. "You look way serious. This will help."

I had gone to my office to be behind a heavy, locked door and to sleep for a while. I had not expected to see O'Neill, but it felt safe and good to be near him, near someone I knew.

We went outside to the middle of the Central Square parking lot, under a streetlight, and started passing the clubs. Even though my hands were cold, and even with everything I owned having just been violently destroyed, I started laughing. O'Neill started laughing too, which caused both of us to lose our focus, and we dropped the juggling clubs. Then we were standing there looking at each other, both of us still laughing. "Like the old days," O'Neill said.

Then, from the shadow outside the streetlight's cone of light, someone started clapping, slow and loud. O'Neill and I stopped laughing and looked. There was XX, and he said, "Brilliant."

I turned away from XX and told O'Neill that we needed to go back inside. XX heard me, though, and said, "Wait a minute, boys," and he walked up to O'Neill and said, "Show me how this works, Mate."

Before I could say anything, O'Neill had knelt and picked up three of the juggling clubs and said, "Here, you hold these," and handed them to XX. O'Neill then saw the tattoos on his neck, wrists, and hands and asked, "Those mean anything?"

"Mementos of a misspent youth," XX said. Then he dropped two of the clubs, held the remaining one in his right hand, and slapped it repeatedly against the open palm of his left hand. He said, "Light. But could still mess a bloke up. Go right through metal detectors."

"Where are you from?" O'Neill asked.

XX looked at him and said, "Passing through. Always passing through." Then he walked back into the shadows and away from us, taking the club with him.

"Hey!" O'Neill shouted.

I put my hand on O'Neill's shoulder and said, "Forget about it. Not worth it."

O'Neill said, "Too much hostile energy. Totally agree. One club isn't worth that."

Neither of us wanted to be outside then, and we went back into the office. I checked the main door's locks, and I went around and closed the window blinds. O'Neill asked me what I was doing, and I said, truer than he would ever know, "That guy gave me the creeps."

"I hear you," O'Neill said. Then he said, "I drank a cappuccino in the afternoon, think I will work a bit more. Then go home and do a soak."

"You and your hot tub," I said, "Now that is establishment."

I went into my office and laid down on the floor, wrapped in a sleeping bag that I kept in the closet. I was thinking about what I should do, about the threats that Tsai and XX had delivered and acted on. Dave Cheat was dead. My house was trashed. Because I hadn't done what Tsai had told me to do. But I did not think there was another immediate urgency. I decided that I would call XX at noon as he and his note had told me to. I would also try to reach Tsai and talk. Maybe Dave Cheat's wreck had been a coincidence. And all my possessions didn't add up to much value. I even tried to smile about XX walking away with a plastic juggling club, thinking he was just messing with our juggling break.

I fell asleep listening to the chattering of O'Neill's typing from down the hallway, the "pressing of buttons," the pounding of code. And then I dreamt of nothing except click, click, click.

The thin detective woke me up by kicking at my shoulder with the tip of his boot. Next to him was a uniformed cop. I sat up. In the hallway, I also saw Suzzy. She had a terrified and bewildered expression. I looked at the clock on the wall. It was eight in the morning. Saturday morning.

"Awake?" Thin asked.

"Stop kicking me," I said. I got up, sat in a chair, and put on my shoes. Then I asked Thin why he was there.

Thin said, "We were at your house. When were you last there?"

"Yesterday morning," I lied. "I worked late and spent the night here. Why?"

Thin asked, "When did you last see Nate O'Neill?"

I answered, "He was here, at the office, when I fell asleep last night, about midnight."

I looked past the police to Suzzy, who was still in the hallway. She had started crying. I asked her what was wrong, and she said, "They called me..." but then the uniformed cop put his hand near Suzzy's face and said, "Shhhh," and walked her down the hallway.

Thin said to me, "I knew you worked down here. I called your assistant. She's the one listed by the alarm company as the person to contact to get in. We found your partner dead this morning."

What!? Dead!?

Thin continued, "Neighbor of his, a few hours ago, heard something. But that's all I am going to tell you now. I'm thinking you should tell me a lot more."

I stayed silent.

Thin then told me that after finding O'Neill, they went to my house looking for me. He asked, "Sure you haven't been to your house since yesterday morning? Now would be the time to say so."

"No," I lied again. Then I asked the detective if I was under arrest.

He said, "Almost. But I want you to take a drive with me. I might arrest you if you say no."

On the way out of the building, I squeezed Suzzy's arm and told her that things would be okay. She said, questioning, "How?"

How? Why?

All four of us got into a patrol car. Thin and me in the back, and the patrolman and Suzzy up front. On the way, they dropped Suzzy off at her home, then the patrolman started to drive again, and Thin asked me, "Know where we are going?"

"To Nate's, I guess," since O'Neill lives in the same direction as my house.

Thin stared straight ahead and said, "One homicide detective in town, and I am it. Three, four cases a year. Five tops. Past month three murders, and each has your line on it."

The patrol car did not go to O'Neill's. It stopped in front of my house. I saw Thin looking at me for any response I might have given away. Then the patrolman let both of us out of the back seat. Thin asked if he could look around inside my place.

"No," I said. "You need a warrant to go in."

He nodded. Then he said, "Normally. But Lars was already in," he nodded toward the patrolman, whose name on his badge was 'Larson.'

"No warrant necessary when there is active crime visible from outside the premises, or some such legal blah-blah." He looked closely at me again. Then he said, "Go and take a look yourself."

I was terrified then that O'Neill's body would now be in there, tossed onto the growing mountain of my ruin. But I went up to the front door. Standing at the top of the steps, I saw what Lars would have seen through the kitchen window, the shattered dishes, torn blinds, and the house paint that was poured over it all.

"Uggg!" I yelled and said to Thin, "You said that O'Neill has been killed. Is he in here? I don't want to go in."

"He's been killed. But not here," the detective said. Go on in. Lars has already been through the place. It's nice in there."

I opened the door, stood for a moment, then asked both policemen to come in with me.

"Now you invite us in, now you want us," Lars said with a smirk.

The three of us walked in together. Water was running across the floor from the shattered sink and toilet, and I heard it dripping through the floorboards into the crawl space beneath the house.

Thin asked, "Can you explain this?" He was standing by the undamaged chair, desk, and computer above the blinking lights of the working internet router.

I said, "This is awful. I have no idea why anyone would do this."

Lars sarcastically said, "Hope you have tsunami insurance." Then he asked, with a laugh, "You want to report a burglary?"

I was overcome with sorrow and overwhelmed by the wet wasp-spray fumes. I rushed outside and was sick. But this time, not in a shared hallway-toilet way, but loudly and into the open, cold air.

"You saved yourself an arrest. For now." Thin said as I was wiping my face off with a handful of snow.

"Come on," he said to Lars, and the two walked out of my yard. Thin stopped before he got into the patrol car and yelled back at me, "Just for you, we'll call your burglary in. An officer might get up here sometime in the next day or so."

Then the two of them were gone.

I went down into the dripping crawl space and turned the water off. I thought about calling the insurance company. I also thought about driving out of Montana. But mostly, I was thinking about what could have happened to O'Neill between the time I fell asleep and when I was kicked awake by Thin. I also was thinking about what XX would say to me if I did call him at the number he had left.

And then I thought about Suzzy.

Suzzy!

Tsai had said to me, "They will start with your business partner. Then the one who answers your phones. They won't stop."

I came up out of the crawl space and looked at the mess. There was nothing I wanted to try to salvage or save. I left the house, walked to the Subaru, and drove downtown, toward the vacant river frontage.

Pascal's truck was parked there. I parked next to it, got out, and banged on the camper shell. It was still early. I banged again.

I saw the curtains move at the camper's window. Pascal looked out at me. He didn't ask what I wanted or why I was there, he yelled, "Give this Fella a moment."

The camper's topper was the same height as the top of the pickup's cab. Pascal reached out the back and dropped the truck's tailgate, which he then swung his legs over and sat on. He yawned, stretched, and reached back into the camper for his cowboy boots and hat and put them on. He was already wearing his long winter coat. "Please tell me a Fella has brought a cup of coffee," he said.

I told him that I hadn't and had an emergency that I needed to ask him about.

He asked, "Can it wait until after some caffeine?"

I shook my head no and said, "I don't think so."

"Who is it this time?" he asked.

I said, "I'm in trouble. But that's not the emergency."

Pascal didn't say anything. He was waiting for me to say more.

"I think someone is going to try to kill..." and I paused and said, "... a friend of mine."

Pascal waited.

I asked, "Will you sell me that gun, the one you taught me to use?"

"The 1911," he said. He was quiet for a bit, and then he said, "A gun would make whatever troubles a Fella has worse. A first rule for guns is: No Fuckin' Way!"

I sat down on the edge of the tailgate.

Pascal said, "Tell me about this friend. Who is going to kill him? And why."

"She," I said. "And she has nothing to do with anything. But last night someone killed another friend of mine. And I think I have until about noon today before they might try to kill her."

I asked, "How much should I tell you?"

"Well," Pascal said, "Normally, I don't want to know anything other than how much a Fella has in his bank account. Or if there is a house deed with a Fella's name on it. But in this case, sure. Talk away."

I didn't know where to start. Instead, I said, "You would not want the house." Then I stood up from the tailgate and said, "Let me show you something like a bank account," and I motioned to Pascal to follow me. "Ok. Persistent again, for sure." Then he walked with me to the back of the Subaru.

I saw Pascal noticing the out-of-state plates. "It's a burner," I said.

Then I opened the Subaru and said, "This might help get the explanations going," and I moved the blanket that was covering the two daypacks and unzipped the top of one of them. "There's about a million dollars in these two bags. It's threat money. Money that I didn't want and didn't ask for." Then I zipped the bag closed, covered the bags up again, and closed the Subaru's back hatch.

Pascal said, "A Fella has surprises. But a gun is still not the answer." Then he said, "Now I know I need some caffeine," and he walked back to the open tailgate of his truck, pulled out a propane camp stove, turned it on, and said, "Fella can do some explaining. While the water boils."

I said, "I won't tell you anything that will get you in trouble, but I won't lie to you either. Someone gave me money to write software for them. Which I did. But then they wanted me to do more. And when I wouldn't, they killed someone I knew, in another city, and they gave me more money," and I pointed toward the Subaru.

I waited for Pascal to ask questions, but he didn't, so I continued. "Police woke me up an hour ago and told me that my business partner is dead. I think the people who gave me the cash that I showed you, I think they killed him. And I think they might kill another person I know unless I do what they are demanding and write their software fast. Or unless I stop them faster."

"You tell the police this?" Pascal asked.

"No," I said.

"The gal in jail, she part of this?"

"No," I said, "not in any way. But the cops probably think there is a connection." I didn't want to explain anymore. I didn't say anything about Tsai, and I didn't describe XX. Or my house.

"I like that bank account. But I'll tell a Fella again, gun is not the answer. Fella going to wild west someone on the street at high noon?"

We were both quiet.

"Give the money back to them an option?" Pascal asked.

"I've offered. All they want is the software. The code."

"Why not give them the software then?" he asked.

"If I do, it won't end. Mistake was that I started."

"That's the truth," Pascal said, "all mistakes start by starting."

I sarcastically said, "Wise." Then I said, "And all criminals drank milk when they were babies."

Pascal smiled then too.

"The bad guys I've known," he said, "usually are after getting money. Never knew one who was about giving it away. Shows I don't understand this Fella's problem much."

Then he was quiet for a long time, drinking coffee from a paper cup. When the cup was empty, he crumpled it and threw it back into the camper, and said, "I've been wrong a lot. I was wrong about that gal of yours too. Stay put a bit," and he crawled under the topper.

He had the 1911 wrapped in a black bandana when he came out and said, "I wiped it down. Wiped the shells too. A Fella did not get this from me. And if asked, a Fella got it at the August gun show at the fieldhouse. No ID needed. Remember that story. Now a Fella also needs to remember some more 'number one' rules. And all gun rules are 'number one' rules. 'Rule number one', guns are always loaded. And this here one is for sure. Round in the chamber. Flip the safety off, pull the trigger, it goes. And another 'number one rule', never point at what a Fella isn't trying to put a hole into. And the last 'number one rule.' Here in Montana, it helps if someone is trying to kill a Fella first before he puts that hole in them. But if a Fella does shoot someone, a Fella will probably still go to jail. At least for a while. I wouldn't be carrying this in a pocket. I'd carry it in a small bag. Law is vague about guns in a shoulder bag. Especially if a Fella remembers to say they were heading out to where they can use a fishing license. Again, Fella did not get this, or any advice, from me."

I went back and opened the Subaru and dumped all the cash out of a school daypack. I put the .45 into the empty daypack, picked up four ten-thousand-dollar bundles, covered the other bag and the loose bundles, closed the car, and went back to the truck.

When I gave Pascal the cash, I said, "And you did not get this from me."

Like cards in a deck, Pascal thumbed the bills of the banded bundles and said, "Waaay too much. Buy a couple arsenals with all this. That gun is only worth about six hundred. Fella can have it for seven."

"You can have it. More if you want. Maybe you will bail me out if there is some extra."

He laughed and said, "Then it's waaay not enough. Again, let me tell a Fella, gun is no answer."

He put the cash in his coat pocket and said, "Sure a Fella won't consider the obvious? Nine-one-one? Calling for help has been known to work."

"Not this time," I said to Pascal, and I got back into the Subaru and drove toward Suzzy's. I needed to try to break the iteration with some simple algebra. Like X minus one. Or Tsai minus XX.

Chapter 13 – A Brick

It was ten on Saturday morning when I drove to Suzzy's house. I parked, put the daypack with the 1911 over my shoulder, and walked to her front door Suzzy was married to another woman, Rachel, who worked as a white-water river guide during the spring and summer, a hunting guide during the autumn, and, as Suzzy has laughingly said, "a beer drinker all year long."

I had been inside Suzzy and Rachel's house twice for parties that Suzzy had hosted. The parties were dress-themed for the season Rachel was in. Almost everyone that I worked with in Missoula would be there, as well as several dozen of Suzzy and Rachel's friends, many with their children. And almost everyone wore themed clothing. At the hunting party a year before, the theme was plaid with orange vests. At the river party, in the summer, it had been shorts and flip-flops. But each time, I dressed as I usually do.

I knocked on the door. Rachel answered, said, "Hey Enzi, the black tee shirt is appropriate today," and invited me in. Suzzy was sitting on the couch, holding a box of tissues. Her eyes were red from crying. She asked, "Enzi, do you know anything?"

I said that I only knew what the police had told me, that O'Neill had been killed. I asked her if she knew more. She nodded yes and said, "We were woken up this morning by police, and they asked questions about how to find you. Then they asked me to go with them to let them into the office and told me that Nate was dead. It was awful. They didn't give me any details, but while I was gone, Nate's neighbor called and talked to Rachel."

Rachel said, "My friend Carl lives next to Nate. He's the one who called the police. Carl called me two hours ago. Freaked out. He told me that he was woken up last night when Nate turned on his hot tub. They had an agreement that Nate wouldn't run the jets at night. The tub is by Carl's bedroom window. But the jets kept running. Carl told me he got angry, yelled out his window, and then went out there and found Nate floating in the hot tub."

Rachel looked at Suzzy, then back at me, then continued, "Carl told me that Nate's face was battered. Carl said that he thought a red light was on in the tub but then realized that the water was red because of blood. Carl also said there was a juggling club floating there. The sort that Nate used."

Three months before, O'Neill had shown up at the summer party wearing a Hawaiian shirt and carrying his bag of juggling balls and clubs. He juggled in Suzzy and Rachel's backyard, surrounded by kids and dogs. I remember that O'Neill had also been teaching people how to juggle. Rachel and Suzzy had been interested in the clubs, and O'Neill had them start by tossing a club straight up from one hand and catching it in the other. But Rachel was holding a beer and had said to O'Neill, "You're asking a lot, for both hands," and told O'Neill, "I don't get to use this line often enough, 'here, hold my beer and watch this.'" And everyone had laughed.

"We were juggling last night," I said. "Less than twelve hours ago." I paused and looked at Suzzy. I was thinking that other than our work interactions about who was trying to reach me, and discussions about new hires and times for meetings, I had only spoken with Suzzy at her parties. And I realized that I had never seen Suzzy look sad and rarely had seen her looking serious, either. And now she was both.

"Last night," I said, "a man with a British accent, tattoos on his neck and hands, he took one of Nate's juggling clubs. A stocky, short guy, shaved head. He was watching us juggle in the lot at work. Came up and stole a club and walked away."

"What??" Suzzy exclaimed, "Did you tell the police this?"

"I had never seen him before," I lied. "I didn't think it mattered. I thought he was a drunk from the bars. Didn't think much about it."

Rachel said, "You need to call the police and tell them this, now."

"I will," I answered, "but there's more. Maybe not related. But you need to know. After the police dropped you off here, they took me to my house."

Rachel was standing next to where Suzzy was sitting. They were both looking at me intensely, waiting.

I continued, "My place was torn apart." Then I lied, "my house was searched. I don't know why or for what. I don't know who did it."

"Is this about the work you all do?" Rachel asked angrily, "Nate gets killed the same night someone searches your place? That's messed up."

I said, "The police told me that after they found Nate, they looked for me. Then they must have come here, and then you," I nodded toward Suzzy, "found me sleeping in my office."

"Why would they look for you right away?" Rachel asked. "What's the connection?"

Lying again, I answered, "I don't know." I didn't mention anything about the thin detective or how he had been trying to connect me with Kaori's murders.

Rachel asked, "Should we be worried? Someone going to break in here because of Suzzy working with you and Nate?"

I wanted to tell them not to worry, but I said, truthfully, "I think maybe. I think we need to be worried."

Suzzy's look shifted between sad, serious, and confused. She quietly started shaking her head back and forth. As Suzzy was doing this, Rachel walked into another room and returned moments later, holding a shotgun by its barrel. She walked to the front door and leaned the gun against the wall. She said, "I think 'Big Blaster' will stay here for a while." Then she said, "I need to listen to you call the police right now." She said this with a sternness that I imagined she used with her white water and hunting clients when they were behaving dangerously stupid.

With Rachel watching, I called 911 and explained to the emergency operator that I was calling about last night's homicide and had new, important information for either Larson or the thin detective. The 911 operator took my name and number and said they would call me back. When I hung up, Rachel said, "As soon as you talk with someone, you let us know." Then she said, "I think you need to go now." I heard her locking the door behind me as I left.

As I was driving, the phone rang. I pulled over and answered. It was Thin. I told him that I had visited Suzzy and her partner, who told me how O'Neill was found. I also told him what O'Neill's neighbor had told them about the juggling club floating in the hot tub with O'Neill's body.

Thin said, "People talk about the dead when they aren't supposed to." Then he asked, "And?"

I told Thin what I told Suzzy and Rachel about the Brit. About him walking up to O'Neill and me last night, taking a juggling club, and leaving.

I said, "It might be connected."

"Might be!?" Thin asked angrily. "Why didn't you mention this earlier?"

"It didn't seem relevant," I said. "Drunks from the bar watch us when we juggle. The bar is next to the parking lot. The Rhino. They come out. I would have told you if you had told me that O'Neill was beaten to death with one of his own clubs!"

Thin, calming down, asked me to describe the Brit. He then told me to come to the police station. Said, "We need to make this formal. Right now."

I told him that I would, then we hung up. I knew I might be arrested or detained, but I still headed downtown. I parked the Subaru a few blocks from city hall, and put the daypack with the loaded .45 in the back next to the cash. Half the cash was in the other school daypack, the other half being the loose bundles I had dumped out. I covered it all up again with the blanket. A million dollars. Less the forty thousand I had given to Pascal. Either way, it still rounded up to a pile of problems. Then I walked into city hall.

Thin met me at the police desk and asked if I would talk with him. Then he escorted me into a bleak interview room where the walls looked like they had absorbed decades of tears and lies. I asked, "No timelines?" but he didn't reply. Instead, he turned on a recorder and told me to repeat what I had told him on the phone about the man from the night before. He asked me several times to repeat my descriptions of the Brit and his actions. Several times he asked if I had ever seen or talked with him before, and each time I lied and said "No."

I told him that the man had a lot of tattoos. Thin asked me to describe them. I told him about the "X" on each of his knuckles. Thin asked, "You saw each of his knuckles? How close to you was he? How much light was there?"

I answered, saying, "Yes. Close. A lot."

But I wanted to stop the questions, stop my talking, so I asked Thin a question. "Do you think the person who killed O'Neill also vandalized my house?"

Thin answered, "You tell me." Then, when I didn't answer, Thin asked, "Your Texas buddy know this British-sounding character?"

I forgot my right, and instead of staying silent, I asked, "Why would he?"

Thin shrugged, then said, "The lines will tell me. Matter of time. When they do, I'll let you know." He turned off the recording device and walked out of the interview room without telling me to stay or go. I got up and left, and no one stopped me.

I drove to my house, again parking the Subaru a few blocks away. I walked past my neighbors' homes. Someone I recognized was checking their mailbox and said hello to me. Children went past on their bicycles, capturing some of the late autumn weather before the coming of more snow. The sun was shining, and the air was clear. It was a good place to live. But my house was never a home. It was a ruin even before XX's visit.

At my house, I opened all the doors and windows. Then I went into the backyard, where there was a view of the hills. I wanted to yell. To scream. Or I wanted to be a st-stutterer again, sitting quietly in the back of a classroom, or walking alone in the far away suburban woods. What I didn't want was to figure out what to do next.

Believing that we are doing the right thing, even when it is wrong, that is a big part of the lie.

Kaori's one love is dead. And if I hadn't bailed her out of jail, he and his new girlfriend would both still be alive. I listened to Tsai, and Dave Cheat died. Then I ignored Tsai. Now O'Neill is dead.

How do I unbend the wheel?

The best literature teaches. I wondered if a book or a story I had read could show me a direction out of my predicament. I thought of books. I thought of graphic novels. I thought of movies. Then I remembered the scene in the film 'Blade Runner' where the 'super genius' got his head crushed because he wanted to show everyone in the room how smart he was.

In the film, androids had been bioengineered to live only four years, and they were enslaved in deadly work. Several androids escaped, and one, "Roy," made it into the bedroom of his creator, the 'super genius' Tyrell. Roy told Tyrell that he wanted one thing: to live. But Tyrell told Roy, "Nope, not possible. Four years is all you get."

Instead of Roy thinking, "Well, this was a wasted attempt," Roy offered ideas to modify his programmed genetics. Roy was technical and specific because, as an engineered android, he was also brilliant. Tyrell, though, shot down Roy's suggestions one after another, saying, "Nope. We tried that. Nope. That won't work."

So, Roy's response to the 'super genius' was to kiss Tyrell goodbye and crush his eyes and skull with his two hands, the hands which Tyrell had bioengineered.

Tyrell could have responded to any of Roy's ideas with, "Wow! That's interesting. That could work!" Then Roy might have let Tyrell live, at least long enough for the two of them to go into a lab someplace to collaborate on the idea. A lab where Tyrell might have found a convenient brick to bash Roy with and escape. Instead, the 'super genius' died while trying to be the smartest person in the room.

Then I remembered what Tsai had said to me: "Say 'yes' to everyone who wants to hear a 'yes'. Never say 'no'. You can always get out of a 'yes' later, but when you say 'no' you will never be asked in again."

Then I knew what I would do. I would say 'yes'. I would activate the backdoor again so Tsai and his partners would keep stealing the early financial reports and making their multi-million-dollar trades. But my 'yes' would not last. I would also build a backdoor to their backdoor. And as I had never wanted to be the smartest person in any room, the doors I would build would close quietly as I left, hopefully unnoticed.

I would also try to make sure that I had a good brick within reach.

Precisely at noon, I called the number that XX left in the daypack on my keyboard. The phone clicked into silence, but I talked anyway. I said, "You've made your points. Tell our mutual friend that I am doing what he wants. But then tell him that I am done."

I waited, listening to the phone's silence. Then I heard XX say, "Do it fast, Mate. Watching you." Then the line went dead.

I called Tsai's burner, which rang with no answer, not even a voicemail prompt. I went back into the house, stepping over the wreckage of my possessions, sat down at the computer, and turned it on.

I did a scan for spyware that XX might have installed, and I found some. They were tracking my actions closely. XX was more than a thug. He was dangerously technical. I was now convinced that he was involved with killing Dave Cheat.

It took me an hour to determine how to disable the spyware secretly, but I left it running while I logged into SLAM and did the first steps of reinstalling the backdoor. Just as I had done in Seattle a few days before. But then, before I checked in the code, which would have turned on the backdoor again, I disabled XX's spyware and started pounding.

I had to do much more than what I had done in Seattle. I had to write a virus, and leave small traces of that virus pointing back to Dave Cheat. Pointing back to when and where he sat, in his cubicle, next to his shelf of beer mugs and photographs. Pushing keys. Doing honest, good work.

I pounded. Click. Click. Click. And the keystrokes flowed together and became math in the Aether, instructions to mess with Tsai's plans. And what were those plans? My backdoor had let Tsai and his accomplices slide in at the front of the line to read dull reports of profits and losses. Those lists of numbers that moved the stock market up or crashed it down. This company is selling more than the pundits expected. That company is selling less. Find out before anyone else and get your bets in first. Make a killing. Like bullets through paper. Small holes. And no danger. Unless you are standing behind the target. How loud is the noise of something that moves faster than the speed of greed? Click. Click. Click. Bam. Small holes and loud noises.

Fritter had given me access to all the computers on his sprawling company network. I used that access to create fictitious users and 'daemon' programs designed and coded to run constantly on the company servers in Seattle and London. I modified the ownership and the touch-dates of the files that I created and used Dave Cheat's credentials for some of them, Fritter's for others. My new code then used those newly created access points to find the network paths required to install itself on every computer using the backdoor; anyone who went through it would then get infected. Click, click, click.

As I did before, I hid the new code in SLAM's corporate logos, as well as in the smiling photos of executives. The sort of photos that people who strive to be the smart ones save on their computers and copy into their resumes and social media profiles. Executives, like Fritter, who might be partners with Tsai, and who might be the ones looking for easy ways to 'smart money'.

I pounded all through the night. Then I checked in my work in a way that made it appear exactly as Fritter had requested. Code that appeared legitimate and would become part of the BGT deal. And the backdoor. The code that Tsai had demanded. The code that XX had killed for. But code that had a little bit more. A bit of the click, click, click that I hoped no one would notice for a while.

It was seven in the morning. It had taken nineteen non-stop hours of "pushing buttons" to create a trap that might topple an ongoing, billion-dollar heist.

Each time anyone accessed the backdoor, no matter where their computer was located, they would turn on code which would then start copying and streaming their files and logging their keystrokes onto remote cloud servers. Those files and logs would be proof enough for any good cyber security cop to start investigations into those who had been accessing data illegally. Investigations would be triggered when the files and the logs started being delivered through SLAM's email systems to everyone on their huge mailing lists of employees, vendors, media outlets, and competitors. The email would start being delivered after I sent a text message to an automated bit of "pushed buttons." Pound. Code. Math. Recurse. Click. Click. Click.

Then I emailed a formal letter to the HR department at SLAM, explaining that the death of O'Neill had been so upsetting that I could not return to work and that I was resigning and leaving on an extended road trip. Then I began a wipe-erase of my computer's hard drive.

That was the end of my technical work. After that, I left the house to look for the rest of the "good brick" that needed to be in reach.

I went into Walmart and bought a tent and other camping gear, some groceries, and a big bag of potato chips. I also bought soft clothing. A warm puffy jacket, and an extra-large, bright purple, fuzzy pull-over hoodie, which was decorated with a large, yellow smiley-face. The hoodie had a loose uni-pocket, the type where you can put your hands in on both sides. I bought a pair of sweatpants with stripes on the side and a folding camp chair with a woodsy design like the ones retirees use next to their camper trailers while they catch up on their reading. I also bought a box of white plastic trash bags, a pair of thin leather gloves, and sneakers.

I drove east along the interstate to Clinton and got off on the frontage road. After several miles, I turned and drove into the woods on a forest service road. A mile further, there was a camping spot where I had been before, one where I knew there was cellphone reception. There was no snow left on the road. There was no close-by house.

I set up the tent, but I didn't plan on sleeping in it. I unfolded the camp chair and placed it near the tent. I opened the bag of potato chips and put it on the ground near the chair. I changed clothes, putting on the striped sweatpants, the sneakers, and the puffy jacket. Over that, I pulled on the fuzzy hoodie with the smiley face. Wearing gloves, I dumped the contents of the daypack, all its ten-thousand-dollar bundles, into a plastic garbage bag which I then left in the back of the Subaru.

I took the 1911 out of its daypack, flipped off its safety, and put the gun into the hoodie's pocket. I put one of my boots into each of the now-empty daypacks and put both daypacks on the ground under the chair.

Nine on Sunday morning, I called XX, and the same as when I called him the day before at noon, there was a click. Then silence. I spoke to the silence and said I had done what our mutual friend demanded. I also told the silence that I didn't want the last "presents" that I was given. I said, "You can have it all in exchange for leaving my friends and me alone. No one needs to know about this. Take it all. But I'm going." Then I hung up.

A few minutes later, I received a text with a new phone number, which I called.

"Hey, Mate," XX answered. Then he said, "Keep this brief."

I said to him, "I did it. It's done. But I'm not doing anything else. And I'm leaving." I tried to sound frantic and scared, which was easy because I was frantic and scared.

He said, "Listening…."

"You can have everything that was in both the bags you gave me. No one needs to know. Take it all, then leave me alone."

He said, "Interesting. Stay where you are. I'll come to you."

"When? I'm not at my house. I don't want to go back there."

"I know where you are, Mate. See you soon."

Then the phone clicked dead.

I took off the gloves and sat down in the camp chair with a thick, hardback book.I checked again that both the burner and my legit phone were on and that I still had cell coverage. Then I waited. I did not touch the potato chips. I did not read the book. I did not fall asleep. I waited.

Chapter 14 – Into The Aether

I thought I'd have to wait and stay awake all day, and maybe through the night, but after about three hours, a jellybean of a car, an airport rental, drove up on the forest service road and stopped fifty feet away from me. I thought he would have snuck up, parked further away, and walked, and I thought he would've come in the dark. XX looked at me through the rental car's windshield. Looked at me sitting there on the camp chair wearing my fuzzy smiley-face hoodie, reading a book. As I was looking at him, I reached into the bag of potato chips, took one out, and ate it. Then, I gave him a wave and pointed at the shoulder bags under the chair. His car started moving again, and he pulled off the road close to where I was sitting, stopped, and rolled down his driver's side window. I saw him looking at me again and looking at the shoulder bags by my feet. I closed the book and stood up, holding the book with my left hand loosely over the hoodie's pocket. I said, "Take these," and I gestured to the book bags, "then go!" I made sure that all the fear I felt was in the tone of my voice, "Take them and go!" I repeated. "Please, leave me alone!"

He said, "Not so easy, Mate." Then, with his left hand, he lifted a flip phone, a burner, which was already open, held it to his head, and said, "Found him." And, addressing me, "Mutual friend wants a word." Then XX held the phone out the open window while leaving his right hand on the steering wheel of the running car.

I was standing, and we were about six feet apart. XX hadn't given any indication that he was worried about me, a coder, someone he had thrown onto a floor. I took two steps toward him, still holding the book in my left hand. When I was close enough to take the phone that he was offering me, I reached into the hoodie pocket, grasped the 1911, brought it out, and leveled it, as smoothly as catching and returning a juggling club in its spinning, fluid cycle.

As the gun was leveling, I was pulling the trigger, and the surprise of the gun's kick hit me at the same time as XX's realization that he had underestimated someone.

His head jerked abruptly, and he slumped sideways. He hadn't turned off the engine or taken it out of drive, and the car started moving forward and drove itself through the level camp spot and stopped as it ran slowly into a ponderosa. The engine automatically revved a few times and stalled. It would have been a quiet moment, except for the roar that was ringing in my ears. It would have also been a tranquil setting, except that there had been a horrific spray of blood that had splashed on the hoodie, the book that I was still holding, and my face.

I heard a small voice coming from the flip phone at my feet. I picked it up and heard Tsai yelling, "What was that? What was that?" I closed the phone and wiped it with the hoodie.

I looked up and down the road. I listened. Then I went over to the jellybean car. I didn't want to look at him. But I did look. For an indelible moment. It wasn't a small hole. It wasn't one of Pascal's paper targets. It was a person. A dead person. He had beaten and killed O'Neill and had probably taken part in killing Dave Cheat. And he probably would have kept killing other people. Suzzy. Maybe Rachel. And he would have kept doing anything else Tsai demanded of him. He hadn't come to where I was to get himself a million dollars. He was on the phone with Tsai when I shot him. He had come to make sure that I was aware that the pressure would never let up. But still, it was not right that I had killed him. For me to think otherwise was part of the lie. A wrong that tries to make a right out of greed gone wrong.

I dropped the flip phone into the jellybean and walked back to where I had shot the gun. I found the spent shell casing on the ground one pace to the right of where I had been standing. I picked it up and put it into the hoodie's pocket. I took down my tent, packed it, the chair, the two daypacks, the bag of potato chips – everything that had been part of my relaxed setup – back into the Subaru. Still, no one had driven by. And at that time of year, hunting season, a random gunshot would not arouse much suspicion.

I put the gloves back on, and from the back of the Subaru, picked up the trash bag holding half the cash. Even though it only weighed about ten pounds, it was dense and heavy. The other ten pounds of bundled cash was loose in the back of the Subaru under the blanket. Twenty pounds cash. About the same weight as a human skeleton. I wondered if whoever had dug Tsai's grandfathers' skeletons from their Butte graves had thought those bones heavy. Two skeletons would have been forty pounds of bone. How many feet of wire would forty pounds of copper make? Enough to light up one mansion on the richest hill? How many pounds of bone was needed to dig up a mountain of copper? How many skeletons had it cost to wire the country?

The networks between New York and London were microwave signals and glass fiber wrapped in plastic. How many keystrokes did it take to create that Aether? How many other bags of cash had Tsai planned on having to keep throwing at me? How many keystrokes for a life?

The thick book that I had used to help hide the gun -- the book that I had been holding when I pulled the trigger -- had several splashes of wet blood on it, which I dabbed onto one side of the trash bag that held the ten-thousand-dollar bundles. Then I went to XX's car and placed the trash bag on the floor by the back seat. I was leaving a half-million-dollar confused mess for Thin.

I got in the Subaru and left. Before getting back on the paved frontage road, I stopped, turned off my phones, and changed my clothes. I put the blood-spattered book and everything I had been wearing into a new trash bag. Then I headed back toward Missoula.

I stayed on the frontage road, and a few miles west of Clinton, where the road dipped close to the Clark Fork River, I pulled over. After removing its clip and ejecting the live round, I threw the 1911 into the middle of the river. It made a splash like a brick being dropped onto a wet sponge.

Then I called Suzzy at her office number, knowing, because it was Sunday, that the call would go to her voicemail. I left her a message saying what I had written earlier in my resignation letter and added that I had told the police about the tattooed man who had stolen the juggling club. I said, "I think he might have thought that Nate and I were drug dealers because of the juggling, I guess. Maybe saw us a few weeks ago juggling at the farmer's market. I think maybe he had been watching me since then and could have searched my house for drugs. Then maybe he went down to the office and saw Nate and me juggling. It's horrible, but I don't think it's work-related. I think they will catch him soon. I gave a good description. I'm getting out of town for a while. But there's nothing for you to worry about."

I hung up, turned off the phone again, and continued to Missoula.

I drove to the Sweet Rest Motel. The place was even more forlorn than it had been when I had taken Helen to the river behind it. The walls in the motel's office were decorated with all the standard 'No' signs. No Smoking. No Credit. No Drugs. But they took cash and gave me a key.

I went into the room and took a shower. Then I went back to the Subaru, got the trash bag that contained the clothes I had been wearing and the book that I had been holding, and walked behind the motel and to the river's edge, which still had not started icing over. I tried to find the rock where Helen had stood, spun, and fallen, but the river and time had done what rivers and time do. They had both meandered and moved, and the bank was not the same as it had been, and neither was the town. Missoula had once been beautiful. Now it looked like a place to run from.

I reached into the trash bag and, one at a time, threw the items into the river, starting with the hoodie, then the shell casing, then the book, the jacket, the sneakers, the gloves, the sweatpants. The last thing I threw in was the empty plastic bag, which floated near the riverbank for a while before being swirled further out into the current. It was the first time I had littered, and I didn't know what was bothering me more: the clothing and plastic I was sending downriver or the bullet I had sent through XX's head.

A man wearing an army field jacket stained with woodsmoke and sweat into a homeless brown color walked up the riverbank to me and asked what I was doing. I told him, "Getting rid of my past." He stood next to me, and we both watched my littering items drift out of sight. He said, "You ain't the first. Lotsa' regrets thrown in from this spot. I've seen 'em float by." He didn't say anything else. I asked if he needed any money, he said, "Nah, I'm good," and then he continued walking up the riverbank.

It was two in the afternoon when I went back into the motel room, pulled down the blinds, and laid down on the bed.

I don't remember falling asleep, but I was woken up by yelling from the next room. The arguing between two people who probably once had been in love but now sounded like they were both looking at the walls of the Sweet Rest and blaming each other. The bedside clock read 8:16 pm.

I left the room, dropping the key in the return slot by the check-in office, and drove to the river lot where I had met with Pascal before. He was there, sitting in the cab of his truck and reading a book under the truck's dome light.

I parked and got out of the Subaru. He saw me and waved, put on his cowboy hat, and stepped out of the truck.

"What sort of trouble is it now?" he asked.

I told him that there was no more trouble and that I was fine.

He said, "Well, that's unlikely, but I'll believe a Fella."

Then he told me, "Detective came down here and talked to me yesterday about a Fella," and he said Thin's name. "I found and reported those two bodies. Thought he was here to ask more about that. But he asked what I know about a Fella."

"What did you say?" I asked.

"Told him what I know. Fella used my services. Didn't say much else. Might have told him that I suspect that a Fella was dumb in love," and Pascal pointed his thumb and finger at me like a cocked revolver and said, "Bang."

I nodded, and Pascal went on, "I know this one. He is always angry. Looking for cop-show conspiracies instead of seeing more Montana bull crap. But he usually gives up fast after an arrest. I don't think the Fella will be bothered by him."

Then I told Pascal that I felt responsible for Kaori having killed the two people since Kaori killed them after we had bailed her out.

Pascal said, "A Fella knows what? I'm almost always feeling responsible. Every time someone I help bail goes and messes up, and most do. Most go and keep messing up. But she would have called someone else if she hadn't reached out to a Fella. Her family, or some other bondsman."

Then Pascal tapped my chest and continued, "The difference is a Fella was fallen for her. Always the ones who try in the best way, those ones get their lights punched out. And I'm not talking about that busted nose."

Then I told Pascal that I was about to drive south. "Maybe live in the car and tent through the winter. Find a place where no one will bother me."

He didn't seem surprised, but he did say, "Be watchful with that money a Fella showed me. Don't be flashing that around."

I asked him if he wanted some of it. Then I said, "Actually, do you want all of it?"

Pascal took off his cowboy hat and scratched his head. Then he shrugged and said, "No. I think a Fella might need it more than I would. And I have a feeling that taking it from a Fella would become a whole stink load of disaster." And he added, "No. I'm good," the same thing the homeless-looking man by the riverbank had said to me earlier in the day.

"Well then," I said, "Again someday, right?"

Pascal said, "For certain," and he put his hat back on and got back into the cab of his truck, turned on the dome light, and picked up the book he had been reading.

I got in the Subaru and was about to drive away, but first, I decided to call Tsai one last time from Missoula. I turned on the burner and called him. This time he answered, and he asked, "What have you been up to?"

"Took a while, but what you wanted is working again," I said.

Tsai answered, "Saw that."

It was probably too soon for him to know that XX was dead, but I knew that Tsai had been on the phone when I fired the shot. So it would have been impossible for him not to suspect something. And from that call, Tsai would certainly know the location where I killed XX.

"I have been having trouble reaching a mutual friend of ours," Tsai said. "Know anything about that?" he asked.

"I know he trashed my house. I know he killed my business partner and helped kill Dave Cheat. I know Fritter is a partner of yours. You want to know more about what I know?" I said this fast, still with fear, but now with anger in my voice as well.

Tsai said, "Don't know what you are talking about."

"I know you do," I said, "but you need to leave me alone now. I am done. I'm gone."

"Enzi…" Tsai started to say, but I hung up and turned off the phone. Then I got out of the car and walked down to the river. I threw both my phones in, one after the other. The splashing sounds they made in the dark were like two trout rising for stoneflies. Trout that sleep in the eddies behind round river boulders. Trout that wake up at dawn and hide all day by pretending to be shadows.

When I walked back to the car, Pascal was standing there again.

"Wanted to give a Fella two somethings for his travels," he said, "Just now finished this one," and he handed me the book that he had been reading by Primo Levi. "A Fella might relate. And this one too," and he gave me a thick and tattered road guide to free and unregistered campsites throughout the west. "Think a Fella might need this here for a while. Drive slow. Think a lot. Stay put when the staying is good."

I thanked Pascal and said goodbye again. Then, in the rearview mirror, I watched him touch the rim of his hat as I drove away from the dim lights and toward the innumerable bright stars.

Chapter 15 - Rocks and Sky

Half a year later, at the end of spring in the desert southwest.

On a windy day, I was in a café at a crossroad near where I had been camping. I was having breakfast and reading the local weekly newspaper. I turned a page and saw words and photos that made my hands shake. It was an article from the Associated Press with two photos: one of Kaori in a Missoula courtroom and another showing one of her drawings. The caption read, "Artist Sentenced to Life for Double Murder." The article luridly described the events that led Kaori from Tokyo to Missoula and detailed that her confessions had been illustrated by her own drawings. She was quoted as saying, "My art was for my one love."

I had not been her one, and her art had never been meant for me. But I had unwittingly helped give her some of what she wanted. I had bailed her out of jail, and she had murdered, and now she was famous.

I put down the paper. I let my hands steady themselves by holding a cup of coffee, and I looked out the café's window. There were no trees outside, no tall buildings, only a landscape of rock and blowing dust.

Then, two weeks later, at the same café. A bright, windless day. Another breakfast, another cup of coffee, and another article. This time, as I read, my hands did not shake. The article was about an ongoing investigation into a massive insider trading scheme. There had been recent arrests of seventeen prominent executives, including Fritter and Tsai, at a dozen different public companies worldwide. The arrests were causing a shake-up of the entire stock market. The article said that the discovery and arrests had been possible because of a computer virus that had tracked the inside trader's activity. It noted that the tracking virus had been created by a network security engineer at SLAM who had died under mysterious circumstances in a car wreck six months earlier. There was a color photo of Dave's wrecked and burnt Tesla, with the caption "Whistleblower's Wreck."

I do not know if Tsai or Fritter have talked about me, and I do not know if they realize that I was their downfall or if they think it came from Dave Cheat. And I don't know if the lines on Thin's scrolls are still converging, but his logic will probably follow Zeno's forever path of getting closer while never arriving. My line touched Kaori's, traveled with Tsai's, moved away from O'Neill's, and crossed XX's. But it started earlier, on scrolls that Thin will never see. My line began in the Aether, in that flowing substance that connects present to past, in the invisible network where my words now navigate, reaching for the glowing screens.

I put the newspaper down. My hands had been steady, but again I picked up and held the cup of coffee, breathed in its good steam, and calmly looked out the same café window at the same desert landscape. The patterns I saw in the rocks merged up into the sky. Up, towards the mathematics of happiness. Up, towards an impossible place without failure or greed, a place of true dreams.

#

Thank you for reading *Paper Targets*. Writers hope for honest reviews. Yet only the rare reader leaves any review. Thus, *Dear Reader*, will you consider going to Amazon (the site where reviews help the most) and leaving an honest short review, or ask your favorite bookstore or library to stock *Paper Targets*? - *steve*

Steve S. Saroff is the author of *Paper Targets* and *The Long Line of Elk* and numerous traditionally published short stories that appeared in *Redbook* and other national magazines. A runaway who became a coder who started and sold successful tech companies, he has helped artists, writers, musicians, and a few good actors start careers. He also helped launch Submittable, the submission system used by many publishers, and he founded FreeMail Inc, the first commercially successful web-based email system (FreeMail was acquired just before WorldCom and Enron's multi-billion-dollar criminal fraud and collapse). Steve S. Saroff hosts the podcast *Montana Voice*.

Printed in Great Britain
by Amazon

55632316R00138